LATEST EDITION

ABSOLUTE CHOICE

THE INFINITY TRILOGY
BOOK ONE

DONIELLE INGERSOLL

ISBN Paperback   978-1-965126-18-9
ISBN Hardcover   978-1-965126-19-6
ISBN eBook   978-1-965126-25-7

Printed in the United States of America.

www.eastwenatcheepublishing.com

Contents

INTRODUCTION

I would like you to use your imagination for a little bit. Suppose you were going about your life as usual and discovered a bottle. When you opened it, a genie popped out and granted you, 12 wishes. You could have anything you want in this world, perhaps even in otherworldly places also. Not even the sky would be limited. You could venture anywhere you liked and beyond. If you could imagine it, you could possess it. Would you like an opportunity like that? What would be your first wish? Perhaps you would wish for instant wealth. You could be dirt poor one minute and a billionaire the next with your own privet jet or yacht. It could be filled with the most beautiful women or sexiest men all waiting to do your bidding. You would never have to lift a finger again to do anything you did not want to do. You could buy your way into paradise. You could have unlimited power only imagined before over people and events in life. Just give a command and you would have others do what you commanded. Snap your fingers and it would be done. If anyone had wronged you in the past, you could even up the score and reduce them to nothing. If you somehow lost a loved one, you could go back in time and bring them to your present reality. You could reverse bad choices you made. You could have hundreds of friends around praising you and applauding your every action like some celebrity or rock star. You could eat whatever food you wanted and always retain a powerful, healthy, sexy body filled with vitality and energy. The fountain of youth would be yours. You would own it. And if you chose, you could pass this bright future on to your offspring. Would you like to live the life of an immortal who could transcend the boundaries of time and space?

Art, the main character in this book stumbled upon something that would give all the above wishes to him. He could have whatever he wanted whenever he wanted it. There was only one problem. He never discovered what he truly had until it was too late. His twelve wishes were forever gone, or were they? One little device in his pocket might change his disadvantaged position forever. Will he discover the secret of the little pyramid or be forced to go through several trying ordeals that could plunge him deeper into trouble or lead him out of the darkness into the light?

Venture with Art in this first of three novels as he travels in a window of time and matter-a liquid universes enabling him to slip between realities, explore parallel universes, create substance from his thoughts and meet the love of his life. What will Art do with the power of ABSOLUTE Choice? What would you do with it? It may be nearer than you think. Perhaps even tonight you can go to this place of wonder where reality and imagination merge. The cosmos is waiting for you. Choose wisely.

The M.A.P Phenomenon
Absolute Choice

*A book by **Donielle Ingersoll***

Again, I tell you that if two of you on earth agree about anything you ask for, it will be done for you by my Father in heaven.
Matthew 18:19

Chapter 1

Art sat alone in his basement. He was discouraged. After three years of intense experimentation, he seemed no closer to his goal of creating an anti-gravity, propulsion unit than when he started. He had made some progress, but it was not what he wanted. During the process he managed to tap into the magnetic fields that existed around the planet but as, yet he could not master them. He had also been able to map them. His goal was to create a land and air vehicle that would be propelled by these same magnetic forces. Many of the futuristic, science fiction movies showed air vehicles flying at multiple levels. Some flicks had shoes that allowed the wearer to fly. His engine would make that a reality. Currently he was trying to isolate antimatter in the magnetic fields. Antimatter was supposed to defy gravity. Every time it was released however, it ended up getting smashed to bits. If he could only channel it, direct it somehow through a molecular pipeline or nana tube then his searching would be over. He could design the craft that would form the next Ford or GM Company. He would be the Henry Ford of this century and build a multibillion-dollar empire.

He was staring blankly into the area between some of the conductors on his device when he chanced to see a small, gray, button sized, cylinder shaped object floating in the space. He picked up a pencil and poked it. He was surprised when it moved to avoid contact with the lead. He tried several times to touch it, but it always managed to evade the point. One thing was clear though, whatever it was, it was trapped in the electromagnetic field between the conductors. He adjusted four of the conductors in a circle around the object. When the fourth conductor was put in place the object went to the center of the group instantly and stayed there. He moved one conductor out some and the object moved ever so slightly in the direction that conductor moved. The other three units continued to exert a magnetic influence on the object, however.

Now that the object was trapped what would happen to it if it were poked? He took the pencil and poked it to find out. It was a little larger around than the pencil. It was not made up of a solid substance. The tip of the pencil penetrated it. No! It absorbed it. The tip of the pencil disappeared within the substance. He poked it in further and more of the pencil disappeared. He pulled the pencil out and as he did, so it resumed its original shape. This was a most intriguing phenomenon. He tried a metal pen that was resting on his desk. The gray object absorbed the tip of that pen also. He pushed it in all the way to the pocket clip and held it there. Although the gray button was only a few centimeters thick, the end of the pen disappeared within it. While holding the pen in that position with a small spring clamp on the end of a rod, he walked around to the other side of the unit to see if the end of the pen was protruding out, but it was not. The end had simply disappeared. When he pulled the pen out it too resumed its shape. He took the retrieved pen and scribbled on a scrap of paper. It wrote well. But where had the end gone when it entered the gray cylinder?

He tried to bring the pen up, out of the gray mass through the top but he could not. Some sort of solid force field he guessed, or shell prevented him from doing that. No matter how hard he pushed up or pulled down, the pen could not pass out through the edge of the cylinder. The cylinder would move a little in the direction it was pushed but not extremely far. When the pressure stopped, the cylinder moved back to the center and stayed there. The inside though was different. He pushed the pen through the cylinder at an angle and there was no resistance inside. The resistance was only at the entrance of the mass and then only on the edges. There was no resistance at the center, but the tension increased dramatically as he neared the edges until it stopped at some invisible wall. Perhaps if he modified this thing some way, he could create the molecular tubes he needed to direct antimatter. Could antimatter pass through the edge of the cylinder?

Art understood this accidental discovery was extraordinary. He was an avid student of science and this defied the common laws of physics. He determined then and there to experiment with it in the proper way. He ran upstairs and retrieved a digital camera from the closet. He stopped at his study and brought his laptop computer down with the power cord and when everything was set up, he wrote down what he had done so far, took pictures of the gray button from both sides of the space it was trapped in and took pictures of both the pencil and the pen as the portion of each penetrated the object and disappeared. His next experiment was similar but different. He attached the pen to the clamp at the ballpoint and pushed it all the way into the object until the tip of the clamp disappeared. He took a picture and pulled it back out. The pen emerged from the device completely unharmed. He sat back and thought. What should he try next? He did not know why he decided to move the conductors but perhaps his subconscious mind had kicked in to direct the event. He moved all four conductors outward and decreased the electrical output of each. Art was surprised to see that the gray button expanded. It grew to the size of a quarter. He took pictures and decreased the voltage even more to the conductors. He again moved them further apart. He kept doing this until the button became about twenty inches in diameter.

Next, he inserted objects of a larger diameter composed of different materials. The gray blob absorbed everything he gave it. Each object would go into the mass and the portion that went in would disappear as if someone had cut it off but when the objects were pulled back out, they were completely whole and unharmed. He thought about this for some time then a question came to mind. So far, all the objects he had inserted into the mass did not contain any living cells. What effect if any, would the mass have on living cells? He would have to find out. From his window he retrieved a leaf from an ivy plant. He poked it into the hole and pulled it out. He half-expected it to be dried or wilted but it emerged unharmed. Should he try his finger next? He looked at all ten fingers. If he had to live without one of them, which would it be? He finally decided on the little finger of his left hand. He slowly moved it toward the mass. What would the temperature be? He pulled his finger back before touching the globe. Upstairs there was a thermometer. It would probably be best to take the temperature inside the mass before subjecting his finger to it. After retrieving the thermometer, he looked at the dial. It read 72 degrees. He recorded that on the computer and took a picture of it then poked it into the center of the mass and left it there for about three minutes. When he pulled it out there was a small change. It registered 68 degrees. He took another picture and then thought about the camera. Perhaps before he poked a finger in there it might be best to see if the camera could go inside and take a picture of what was there. The camera he had was a rather expensive one. There was a cheap one he purchased several years earlier. He would try the inexpensive model first, though the quality of the picture would be considerably less. When he retrieved that camera, he cleaned out all the images in the memory card and rigged up a device so he could push the shutter button once the camera was within the mass. OK! It was time to see what if anything was inside. The gray blob absorbed the camera completely as it had all the other objects. When he pressed the trigger to activate the shutter within the mass, he heard no reassuring click, no sound escaped the mass. He decided he would stick a radio in next to test that theory.

He took several pictures moving the arm that held the camera in different directions before pulling it out. When he had retrieved it fully, he looked at the meter. It showed that six pictures had been taken. With trembling hands, he removed the card from the camera and inserted it into the proper slot on the laptop. A little window came with several options. He scrolled down to open file to view images and left clicked the button. Six pictures appeared on the screen. He was disappointed though as the pictures appeared to be of the different angles of the room from which he had moved the camera within the mass. One showed his desk with the laptop. Another showed the machine with the conductors. It was as if he had taken the photos normally with no gray blob having absorbed the camera. The only change he noticed was a decrease in clarity. The images appeared to have been taken with a special mist effect lens. It was time for the finger trick. Without hesitation he approached the gray cylinder with his little finger and poked the tip of it in. He felt a little resistance and his fingertip within the cylinder felt cooler. He pushed it in a little further, so part of the nail disappeared and pulled it out quickly. His finger was as normal as any of the others. Next, he crunched his fingers together and thrust three of them into the mass. Like everything else they disappeared only to appear again when he pulled them out completely unharmed. The slight resistance he felt covered the entire portion of the hand that he inserted. Next, he curled his index finger up around the edge of the mass like one would curl it around the curve of a coat hanger. He tried to pull the twenty-inch ring from the center of the space in which it was trapped. It moved only slightly in the direction of the applied force.

He went and got a small radio. Would sound escape the gray mass or would it also be absorbed? He tuned the radio to the ball game that was playing and after attaching it to the arm, poked it through the hole. One minute he heard the announcer all excited over the three-run homer the player made, the next minute everything was silent. He left the radio in for a couple of minutes then pulled it out. As soon as it emerged the ball game resumed. The other team was up to bat now, so the radio had not stopped. He turned the volume up full force. He pushed the radio into the gray mass again, and again the mass absorbed the sound. When he pulled the radio back out the volume was as loud as ever. What should he do next? He noticed a cup he had brought down sometime during the last week. There was still a little water in the bottom. What would happen if he put the cup through the center of the mass and turned it over? Would the water pour out? If it did, where would it go? Would the floor become wet?

He grasped the handle of the cup and proceeded to carry out his intentions. After the mass absorbed the cup in his hand, he turned it over and pulled it back out. He looked in the cup. There was no water in it. So, the gray mass had absorbed the water. He looked on the floor. There was no water there so the water had stayed inside the mass. This was becoming more of a mystery all the time. So, objects dropped within the circle were not lost or at least appeared not to be. He would see. He took a penny from his pocket and holding it with two fingers dropped it just inside the gray cylinder. He looked at the floor. There was no penny just like the water. Somehow the gray circle seemed to absorb motion or movement as well as objects.

So far in his experimentation he had inserted the objects from one side of the gray mass only. Why not see what would happen if he inserted something from the back side of the mass? No, he would not insert anything else. He would drop the penny inside from the other side. He took the spring clamp from the arm on the machine and clamped onto the penny. He was not surprised to see that the penny disappeared as before. To find it, he would need to insert a camera from that side. He gently pulled the spring clamp from the cylinder and sat down in his chair to ponder this strange object with its unearthly qualities. What he found so far was that objects inserted from the front and back both disappeared. What Art really needed now was a tiny video camera that he could insert in the mass to record what happened to the movement of the objects he dropped or any other thing it might reveal. To see everything through a fisheye lens would probably give the best view. He decided to go down to a local department store and pick up something inexpensive.

Before he went to purchase the camera, he wanted to be assured that the gray mass would not go away. If he had trapped it by chance, he could not afford to lose it. If the power went off and the conductors lost their charge, the gray cylinder with its fascinating qualities could be lost to him forever. He had to make sure that did not happen. During the next half hour or so he added a battery backup to the machine. Now if the electricity chanced to go off, the batteries would kick in to keep the charge active. He was feeling much better about going out now. The more he discovered about the object the more he realized he had to learn. All sorts of hypotheses were forming in his mind as to what this was. Each would require careful testing. The miniature video camera would help him do further testing more than anything else he could think of at this time. With that he could make more careful observations. He could also record his experiments on SD Cards. Once the card's memory was full, he could store the data to a DVD disk for more permanent preservation. This was especially important because of all the magnetic energy that seemed to permeate the area around his machine.

A couple of hours passed before Art returned with the camera. Another hour passed before he had everything set up and ready. For assurance he placed the recorder in another room and hooked up some hard wire controls so he could activate the recording process at will. He set up a monitor in the basement about 10 feet from the gray mass. Would a video camera work inside the mass? Things inside the gray cylinder appeared from the outside to absorb movement. Was there movement within? There had to be, but could it be recorded? Art hooked the tiny camera with its fisheye lens to the arm with the spring clamp, turned on the monitor and watched as the lens approached the blob. The fisheye lens distorted it quite a bit. He could see the whole room revolving around the mass. Then the lens was inside. He could still see the room. It was just like the other camera. He took a quick look at the floor. There was a penny on it and a wet spot where the water had fallen out of the cup. He pulled the video camera out and changed the lens to a wide angle one. Now things within the cylinder appeared more normal with less distortion. Perhaps this lens was better.

Art's next test was to see what happened to the penny when it was dropped. To record this, he attached a small stick to the bottom of the video camera and placed the penny on it. Once inside the cylinder he turned the stick over and watched as the penny fell to the floor. Though he could not see the penny fall from the stick outside of the cylinder, he could record it falling to the floor on the inside. Again, there was no trace of it outside the mass. Was it possible to do what he really wanted to do and was being pulled to do? If he enlarged the gray cylinder, would it be possible for him to stick his head through and if he could, would it be possible to physically enter through the mass? How would he be assured of enlarging the cylinder enough for him to enter? What would happen if he subjected his brain to the charges that were being emitted from the conductors? Would he need more conductors than four? How much voltage would be needed to hold and indeed enlarge the cylinder enough to step through it? If he did manage to enlarge it enough to enter, could he return? If he entered entirely, would he still exist in there? Where would he go once, he was inside? Could he go upstairs and move things around, then come back down and re-enter the basement through the cylinder? Could he then go back upstairs and find that the object he moved inside had indeed been moved outside? How stable was this mass? He did not want to lose it. If he made even one wrong mistake, it could be gone forever and with it a million questions waiting to be answered.

Art decided that before he physically attempted to enter the cylinder, he would do a lot more testing. He would test the charges needed to stretch the size of the mass. He would send the camera in and do several things inside while recording it all. After he was sure that everything was safe, he would send in a laboratory mouse from the college where he taught. If the mouse survived and was able to move around within, then and only then would Art attempted to enter himself. Over the next several days he practically lived in the basement. He would work until he dropped exhausted into the large reclining chair not far from his desk and as soon as he woke up would start again. He was discovering that inside the cylinder things were in a different state of existence than outside. For instance, objects within the cylinder appeared to be more in a liquid state, not a liquid state like water, but like a dry liquid. It was like liquid energy. The universe within the cylinder was compressed a lot more than the one outside. It was not compressed enough to form a solid substance though. Solid objects from the outside became liquid and decreased in size when inside. He discovered that when he placed a penny on a quarter and watched the monitor as he flipped the coins in the air, they appeared to pass through each other as they twirled but still retained their shape. When he placed his two fingers in and pinched them together, they appeared to pass through each other a little, but whenever he pulled them out, they were normal. When held perfectly still the picture within matched that of the room without. Only the size and clarity changed. When things moved around though they seemed to emerge and converge slightly into each other. Objects moved slower within and there was a slight delay in action.

One day he decided to put the radio back into the cylinder and record what happened. He was surprised when he did. The various objects within the mass all seemed to vibrate with the music. Looking at the video from within the gray mass, he could see the forms of everything changing shape. They were distorted in different ways as louder or softer sounds or beats came from the radio. The best way he could describe it for example was watching one's reflection in the water. If a pebble were dropped in, the rippling effect of the water distorted the image reflected there. If a microphone were inserted within the cylinder, he could hear sounds from inside and record them on the video. They were a bit altered but not all that bad. One thing was certain, within the mass the substance of everything became similar. Solids, liquids, gasses, sounds all became a flexible, liquid energy that could be distorted and manipulated while keeping their identifying form. One thing was certain, time from within the cylinder and time from without were different. That is when he wondered if perchance, he had discovered a primitive form of time travel?

Chapter 2

The mouse stood trembling in its tiny cage as Art eased it toward the gray mass. He had set up a video camera to record the outside as well as the inside. He split the monitor so there were two cameras recording the event on the same screen. One was recording the tail end of the mouse. The other camera within the cylinder was recording the front. The moment finally came when the nose of the mouse passed through the gray door. Art could see it emerge. The mouse quivered slightly as the nose felt the mild pressure from within. Soon his head appeared. Finally, his whole body was within. The camera inside showed the mouse moving around. It was alive. He left it in for several minutes. Would the mouse die when it came back through the opening? He brought the cage back down and out of the hole. The mouse appeared normal in every way. This was the final test. If the mouse could survive within, so could a man. It was time to enter or perhaps he should wait a few days and see if the condition of the mouse changed any.

Art decided to wait a few days and see how the mouse fared. He would experiment with enlarging the opening and see if he could make it easier to enter. Over the next several days he modified the conductors. He created a portable unit that expanded or collapsed the gray button to any size he desired. It was small enough to fit in an aluminum case. Basically, each section of this portable unit was a large battery. When all the sections were combined, the circuit was completed and the large amount of power necessary to maintain the mass assured. The battery sections were designed in such a way to allow them to telescope in and out. As far as the mass inside was concerned, when in its most compact form, the gray cylinder in the center was nearly invisible, no larger than the head of a pin. When enlarged and the power modified, it became any size he desired. He had successfully transferred the gray mass back and forth between the stationery and portable units. In doing this he discovered to his relief that the little gray cylinder apparently had many brothers and sisters. When fully charged, the portable unit attracted its own gray button. He had to put the unit on maximum power at first, then a gray cylinder would be trapped in the center just like the stationery unit. After it was trapped, he would power down to a minimum level and if there was any flow passing through the conductors, the button remained. Just to be safe though he always had one active unit suspended somewhere as a backup. He needed a name for this thing. Gray cylinder, button, mass, blob just did not cut it. He thought for a moment. Finally, he came up with one. He would call this invention a rather common sounding name, Metaphysical Acceleration Processor, MAP for short. He chose the stationery unit for his first adventure into the unknown after seeing that the mouse appeared normal in every respect.

Art had stuck his head through a few times but never entered entirely. He adjusted the MAP, so its trapped mass was easy to step through. He set his watch exactly to the clock on his desk and was soon at the opening. He put one foot through and then ducked down and put his head through before pulling in his other leg. Once inside he stood up. It was a different world in there. He could think clearly. He could see. He could move, but his surroundings and physical existence were more liquid than solid. Though the surfaces above, around, and below him gave way slightly at his touch, they still had a quality of solidity about them. He could jump but when he landed his feet penetrated the floor a few inches. He noticed there was more resistance to movement within. He was constantly pushing against a greater pressure than the outside world. The atmospheric pressure was greater. It would be best described as walking through water or air with several hundred percentage points of humidity, it felt heavy in his lungs. He stayed in only for a couple of minutes before going back out into the room. Once outside he took note of his physical person. For all practical purposes he was unaffected.

Art decided to enter again and this time, do more activities once inside. He would go upstairs and move some things around in the kitchen then come down, exit, and go up and see if they remained moved or not. In the kitchen he changed the forks and the spoons in the silverware drawer and moved a glass of water from one side of the table to the other. There was an unopened box of candy on the counter. Would he be able to taste things in this world? He opened the box and reached for a piece of candy. His fingers penetrated it but when he lifted them up the piece of candy came with them. He popped it into his mouth. He tried to taste and though some of the flavor finally came through it was as though his mind tasted it rather than his tongue. The sense of touch was more sensitive in his mouth. As the candy dissolved it did not seem to be contained within. The whole area around his head seemed to absorb it. Could he feel temperature change in this world? He opened the refrigerator and touched the freezer box. Only the slightest sensation of cold came. It was greatly lessened but still there. In this world he would have to fine-tune his senses and be more on guard as things could happen. For example, if he touched a hot element on the stove, he could get a bad burn and not realize it until he came back into the physical world.

All movement from within was by delayed action. It took time before a slight sensation came through. After turning on the radio and testing his hearing, he went downstairs and again exited the opening. He then proceeded to go upstairs and check on the activities he had done. He was not surprised to see that the objects he moved while inside the mass were not in their new locations when he went up after coming out. The candy was not missing from the box. He could not see a fingerprint where he had touched the ice box.

He entered again and again and found that it did not take long to adjust to the more liquid state of existence from within. The sounds were muffled in this world and mixed with a humming and buzzing. There seemed to be a lot of static in the air. He could hear it crackling and interacting with the environment. The sounds were what one would expect if they were under water, hearing from a liquid environment and amplified a little. The static and crackling sounds were electrical in nature. Though things seemed in a liquid state within, it was a dry liquid. That much was sure. After going in and out and trying all kinds of things, he even ventured to drive around the block once in his car though it seemed strange to see his hand merged with the steering wheel while in the liquid universe.

He observed people from within, but they appeared not to notice or interact with him. He even talked to them, but they heard nothing. It was like the radio that was silenced when it passed through the cylinder. The sound of his voice was absorbed somehow and so were his movements. He touched one man on the back, but he did not even flinch. He could walk into his neighbor's house and no one would see him.

It is a good thing I am honest man, Art thought to himself, I could steal anyone blind and they would never know it. One could be a pick pocket and be a block away before the loss was ever felt or discovered by the unfortunate owner of the wallet. He shuddered at the power this gave him. He found that he could change the shape of objects from within, but they would not be changed when he came out. When he cut a piece of toast in half from within, it was not in half when he went back to the physical universe. This led him back to his pick pocket idea. If he did pick pocket someone, he would have their wallet from within, but would it still appear to be in their back pocket without? Would it still have money in it?

At first it was interesting noting the differences in the two dimensions, but they really were not all that dissimilar once it was all summed up. The discovery could have many commercial uses but somehow, he knew this discovery could never become common knowledge. Nothing would be safe. Humanity was just to evil. If commercial applications were discovered, they would have to be contained within single unit inventions. Humankind must never be free to enter the doors he had discovered.

Though there was more resistance within, friction was reduced. He found that out when from within the cylinder he went and cut down a small tree. The hatchet met with much less resistance than in the normal universe but seemed to cut in equally as fast as it would on the outside. Though objects moving from one location to another met with some resistance, their velocity was greater to make up for it. Things could bump into each other without forming scratches within unless really slammed together with great force. When checked from without they showed no marks of contact.

His eyes saw things from within differently than the cameras he had used. The mouse for instance had what appeared to be a pink aurora around it like a neon light. Plants had a golden green luminescence around them. He noted violet and blue auroras animating from his kitchen counters. He assumed these were microscopic, living organisms. A sponge on the sink radiated every shade of color in the spectrum. There were blotches of multicolored green and blue. The colors radiating around the sponge looked dirty though as if peeking out through miniature towers of grime and waste. All life gave off one form of neon color or another. He captured a spider and placed it in a jar and just for observations sake, sprayed it with a bug killer. He took note of the luminescence. It started out as a deep violet but grew dimmer, finally disappearing as the life of the spider expired. He pulled some Lysol out from under the sink and sprayed a section of the counter. The colors there faded and died. So, one could see a difference between that which contained life and that which did not. For the first time he could really tell what sterol was. This could mean millions of dollars placed in his pocket if a commercial application of some unit were applied.

He looked at himself in the mirror. His own body radiated a golden color. Sometime during developing his portable unit, he had smashed a finger. He looked at it now. The halo around the soar finger was not golden like the rest of his body but orange. It became red where the hurt was the worst. He wondered if colors could give the medical field some form of idea how healthy the host that housed life was? He was sure it could. This alone if fully developed could bring him wealth without measure. He would build a medical diagnosing unit and patent it. This is where he would start. No. that would take too long and besides there was technology in existence that did about the same thing already. It would take less time to develop a sanitizing unit that could be used by the cleaning industry or the household perfectionist. There were a hundred places to start. He would put in for his resignation at the university. He no longer needed to hassle with aggravating students.

Art wondered one day if he could light a fire inside. Would a match strike? Would the universe inside explode if subjected to fire? He decided to check it out but from a distance. He got a ten-foot pole and put a match on the end of it. He would use his portable unit and set it up close to the door. That way if there was an explosion, he might have a better chance of escaping harm. With the match lite, he slowly approached the mass. He would put it in and pull it out as quickly as possible. Upon doing this he found the flame was extinguished the second it hit the opening. He rigged up a way to strike the match while it was inside, but he was not. It would not spark even from within. So perhaps this WAS a liquid universe? The temperature differences within were not nearly as apparent as those in the normal world. He recorded all this and recorded it on his laptop.

One evening before drifting off to sleep, Art asked his subconscious to see if it could figure out how to make objects he moved inside be moved outside. The next day while in the process of looking for a pen, he ran across a taser he purchased at some point in the past. It had a dial on it that would allow one to go from a few thousand up to a million volts. What would it do within? Again, he rigged up a way to activate it inside and had his camera observe what happened. To his delight the unit sparked. This made sense. The electronics he placed within still functioned in there. His subconscious told him to use the taser. He did not ask why? What would happen if he moved a fork then tasered it? Would that reset its location? First, he would see what happened when he personally pushed the button. He would put as small amount of his hand in as possible to do this so if there was a burn, or a shock, most of him would be outside. Presto. His hand inside was able to activate the taser. So, he went in, moved the fork, tasered it and came back out. This time much to his delight the fork was in its new location. Somehow applying an electrical shock to it from within after moving it set it in its new position outside. Otherwise, there was no change in location. Now he could go somewhere, move things around, taser them and they would be moved on the outside. He recorded the spot while inside and checked the camera. There was a blue flash from out of nowhere in front of the camera and then the fork appeared. He fooled with the voltage and found out that the larger the object, the more volts were required to set it in its new location. A million volts, however, could set a good-sized object. Sometimes the auroras got wiped out during tasering. That meant the high voltage sometimes killed certain biological forms of life. There was no movement on the outside recorded, the object simply appeared in its new location. Amazing! Wow! He could think of thousands of things to do now with this unique trait. But suppose while inside an unexpected electrical charge touched something that it was not supposed to? He would need to be incredibly careful, especially if using electrical equipment.

When Art had put things from the back or negative side of the unit, the objects appeared to be a little ahead of time. What would happen if he entered the unit from that side? He set up the cameras and decided to give it a try. The camera recorded nothing but the room in the physical world. A cricket, however walked across the wall. The camera recorded it both from within and without. The movement of cricket on the inside of the device appeared to be a split second faster than the movement of the cricket outside. There was one event that perhaps happened? Just before he exited, Art thought he caught a quick, view of a grey alien. No! That was not possible. He did not believe in that UFO stuff. He had never had any encounters with any. Right now, his mind was more enthralled on being able to transverse the world, undetected. To him, that had many more applications. Perhaps those applications were endless? Time would tell, that is if he survived long enough. Still the greys sighting, if it were real, left an uneasy impression way back in some corner of his subconscious. Entering the liquid universe from that side of the unit might be more dangerous. He determined to mark the portable apparatus clearly as to which side was which incase, he happened to need to enter or exit quickly and forgot to check.

One day from within he took out the old family album and looked at the pictures. He saw his wife and their 7-year-old son looking back at him. The photos were uncanny, almost real. After studying them closer, he isolated the eyes. The eyes in the photos looked so real. They unnerved him. He could almost see them blink. Art thought back over the 11 wonderful years he and his wife had shared. Somewhere along the way, they had been lost to him. He and his wife had been so much in love. Their deaths had not been accidental. He knew it. His lawyer knew it. The killer knew it also but got away scot free. He was a smart actor. He had played the jury right into his hands. He presented a face of utmost sorrow, empathy, and concern for Art's loss. It was sickening. Art never bought it but most of the jurors were in tears after his phatic plea of remorse and sorrow over the most unfortunate mishap. Phatic, my foot, Art remembered thinking, psychopathic, yes but not phatic. The killer had been his neighbor. All the evidence pointed to him as the one who had done it. Supposedly the neighbor had heard a scream and then nothing. He told the jury he waited about half an hour then when he heard a crash, ran into the house. He found Sandra lying battered on the floor. Sonny was already dead, but the lady was moaning. He told how he called 911 and rode to the hospital with her while the police notified Art who was teaching a late-night class at the time. It was all a nice story and they bought it. It did not happen that way though. The day after the trial was over the neighbor moved away. The murders were intentional and premeditated and that man had done it. Art knew this in the depth of his being. It is there where one's innermost spirit that cannot lie, lies.

He had ventured into the realms of his subconscious, consciously on several occasions. He had isolated the river of plenty that contained all one's needs in life, and infinitely more. He immersed himself in its healing streams and nourished his soul repeatedly. He even found some forgiveness there for the murderer, but it was not complete. He allowed a few, tiny grains of bitterness to remain and when he was not paying attention, he sometimes slipped. At those times he found himself delving into that river of evil from beneath that draws any who harbor such thoughts down the currant of destruction. He would always pull himself away from it though and seek the good then his soul would be washed clean again except for those particles of revenge that he cherished too much to give up. He would always keep these. He deserved that much did not he for all the pain and loss his enemy had caused him to suffer?

He decided now while holding the photos of Sonny and his wife to meditate on those happy days of long ago. He went into his breathing rhythm. As he drew in the breaths of liquid air, he could feel the life flowing into his being, filling him with an energy force unlike anything he had ever experienced on the outside before. Each breath elevated him to a higher realm of existence. Finally, the great river was before him, stretching into the infinity of the universe beyond. He found in the streams of memory, those that reflected his wife and traced them back to a time when she lay in his arms on that very couch. He caressed her with his thoughts. He drew her substance out of the past and kissed her gently. She responded with that tender love that only she could give him. At first, she held their sleeping son on her lap, but as their love grew more intense, she lay him aside and they made passionate love as the time within slipped away.

The chimes on the antique clock roused him out of sleep. It must have rung a dozen times at least. Would it ever stop? It had been a marvelous dream. He had experienced bliss beyond comprehension in this wondrous world of the yet unknown. It had been as real, no; more real than any physical experiences from without. In this world, even one's thoughts were like a river of substance, propelling the traveler to a level of ecstasy impossible to match in the physical realm. At last, he was happy. He could come back and find her here anytime he chose. Perhaps he would just come back one day and stay there forever, locked in her embrace. Could this be heaven? No, heaven was not supposed to have bad things in it like bacteria on his counters. It was not heaven, but a person could probably make this world into a utopia of whatever they desired. Within its realms, the human was for the first time given the power of absolute choice. He could carve his own future. Perhaps even change the past.

Art was upset at the clock. It had taken her away. His conscious mind had come back to take control and screened out the vision. It was impossible so the conscious said, and so it was. He locked his thoughts on the clock and with his mind wrenched it from the wall. He was startled when it fell to the floor and broke into pieces. Then the crashing sounds came with a muffled tone to his ears. That did it. He had to leave this place, or he would go crazy. He bounded down the stairs two at a time and leaped through the opening back into reality. Then he heard crying. He quickly adjusted the conductors down so the MAP was a tiny pinpoint and started toward the sound. It was coming from the next room. He saw her curled up on the couch with a tiny teddy bear held snugly in her arms. He guessed her age to be about four, perhaps five. She looked at him as he entered, then reached her small arms up toward him, signaling to be picked up and held. It was instinctive. He lifted her and cradled her close in his arms while he wondered who this tiny, amazing mortal was? She was a miniature model of his wife. But he and Sandra had brought only a boy into the world. They had wanted a girl but that had never happened. His wife's final words reminded him of that now. He played them over in his mind as he had a hundred times before.

"I know I am dying. I had a great life with you, Art. You were the best husband a woman could ever have." He remembered how she had stopped, caught her breath then coughed up a blotch of blood.

"I have only one regret. I will not be able to give you a daughter, and Sonny a little sister. I know how badly you wanted one." Art had wanted a daughter very much.

"I love you," she whispered. Then she had closed her eyes and was gone. They had not told her Sonny had died. It was something she would not have been able to cope with.

Art was startled out of his thoughts, to the point of almost dropping the girl when she spoke.

"I wish Mommy had not gone away. Daddy. I miss her. I had a bad dream. I dreamed an awful man came to the house and hurt her and Sonny. I watched him. He did not see me. I was hiding from Sonny in the closet. It was awful, Daddy. Do not go away again. Please!"

For a moment longer he remembered that she was not but only for a moment because she truly was his daughter. He held Kanna close until she fell asleep then carried her gently up to her room. He dressed her in her night gown and tucked her in bed. She was so beautiful, just like her mother. She had been his only comfort since the untimely deaths of Sandra and Sonny. He placed the teddy in her arms and kissed her gently on the forehead before tiptoeing out of the room. On the way he passed the old clock. One, two, three, four, five. Six, seven, eight, nine, ten, eleven it chimed. A small crack was seen in the casing.

Chapter 3

Davidson looked at the recently acquired particle beam unit. It had been purchased from the Colonial General Hospital. They had won it in a bid for some government surplus items. It had proved damaged though and not worth the cost of repair. Davidson was a physics major at the local college. This would be the big break that was needed to finish a three-year research project. Back at the lab, the insulating chambers that came with the merchandise were already set up. It only took two hours to install the camera. Then the student put on the radiation gear and plugged the unit in. A bright, blinding light came from the center of the chamber and fragmented through the isolation tube. There was defiantly a problem with the unit. The beam was not focused. Its rays began to scatter only inches from the lens. There were no parts available for this unit. It was too outdated. The Internet had been checked from at least twenty search engines but did not turn up the needed parts. If this were to work, Davidson would have to make the parts. After shutting off power to the unit, the lens was removed.

The scientist was not a young student. An attempt at marriage and a career in mathematics had both failed. Now 30, Davidson had turned again to pursuing studies in the higher sciences. The lens holder would just have to be manufactured in the metal lab. It would be a triple lens unit with a liquid, crystalline fluid injected on either side of the center lens, housed between the front and back lenses. The fluid would have conductors inserted so a positive charge could be given to one side of the lens and a negative charge to the other. A solenoid would also be needed to keep alternating the positive and negative charges back and forth between the two solutions. Once charged the crystals within the solution should align themselves allowing the beam to be directed with exact precision. It would take three days max. Hopefully when it was all done the beam would be focused. It was a new approach, but Gem was sure it would work. By increasing or decreasing the amount of the charge in the alternating solutions, the beam could be narrowed or widened without losing any of its force. Recent studies had revealed a way to make particles travel faster than light. If this could be achieved with the addition of a camera, x-rays could theatrically be taken of images before they were formed. It would be in measurements of the smallest degrees at best, but it was something that had not been done yet.

Meanwhile, back in his basement, Art kept plugging away. He finally had a prototype created for the sanitation unit. It had taken longer than he expected. Though his eyes could see the aurora of life around living matter, he had to delve into new avenues of photography to make a machine see what his eyes saw. After several weeks he had a breakthrough. The process was simple yet complicated at the same time and he was rather tired of it all. He decided when he finished this first device, to put the whole liquid universe project on the shelf and go back to the anti-gravity unit. He could always come back to the Metaphysical Acceleration Processor when he thought of some new, simple fabrication that would not take much time or effort to launch. Sometimes it was best to let his subconscious mind solve problems while he concentrated his efforts on other things. He outlined the characteristics of the invention and sent them with the prototype to his patent attorney. There was one part that only he could provide. It was a rectangular glass filament that held the same atmosphere from within the liquid dimension. He had secured several of these units. When, if ever, a manufacturer started producing them, Art would supply this one part. He was the only one that ever could so long as he controlled the processor. If anyone got snoopy and tried to analyze the substance within the glass, they would come up with nothing. As soon as the glass was opened or broken, the substance expanded and disappeared into the air. This was a safety valve he would put in each invention that might eventually come from MAP. The university had granted his resignation and he would need funds soon. He felt he could get his new unit in production in as little as three months.

What Art failed to put together though was the fact that the discovery of MAP could well be the missing link to his anti-gravity studies. It was hard to understand why he missed this point. If things within the new dimension had less friction and moved with what appeared to be greater and lesser velocity, wasn't that exactly what he needed to help in overcoming the forces of gravity? Also, if things from within the liquid universe were a few split seconds ahead of or behind their counterparts in the physical universe, depending on which side of the cylinder they were inserted, what happened during those few split seconds of difference. If one thought about it, for that brief time the objects in the liquid universe had overcome the force of gravity entirely. They had instantly been moved from one location to another with no resistance whatsoever. They had also moved so fast that they appeared to jump ahead in time. Though it was not much time, could not these split seconds be extended in some way? If the same object could appear to move so fast that it occupied two spaces in time at the same time, could not a machine use this same principal to move at incredible speeds? Logically it seemed there were ways from within the liquid universe of the cylinder to reduce or entirely overcome gravity? But this concept never came to his mind, so he did not turn his studies in that direction.

Several months had passed since Art shelved the Metaphysical Accelerator unit. A manufacturer was mass producing the sanitation units and money was finally coming in. He slowed down some from his work. A typical day's schedule might read like this. Rise at 6:00, shower, start breakfast for Kanna and himself then get her up. She usually ate in her night clothes. She would then brush her teeth and shower. While she was in the bathroom, he would lay out a couple of clothes selections then go back to the kitchen and clean up the breakfast mess. Kanna liked to select her own colors. She was very particular about that, just like her mother. Art found that out when he tried to put an outfit together for her that did not suit her likes. He never tried again. After she was dressed, he would drive her down to the daycare and grab a few things from town if needed then head back home and work in the lab. He would spend the day there then go get Kanna around 4:00. They would go out to eat then. He would spend part of the evening doing things with her. She loved it and looked forward to these special times with Daddy. So, did Art.

One morning after dropping Kanna off at the daycare, Art was reading an article in a scientific journal when he chanced to see a title that caught his attention. Some inventors had sent in a report of his studies on a particle beam unit with an added camera. Supposedly this camera could take pictures in the future a few split seconds before they happened. Normally Art would not have paid that much attention, but something in the back of his mind seemed to link this with the MAP unit. With it, Art had been able from within to take pictures of things a little ahead of their prescribed movement in time. He had done this with a normal camera as well as a digital recorder. He had not needed one that used particles. Perhaps there was some connection between the two? The owner of the particle unit lived in the next town, so Art decided to pay him a visit. Perhaps a particle beam camera could take different pictures of the universe within. It might be just the thing that was needed to discover more about what MAP really was.

It was a pleasant drive to the home of the inventor. Kanna was buckled securely in the car seat behind him. He would drop her off at the daycare then continue to the address he had scribbled on a scrap of paper. Autumn had arrived in all its glory. The hills glowed with reds and golds. The leaves of the quaking aspen had turned yellow and moved in their magical way as a light breeze touched them. It was perfect weather and so far, a perfect day. Art called ahead and informed Davidson of his intent to visit. Both scientists were looking forward to the meeting. Art had spoken a little about his discovery. It was just enough to perk Davidson's interest. Art brought along the portable MAP unit. He discovered that no matter where he went in the physical world, once power was supplied there was always a small, gray cylinder in the center of the field to work with. He also discovered that once inside the Accelerator he could collapse the unit, place it in the aluminum case and travel from within to a new location. He could do whatever he wanted and then assemble it again. Once assembled he could pass back into the physical universe and collapse the unit back down. This was very handy. Most of the time, however he chose to travel in the physical universe.

Davidson was curious indeed. If there was a way for objects and even people to consciously move in time a few split seconds before or after they normally would in the physical universe, then perhaps this camera really could do what had been claimed about it, take pictures a few seconds into the future. The scientist was thinking of several commercial applications for the camera and the potential for an accelerated income when Art turned into the drive.

Art opened the car door and retrieved his case. He rang the doorbell and a short man dressed in radiation gear opened it for him. The man gave him a suit and after Art put it on, the scientist made sure it was sealed. He motioned for Art to follow him into a lab at the back of the home. The camera was mounted on its bracket. There was a strange transparent tube in front of what appeared to be the lens. Along the tube there were several metal bands that were connected to thick cables. Off to the left there was a set of controls. Davidson pushed several switches and the whole apparatus came to life. In time the transparent chamber was filled with a foggy solution. When the camera was switched on, a tiny beam of blue light shot down the center. It bathed the entire room with an eerie glow. Davidson placed a container housing a black rectangular shaped box at the end of the beam and flipped a lever. There was a blinding flash that made even the dark lens in the radiation gear appear brighter than the noon day sun. Then the camera shut itself off and the box was unlatched and removed from the holder. From somewhere a motor came on. Fans seemed to suck the air from the lab. It was replaced with air so fresh Art could have sworn it was the way all nature smelled after a lightning storm.

"It's all clear," Gem called. "We can take off our helmets and I will show you what we just recorded. Art removed his head gear and pushed a lock of his black hair out of his eyes. He had always worn it a little longer than the average man. Davidson removed his helmet also and when she did, Art held his breath before gasping out the first thing that came to his mind.

"My God! he cried. You're a woman and an unbelievably beautiful one too." Then as if he heard what he had just said, he turned a couple of shades of red with embarrassment. Gem flashed him a broad smile and spoke.

"I would tell you that it happens all the time, but I can't lie. I usually do not go around with garb like this covering my face, but I just made a new discovery when you called and got too involved. I was in the lab when I picked up the phone. This helmet altars my voice. I think it makes me sound older. After our talk, I lost track of time and then your car was pulling into the drive. I did not take time to remove my helmet and greet you properly." She held out her hand.

"My name is Gem; how do you do?" Art took her hand in his. It felt warm and alive.

"Fine," he responded. "I'm Art." Gem lead him to what appeared to be an electron microscope of sorts. It had been tinkered with and there were a couple of small patches of aluminum in a couple of places on the housing. These were secured in place by tiny rivets. The unit had black, adjustable eye pieces. Gem placed the black box under the lens and flipped on a switch. The scope made a low humming sound. She looked through the eye pieces into the box and seemed to focus on something. Then she motioned for Art to look.

"What do you think of this?" she asked. Art looked and

saw a series of small round spheres. Gem moved the focus adjustment and Art's whole field of vision was filled with radiating colors. One sphere had obviously exploded and as Gem moved the focusing device the exploded particles began to move. The fragments of the sphere retreated backward until the sphere was again visible, whole, and complete. It was a photograph or x-ray of an anti-explosion recorded in precise detail. Art could not grasp the totality of it all. He removed his gaze from the eye pieces and shook his head.

"You're going to have to enlighten me as to what I just saw. I am totally lost, Gem." She shoved a lock of hair away from her eyes and looked at him. She noticed that his eyes were green. They were an unusual color. She had never seen a green color quite like it in any other eyes.

"What did you see?" she asked gently as she searched his eyes for an answer.

"It looked like you photographed or x-rayed an anti or counter-explosion. That is the best way I can describe it. If a person recorded an explosion in digital format and played it backwards, that is what one would expect to see. It would look something like what you have there in that box."

"That is what you were supposed to see," she responded while looking quickly around the room. "Only I did not play the movie backwards. Do you know what that means?"

"Maybe," he replied, not wanting to sound too enthusiastic. "It could be a trick. You could have flipped the case around before you placed it under the scope."

"No, that didn't happen. What you see is the order in which the explosion was recorded."

"Well then there could be another explanation," Art stated as he searched his mind for just the right words then proceeded to speak slowly as if describing a picture, he saw in his mind. "The beams you sent to record the explosion could have hit up against something at the end of the cylinder and bounced back before crashing into the atom or particle or whatever those little spheres are. If that happened, your unit would record the explosion from backward to forward."

"Now you're getting somewhere. I had the same theory for a while but after repeated testing, discovered something else happened that explains the order of the recording. Only the purple spheres react that way. The red and light green ones do not. They appear to explode from the outside in. The explosions I have recorded with them not only expand and contract, but they contract before they expand. It is different with the purple ones. They explode from the inside out. I think what I am capturing is the movement of anti-matter."

This struck a chord in Art's mind. He had run into something like this repeatedly in his research.

"Come over here and I will show you what I have found. Your camera seems to have just answered the big question that has been preventing my completion of an anti-gravity engine I have been struggling with for the last umpteen years." He put his arm out and placed it gently around her waist as he drew her toward his case on the table. She flinched slightly at his touch then steadied herself as his hand lingered. He pulled out his portable unit and opened it up as he spoke.

"I have been wanting to share this with someone for the last six months but have been afraid to for fear of this technology getting out. If this got in the wrong hands, or if certain entities even knew that something like this existed, my life and the lives of hundreds, perhaps millions of others could be greatly endangered. I have discovered quite by accident, a door to a liquid dimension. Once we enter it, the entire world we take so much for granted, changes. Time seems to slow down. What you are about to see must never be shared with anyone unless you discuss it with me first and we assess the possible pros and cons of the results. Do you understand? If you do not, I will close the case up and not reveal what this is."

"Wow," she responded with a look of skepticism on her face. "You are really protective of this thing, aren't you?"

"I don't mean to be stern, Gem, but yes, I am protective, and I have to be. This really is all that I insinuated and probably a whole lot more. I have not taken nearly enough time in researching the infinite possibilities contained within.

I really cannot do it by myself. I need a confidant. I need a partner who will help me figure out what this is all about. It cannot be just anyone. I need someone who knows the laws of science and physics because from what I can tell, when one enters this dimension, several of those laws diminish or disappear. The phenomenon is otherworldly. Will you promise to follow the directions I have outlined to you and share this with absolutely no one without first consulting me? I need an honest answer before I show it to you."

Gem thought about it for a moment. She was good at keeping secrets. So far as she discerned, no one knew how she had constructed the lens in her camera. Neither did anyone know how she modified the scope to read her recordings. No one knew of the composition of the substance within the plates she installed at the far end of the cylinder to record her experiments. She was good at keeping secrets and she would do her best to keep his.

"I agree to your terms. I have some secrets of my own that I want to keep control over. It is a security measure, you know. I need money to live and if what I have discovered were common knowledge, then they wouldn't need to come to me which would ultimately mean no dolotties."

"Exactly Gem. You seem to know how high the stakes are with things like these." He motioned to her scope and his case as he spoke. "I don't know enough about the ins and outs of your devices to make a judgment call, but I do know that what I have here is potentially extremely dangerous, even deadly in the hands of the wrong people. If the US or any government for that matter knew about this, they would take the device, lock me in a room somewhere and never allow me to see the light of day again. I happen to like my freedom, a lot! They would not be content with my imprisonment, when I was out of the picture, who knows what they would do with this? They could do anything they wanted, and nobody could stop them. They would have in effect the potential for ultimate control over everything and everyone and that is just too much power to place in the hands of anyone, even me. I really should destroy it, but I need it to do some things for me that I can't do without it, so I am willing to take the risk."

He opened the case and set to work. Before long he had the unit set up and the telescoping arms positioned so the gray cylinder in the center was large enough for him to place his hand through. Gem drew close with a look of wonder as she saw the thin, gray cylinder, apparently suspended in space between the conductors. Little streams of blue green electricity danced all around the edge of the dull gray mass. Art adjusted the controls down to where there was little if any power visible. MAP stood stationery, waiting.

"What do you call this?" Gem asked the question quickly with a strange little clip at the end of her sentence as if she had a hick up or were catching her breath. Art looked at her.

"Were you holding your breath or was I just imagining things?"

"Yes," she replied. "I was holding my breath. I do it a lot when I make some new observation, or when I get excited about something. It is a bad habit I have fallen into."

"What caused you to hold your breath this time, observation or excitement?" Art asked the question with a hint of teasing in his voice.

"Both," she answered. Art spoke again choosing how best to proceed to the next step with this intriguing woman.

"I am going to put my hand through the center of the cylinder, and I want you to tell me what you see. Are you ready?"

"Yes, I am very ready," she replied. "Hurry and do it quickly unless you want me to turn blue and pass out from holding my breath." Art smiled as he put his hand through the center of the ring. Gem gasped again.

"Your hand looks like it is cut off. What did you do to make that happen?"

"Nothing," he replied with a matter-of-fact voice. "The cylinder absorbs whatever enters it."

"Does it damage your skin or anything like that?" she

asked looking at the hand that was then returning from the entrance.

"No, it doesn't. Now I will show you something else even more phenomenal." He adjusted the arms further apart and lower the mass almost to ground level then adjusted the power. The cylinder sprang into a four-foot diameter circle and before she could respond, Art stepped through the ring and was gone. Gem let out a scream. He was beside her one moment then he had completely disappeared. She went around to the other side of the unit and looked. He was not there! She tried to investigate the ring, but it was a silvery gray that did not let her see anything.

Meanwhile from within, Art crept around to the back of Gem and placed his hands on her shoulders. She did not seem to notice. He went around and investigated her face. She wore a most distressed look. He saw fear and wonder at the same time. Like his own inner glowing color, she shone with a golden essence. Around her eyes however he saw a ring of violet or purple. He wondered if she had trouble with them. They looked luminescent and beautiful. Gem was staring at the opening and did not move. Art got really close to her. He noticed a small smudge on her chin. The glowing color around it was more golden green than the rest of her face. It could be a spot of bacteria or perhaps a birthmark of some sort. He put his hand through the opening and touched it. Gem screamed again as if she had been struck in the face. She backed quickly away from his touch and bumped into a bookcase. A couple of books went clattering to the floor. Art pulled his hand back in quickly then popped back through the cylinder and was again in the room. She stood white and speechless.

"How did you do that? What is this? What makes it work like that? What happens when you are inside? How does it feel? Please tell me. I have so many questions. There has never been anything like this, has there?"

"Wait just a minute," he smiled, "One question at a time. What question do you want me to answer first?" She responded with a different question than any of the others she had asked before.

"What is it like when two people are in there together?" Art had taken Kanna in a couple of times, so he knew the answer somewhat, but it was better experienced than described.

"Come inside with me and I will show you."

"No way," she responded quickly with that little clip again before she had time to think. "I don't even know you. When did I meet you? Only an hour ago and you are already asking me out?"

"Not out," he responded, "but in. Come now. I promise you will like it. After you go in and out some of those other questions you asked will be answered. I will go in first and you follow. You will see me the moment you put your head through the circle."

"OK. You convinced me but if this doesn't work out, don't ask me for any other favors." Art entered the cylinder again and waited. After a minute or so he saw a finger appear then a hand. He wanted to reach out and grab it, but he did not want to spook her again. The hand was followed by an arm then the arm went back out and the other hand appeared. Later he saw her head.

Gem proceeded slowly. She felt the cool resistance of the matter within the sphere. It was a totally otherworldly sensation. When she got up enough gumption to stick her head through, and while taking a couple of seconds to allow her eyes to adjust to the pressure, she saw Art smiling at her. It was a reflective look. His form seemed to waver back and forth as the whole dimension moved with the rhythm of the sounds from within. Then she was there. She felt her feet. They did not feel much. She seemed to bounce around like a rubber ball. She reached out for him to steady herself, but her hand appeared to penetrate his being before it came to a numbed stop. She turned her back to him and looked at the cylinder-shaped door from within. She wanted to be sure it was there so she could bound out of it quickly if anything spooked her.

"It is darker in here than out there," she commented.

Her voice reached him in haunting echoes and vibrated away as if in a tight walled canyon, "and cooler." He placed his arms around her as if to warm her. She did not resist. It was an innocent moment of awesome discovery and he felt like she needed to share it closely with him. He was right.

"Are you married?" she asked as she gave him a sheepish look. She looked like a ten-year-old peering up at him. Art was startled by the question and took a little time before he responded.

"Was. And you?"

"Was once but it didn't work out. He ran. I think he got scared. Thought I was too smart for him or something."

"Did you have any children, Gem?"

"No," she responded with a bit of sadness. "I didn't have time for any. I was always too caught up in my work. And you? Did you have any children?"

"Two," he replied. Gem pulled herself away from Art and turned so she could look into his eyes.

"Where are they now?"

"One is at the daycare. She is nearly five. Her name is Kanna. The other, a boy is not living anymore. He died with his mother."

"I am so sorry," she replied and even from within Art could see that it was genuine. It brought out a sadness in her, but she had mentioned it with compassion.

"I know, I mean I can see that you really are sorry. It is no big deal I suppose. But it is not the way I wanted things to happen." Gem reached out and placed her hand on his shoulder in an act of sympathy.

"I can tell you suffered, Art." He took her hand in his and kissed it gently. His lips passed through it before they came to rest on her liquid skin. Soft was softer in here than out there. He returned her hand to her side and looked at his watch.

"Time really flies doesn't it? At least out there. In here it almost stands still but I promised the daycare I would not be gone more than a couple of hours. I would like to come back and work with you on a couple of projects if you don't have other plans?" His comment was more of a question than a statement. She did not hesitate to answer.

"I would love it, Art." She made no pretense about wanting him to come back. It had been one of the most amazing days in her life and he was one good-looking man. "I still have a million questions to ask you and that is going to take a long time. You might have to come back repeatedly if you are willing. I know it is a bit of a drive, but I would love to have you back."

"You might come over my way sometime too," he added. "The road goes both ways you know?" They left the interior of MAP and before long Art had the unit back in his case and was shaking her hand goodbye as he headed out the door.

"I had a great time, Art," she commented in a lingering way as if she really did not want him to leave. "I will be eagerly waiting for you tomorrow. By then I will have a couple of hundred more questions."

"Write them down and I will do my best to answer each one, on second thought however, maybe you better not write them down." With that he was in the car and heading out of her driveway.

Chapter 4

Art picked up Kanna. She wore that excited, happy little smile of hers that reminded him so much of her mother. He thought of Sandra, then Gem. Gem had that same excitable spirit. She was carefree like a fleeting breeze on a windswept mountain. She was also intelligent, handy with tools like himself and incredibly beautiful. Mostly beautiful he thought. She had to have modified that unit with a camera in some way and used new technology to record her observations.

"Daddy?" Art was pulled away from his thoughts.

"Yes, Pumpkin."

"Will I ever have another Mommy again?" Art was startled at the question. Was this child insightful of what? He had just been thinking about the most important woman in his past and potentially the most important one who would be in his future when out of the clear blue, his daughter ask about it.

"Would you like another Mommy?" Without hesitating she responded.

"Yes, Daddy."

"What would you like your new Mommy to look like?" Kanna frowned for a minute as if trying to see a picture in her mind, then she answered.

"I would like her to look something like Mommy only with brown hair. She would be very smart, and pretty, and love me very much. She would read me stories and play with me and she would help you too, Daddy, with your work. We would both love her very much and make sure that no bad man ever came and hurt any of us." Art pondered his daughter's description. Gem had brown hair not like Sandra's golden blond color. Gem was very smart and as pretty a woman as he had ever seen. He had no doubt that she would love Kanna very much, play with her, read her stories and defiantly be of great help to him in his work. Did she know? Could Kanna somehow envision his thoughts? The little girl fumbled with her fanny pack. It was a gift her grandmother had given her last Christmas. Grandma had filled it with some miniature dolls and Kanna took them with her everywhere, even to bed, these, and Teddy. She pulled out a painting of a lady with brown hair.

"This is what our new Mommy will look like. I painted it at Linda's house." Art looked at the painting. He was stunned. Not only did the lady have brown hair but she had a violet ring around her eyes and a golden green spot on her chin.

"Where did you get this Kanna?" Art asked the question sterner than he meant to and Kanna almost cried. "I am sorry, Honey. I didn't mean to speak to you like that, but your picture startled me."

"I painted it, Daddy. Just like I said. I saw this pretty lady in my mind and thought she would make a good Mommy for us. Do you like her?"

"Yes, very much. I think she would make a wonderful Mommy for you."

"For us, Daddy. Not just me but you, too. We will be together, and this Mommy will never go away."

Art had to think this through. This whole thing was getting crazier by the minute. It was like a giant magnet pulling him toward a destiny he had no power to control. With MAP he once had thought he had the power of absolute choice but now he wondered? Would that choice be his? Then he realized it might be. He had been making choices and this MAP thing had been turning his thoughts into reality. Not only that, but it had also been mapping if you would, a clear path to make those thoughts reality. He would marry Gem. He knew it somehow and it would not be too long before it happened. Why? Because he wanted it that way and that is how it was working and would work. Kanna would have her Mommy with the long, brown hair.

A stray thought popped into his conscious at that exact moment. Kanna? Who is she? I have no daughter who needs a Mommy. I only had a son, Sonny. The thought flashed only for a moment then whirled away in the mist of infinity. Kanna was talking again.

"Daddy? What is it like to die, to not be any more like what happened to Sonny?" Again, Art was startled. She had perceived his thoughts again. She could even grasp some of the most remote ones and that was scary. He took her little hand in his own and answered.

"It is something like when the lights go out at night. You see everything one moment then it is dark, and you do not see anything. But more than that, you do not feel anything either. You do not feel stuff like your hand in mine and I am going to make sure that you do not have to worry about things like Mommy's going away and not coming back. I love you very much."

"I love you too, Daddy. Thank you." Art would have to think about these things, but he must not do it now. He was too physically close to his daughter. Perhaps if she were further away, he could collect his thoughts and try to figure something out. He tried to focus. He let his mind zero in on his daughter. A picture emerged at the fringe of his mind. He saw his mother.

"When are we going to Grandma's house again?" Kanna asked. Art nearly jumped with relief. He could do it too. Kanna had been thinking about Grandma and he had sensed it. There was one difference though. He could discern Kanna's thoughts consciously. Kanna on the other hand discerned his unconsciously. This would give him a little advantage, an edge you might say in raising this unusual child. The telepathy would be stronger in one direction than the other. He would have to make certain of that. He would just have to keep one step ahead of her until she discovered the truth about it herself. He pushed the thought quickly from his mind. Could she discern abstract thought or was it only image thoughts? He spoke rapidly in answer to her question to keep her from listening to the mental conversation he was having with himself. He would try one more experiment in mental telepathy with this little wonder. He consciously thought, would I rather have Sandra back in my life or Gem? I could probably go back in time and prevent the murder. Sandra had been nice but there were a few things about Gem he liked better. If he went back would Kanna be? His thoughts were interrupted by another question from Kanna.

"Daddy, I did not know mommy very well. I think I was too little when she went away. I do not remember much about her. But our new mommy I will get to know very well. That will be nice won't it, Daddy?" It had worked. This was the final proof he needed. He really should get her off to Grandma and Grandpa's house and soon.

"Would you like to go tonight and stay with Grandma and Grandpa for a couple of weeks?"

"That would be fun, Daddy. Do you think I can?

"I will call Grandma on the cell phone and ask right now." He was remembering the number in his mind when she spoke.

"Let me do it, Please, Daddy."

"How can you? You don't know her number."

"You can help me. What is it?" She took the phone and punched four buttons, then three more, then four again and hit the green call button.

"Is that the right order, Daddy?" The phone rang once, and Grandma answered.

"Hi Grandma. How are you?"

"Why fine. How are you Kanna?"

"I am ok. I have the dollies you gave me and Teddy. I play with them every day, and Daddy wants to know if I can come and visit you for a couple of weeks. He has a scientist friend he needs to work with, and they probably would not have time to take care of me because I think what they are working on is important. It is secret. Can I come and see you, Grandma?" Art was stunned at her insight. This would be harder than he imagined. That was exactly what he was thinking in so many words. It was a perfect five-year old's paraphrase of his more technical thoughts. Grandmother's voice came back over the phone.

"I would love to have you come. When can you get here?"

"Tonight, I think. Daddy needs to work with this lady right away. He will be seeing her tomorrow."

"Lady? Kanna. Is the scientist that Daddy is working with a lady?"

"Yes. She is very pretty, and she is going to be my new Mommy, but she does not know it yet. That is one of the secret things she and Daddy need to work out. That is why I need to come to your house."

Art had pulled the car off the road. He had missed his turn. Now he put his head down on the steering wheel and tried to blank all thoughts from his mind, but they were screaming at him and he must not let Kanna hear them. He mentally formed an imaginary ring around them and marked them closed to broadcasting. It worked. Kanna changed her conversation.

"How is the pony Grandpa got for me? Is he big enough to ride yet?"

"Not yet, dear but pretty soon. Grandpa must work with him a little more. He might be ready to ride before you leave." Kanna spoke again.

"Daddy pulled over to the side of the road. I think he wants to talk to you, Grandma. Here he is." At that moment it was the last thing Art wanted to do. He was so rattled, he wanted to collect his thoughts before he did anything but there was the phone.

"Hi, Mom. How are you?"

"I am fine, Son. What is this I hear about your new scientist friend?"

"Nothing much," Art lied. "She developed some device that might help me make the engine I have been working on, workable. I really do not know that much about it, but my intuition tells me she may have the missing link to make it all fit together."

"That is nice, Son. Is that all?"

"So far," he replied.

"That is not what I heard. What is this about a new Mommy? Are you engaged?"

"Not that I am aware of. I just met her for the first time today and engagement or anything like that never came up in our conversations."

"Then what was Kanna talking to me about?"

"It's really complicated, Mom. I do not understand it myself yet, but I really need some time to figure it all out. With all that is at stake here, I am afraid I would not make a very responsible father for the next couple of weeks. If you do not mind, I really need someone to see to Kanna. I may have to go on a trip, and I don't want to worry about her."

"Dad and I will love it, Art. When do you think you will be here? Should I make supper?"

"No, I want to spend a little time with Kanna before I see you. I think we will eat out on the way." Art tuned his mind to Kanna's. "She wants to go to, Humm, McDonald's to eat on the way. We will be there probably around eight p.m."

"That will be fine, Son. Looking forward to seeing both of you. Goodbye."

"Goodbye, Mother." Art pushed the stop button and wiped the perspiration off his forehead with a dirty napkin he pulled off the floor. It left a small streak of dirt where he wiped. He looked at Kanna before turning around to catch the road he had missed.

"How did you know I wanted to go to McDonald's, Daddy?" she asked with a questioning look written all over her face.

"A little bird told me. Sweetie. Come to think of it though, it really was Ronald McDonald himself." Kanna laughed.

"You are funny, Daddy, and don't worry about me. Grandma will take really good care of me. I hope she makes those big sugar cookies of hers. They taste so yummy."

"Maybe she will let you help her make them?"

"I was just thinking about that, Daddy, and how much fun it would be."

"I know, Sweetie," he replied and then thought. I know more than you can possibly know, but then he stopped himself because he really questioned if he could?

Kanna had her little suitcase packed and ready to go five minutes after she got home. Art wondered if she had remembered everything like pajamas, under clothes, toothbrush, and things like that?

"Do you want to check this, Daddy? I think I remembered everything like pajamas, panties, even my toothbrush, but I am not sure?" Why did he know that was coming? She opened the case and he looked. She needed a dress in case Grandpa and Grandma decided to go to church but that was all. Everything else was in there.

"Daddy. Do you think I should take a dress? Grandma likes to take me to church."

"I was just thinking about that, Honey. You probably better get one just in case." He watched the tiny figure head back into her room. What a wonder she was. How would he broach the subject of this child with Gem? What would she think of the unusual gift this girl seemed to have developed? If she could read into everyone's thoughts, then that was one matter. If she could only discern his, then that was another. Could he find out? He wondered? They had to pass not more than three blocks from Gem's house on the way to Mom's. Would it be to forward of him to stop by for a few minutes on the way? If they were indeed intended to be together, how would the issue of Kanna affect the relationship? When would be the best time to introduce her? Instinctively he knew. He must stop there on his way, today. He would observe the reaction between Kanna and Gem. He would know right away if his daughter's gift applied to others aside from himself. He called Gem from the cell phone. She answered and was apparently glad he called.

"I was just thinking about you, Art. Your call came at exactly the right time. I was going out to get a bite to eat and some hardware for my machine. What is on your mind?"

"I am taking my daughter to my folk's home for a couple

of weeks. She is all excited about it. We must pass about three blocks from your house. I was wondering if I could stop in and you two could get acquainted for a couple of minutes." There was no hesitancy in her voice. She came back with a reply immediately.

"I would love that more than you can imagine. Please bring her by. What time do you expect to be here?"

"I promised to take her out to Ronald McDonald's. I thought I would stop by after that. Would an hour and a half from now be a good time?"

"Why don't we make it a date, Art? I will meet you at McDonald's here in town. I have been punching the buttons a lot today and though the meter shows no traces of radiation escaping from the seals, I would not like to endanger anyone. Besides, burgers and fries and apple pies sound like a meal made in heaven. I have not eaten all day and I am starved. Will you be there by 6:30?"

"Precisely, but you scolded me earlier today about asking you out an hour after I saw you. I don't want to impose."

"You aren't asking me out. I am inviting myself out. Don't be late now."

"You neither. Bye."

"Goodbye." Kanna came out of the room with her fanny pack, the little teddy bear, her suitcase, and the miniature dolls Grandma had gotten her. She had changed her clothes. She was dressed in pink slacks and a light pink sweater. She had fixed her hair up or tried to. Somewhere she had found some pink ribbons and had tried to get them even in her hair, but one was a full inch lower than the other. Art took his hands and gently moved the higher ribbon down to match the lower one then he gave her a little peck on the lips.

"You look very pretty, Sweetheart. I see you are all ready to go." She moved her little head up and down as she spoke.

"Yup. All ready. I even have, Teddy." They went down to the car. Art picked up his case. He never went anywhere without it. For security sake he pushed the secret switch to turn off the stationery processor and they left the house.

They arrived at McDonald's at exactly 6:30. Gem pulled up in her red Sudan right beside him. They exited their car doors at the same time and Art helped Kanna out of her child seat.

"This is Kanna, Gem. Kanna, this is Gem. The scientist I am working with."

"How do you do, Ma'am?" Kanna asked in a courteous voice.

"I am fine and, how are you?"

"I'm fine too. Daddy told me you were planning to meet us here. You are very pretty."

"You are very pretty yourself, Kanna."

"Thank you. I am glad you could eat with us."

"I am glad too," Gem responded. They went into the restaurant and placed their orders. Kanna wanted a special meal. Gem and Art settled for a number 3. They ordered three apple pies for desert and were soon seated at a table. Kanna looked up at Gem and spoke.

"Daddy is taking me to Grandma's house. Grandpa got me a pony and I need to see it a lot, so it knows it is mine. Grandma and I will make some of her big, sugar cookies tomorrow then we will probably go to church the next day. It will be really fun."

"It sounds like it, Kanna. Do you like to play on the equipment in the kid's room?"

"I like the bouncing trampoline with all the balls. It is fun to slide down the slide and land in them. Do you like to play?"

"I really do, Kanna. I like to play more than I have taken the time to do lately. Getting out to see you was a particularly good thing for me to do tonight."

"I am pleased that you could come." Kanna was trying to sound very grown up about the whole thing. She was doing a good job at it too. Art wondered at the depth of this girls' actions. Where was he when she was growing up? He had been way too busy to notice her as much as she needed. It was almost like the last five years of her life had been compressed into the last few months or weeks, but he knew they had not. He had a thousand memories. The album was full of pictures. There were more however from when Sandra was there. She always had a camera close by and one never knew when a flash would go off. Gem was enjoying her burger. She was really into it. A little catsup stuck to her chin. Kanna reached up with her napkin and tenderly wiped it clean.

"You had a bit of catsup there and I wiped it off. I hope you didn't mind?" Both Gem and Art burst out laughing, then Kanna started to laugh too. It was the most fun Art had, had in months and he somehow felt that Gem sensed it too. This was the one. This was the one woman in all the world, if not all the universe who could fill the empty void in he and his daughter's life. It had happened just like he had imagined. They played on the play equipment and laughed some more then went back out to their cars. Until now Kanna had been the perfect little girl. She had been sweet, wonderful, loving, and laughing. Everyone was feeling good. Art crossed his fingers in hopes that it would not be spoiled. He conceded that she could not discern any other person's thoughts but his own. He knew he was right. There were some things he just knew. He also knew that he wanted to kiss Gem goodbye in the worst way but did not dare try.

"Gem? May I call you that?"

"Why certainly, Kanna. You sound like you have a question on your mind just ready to explode."

"I do, thank you. We probably need to go soon so we don't keep Grandma and Grandpa up too late, but may I hug you goodbye?"

"I would love that, Kanna." Gem bent down and took the little girl in her arms. Her motherly instincts came screaming to the surface from some buried place way down in the depths of a forgotten corner. She remembered how desperately she had wanted a daughter. For her though it was physically not possible, at least by normal measures. When she found out about it, she took those desires and stifled them. It was part of the reason her marriage had not worked. Her self-imposed guilt over not being able to birth a child just would not quit. She knew in an instance this was her destiny. This little girl needed a mother, and she was awed by the whole thing. She lingered with the hug and nearly cried. A couple of tears sneaked out of her eyes. Kanna looked up at her and wiped one of them away. She had a little tear coming down from one of her own eyes. She gave the lady a sweet, childlike kiss then pulled herself away before Gem could return it. Kanna was speaking again.

"I think my Daddy would like a hug too, but he is afraid to ask." Gem looked up at Art and back to Kanna then to Art again with a wondering question. He could clearly see her thoughts.

"I would like that very much, Gem. May I have the pleasure?" He opened his arms and she slipped into them for a warm embrace. It felt good to Gem. It felt like she had finally come home. They lingered only for a moment more, than exited the building going back to their individual cars. Art unlocked and opened the back door before helping Kanna with her seat belt then went around to the driver's side. He looked at Gem. She was smiling. He could see her forming some words silently with her lips.

"Yes! Yes! Yes!" She got in her car and waved as Art and Kanna pulled out. They waved back at her. Both were smiling.

Chapter 5

Art arrived home a little after midnight. He checked his mail and found an order from Spiffy Clean for 1,700 of his sanitation unites. He whistled softly as he calculated the money he would bank from that order. It would be more than a million dollars. He was not tired, so he picked up the newspaper and started thumbing through it. He came to the real estate section and glanced at the houses. There was a large log home that caught his eye. It did not have an address, but it was lake front property and there was only one lake nearby. He could see it on his way to Gem's house in the morning. He could afford a nice home now and with a possible expanding family, a bigger one would be needed. After half an hour he retired.

The physicist meditated a little before falling off to sleep and entered a dream state while still somewhat conscious. It was a state he did not get too often but in lucid dreaming, the dreamer is supposed to be able to control the dream. If he asked for the dream to solve some problem, it was supposed to do it. He asked his dream how to figure out the Metaphysical Acceleration Processor, but it was too broad a question. There was too much information to pass on. He needed to be more specific. There was one problem that bothered him. He thought back at the penny he had dropped through the hole that first day he discovered the MAP phenomena. Why could he move freely around inside the liquid universe and not be noticed? Then he asked another. Why did a jolt of volts fix items in the physical world? In the physical world only, metallic items would conduct electricity. Within the liquid universe any object would respond to the charge.

In his dream he entered the door. He saw everything glowing with auroras. There were red ones and lavender ones. He saw green and gold ones. He saw orange and blue ones. There were some pastel-colored ones too. Then while still dreaming, he exited the black hole and looked around. There were no colors surrounding anything. A giant penny appeared. On the base of the penny was a spot of violet aurora. The penny went flying through the dark hole. He saw it get smaller and smaller then come hurtling back. Just about the time it was ready to fly out of the hole, a white rat grabbed it. The rat took a bite out of the penny. The penny fell to the floor. When he looked at it, there was no glow at the base, only a chunk missing where the rat had bitten it. He could not make any sense of it. It got foggier and foggier. The next thing he knew the antique clock in the dining room was chiming. One, two, three, four, five, six, seven, eight, nine, ten. Had he slept that long? He was planning to be at Gem's by ten. He jumped out of bed and showered quickly. He did not even take the time to shave or eat breakfast.

It was after 11:30 by the time he got to Gem's house. She came out to meet him. This time she did not have the radiation suit on. She was dressed in tight slacks and a light pink top. She had taken a little time to do something with her hair. It flowed long and shiny down her back. She smiled and waved for lack of something better to do.

"Hi, Art."

"Hello, Gem."

"You got here about the right time. I have been neglecting my housecleaning very badly. I woke up at 6:00. I could not sleep any longer, so I got up and cleaned house. Do you have a pickup?"

"No. Why do you ask?" Gem motioned at a large pile of boxes and stuff in the garage while answering.

"I need to take this to the dump."

"I don't have a pickup, but I have a 4x4 van. The seats in the back will fold down. I think we could get most of it in that. Would you like me to bring it over next time I come?"

"Yes, if it wouldn't be too much of a bother. Are you hungry, Art?"

"Come to think of it, I am. I overslept and didn't take time to eat or shave." Gem looked at his face. There were little whiskers all over his chin. She took her hand and touched them gently. The sensation took Art by surprise. He stiffened.

"You look good to me, Guy." She took her hand away and led him into the kitchen. The room was full of a wonderful smell. She pulled a meatloaf out of the oven and placed it on a potholder resting on the table. She popped another dish in the microwave and got some peas boiling on the stove. In less than ten minutes they were enjoying a meal. She put a couple of chicken dumplings on his plate and spooned some peas over them. She gave him a generous portion of meatloaf and brought out a couple of sodas for them to wash it down with. It was great! Art set to work at it enthusiastically, hardly saying a word. He was thinking about how best to approach this relationship. Finally, he decided that the conversation should be straightforward. He would get his feelings out right from the start and if it scared her off then so be it. They could still work together on a professional level. He was trying to figure the best way to open the subject as he finished his last bite of roast.

"Could we talk a little, Gem, before we start to work?" Gem turned a little pale before she answered.

"Yes. We could go into the living room where it's more comfortable." She put the dishes in the sink and showed him to a soft sofa. She pulled a bean bag chair from the corner and plopped herself down a few feet in front of him.

"I'm ready," she said.

"I have been trying to figure out the best way to tell you this and I must admit, I have gone round and round. I am the type of person who must get things out in the open. I hate playing games. God gave us mouths and a mind and I think He expects us to use them. I was attracted to you the moment you removed your helmet yesterday. Kanna really likes you and I just wanted to say that if, if." Art paused a moment as he searched his mind for the way he wanted to speak the next phrase. "If I am out of line in liking you, then I want you to let me know right up front so I can get over it and we can combine our research and try to help each other find some answers on a more professional level." Gem looked down and waited for what seemed like hours before she responded.

"Are you asking me if I think it is too early for us to start a relationship?" Now it was Art's time to think. This was not going to be easy.

"What kind of a relationship were you thinking of Gem?"

"That is what I was asking you. What is your definition of liking me?"

"I don't make it a habit to womanize," Art responded. "I was very much in love with my wife. When she was taken away, I did not think I would ever find another person whom I could feel for. I tucked my emotions away and tried to forget them. There are certain things that I know deep down inside. I can sense stuff and it is a true sense. It has never failed me yet. I sensed if we allowed ourselves enough space, we could in a rather short time acquire a good relationship that would develop into something wonderful if we let it." Gem looked out the window and a soft smile caused her whole face to glow.

"I really respect the fact that you came right out with this, Art. I will tell you up front that I am not ready to hop into bed with you tonight. I will say however that I am with you on the relationship bit. I want you to be comfortable around me. If we bump into each other or happen to touch, I do not want you to stiffen and feel that it might have been out of place. We can get that out of the way right now."

Gem got up on her knees and crawl, walked over to the sofa. Art had his legs slightly open. She moved them apart, leaned in close and took his scrubby face in her soft hands. She rubbed her left cheek on his whiskers then her lips found his. The kiss was long and passionate. When it was finished, she said.

"Come on guy. I am dying to move to the next dimension with this relationship. Where is your case?" Art blinked back his surprise. He stood up from the couch and caught her just as she turned. He brought her face close again and this time he took the initiative.

"There he said, now we are even." They stayed in a meaningful hug for a few moments longer then headed for the door. He had the unit set up in a matter of minutes.

"What would you like to do now, Gem?" She looked up at him and responded.

"We didn't get far yesterday. The wonder of it got me all emotional and I started blabbering in there, so I really did not get to observe much. Let us start with going in together again and you point out some of the observations you have made that will show me how things are different from the outside."

"That sounds fair enough. Before we enter though I want to show you something that is very puzzling." He pulled a quarter out of his pocket and explained that he was going to drop it just inside the circle. He proceeded to do it. It disappeared.

"This thing seems to absorb movement. If I drop the quarter from this side, it disappears. I must go inside to find it. If on the other hand I drop it from the other side and go in to see it, the camera shows it there before I release it."

"Time is different from one side to the other. One side operates behind our time out here and the other side operates ahead of it."

"That is something like my camera," she exclaimed in an excited tone. Her eyes lit up for a split second then faded just as quickly as a question popped out of nowhere. She was about to ask it, but Art spoke first.

"There is something funny though, Gem. Did you see me walking around yesterday when you were out here, and I was in there?"

"No. You went in but never came out." Art shook his head.

"I didn't come out, but I walked around. I walked up behind you, even got in front of you. You had a little spot of green at the base of your chin. The rest of you was bathed in gold except your eyes. They had a ring of violet around them.

Do you have a birth mark on your chin?" Art looked closely at it. There was nothing visible.

"When I was a small girl, I fell on the ice and a large chunk of skin was ripped out of my chin. They did a skin graft from my stomach. I used a lot of vitamin E oil and the scars are almost invisible."

"Well, that explains what the green mark was then. When we go in there, you will see that all living matter has some sort of aura around it. Animate objects like this quarter do not unless they are dirty enough to have germs on them, then they have a slight glow also. I had a weird dream about that just last night. I was trying to reason this out when a large penny flew into the hole. It had a spot on it. It spun around inside for a while and started to come out, but a white rat stopped it. He bit the penny right where the spot was. When the penny came out, there was no color on it. The bite chunk was missing. I went to sleep before I could figure out what it meant."

"To be frank with you, Art, I don't know enough about your discovery to draw forth any interpretations from dreams. I have one observation though. Something was removed from the quarter while it was inside."

"I could understand that a little." Art placed his hand up and rubbed his chin as a faraway look came into his eyes. In his mind he was seeing a clear picture of his machine with the many colors on surfaces within. "My invention is based on that fact. Living microbes could possibly be absorbed. When I compare the two universes, the one inside seems balanced perfectly while the one without is not."

"I don't mean to change the subject but what did you name this phenomenon, Art?" She pointed to the accelerator as she asked the question that had popped unexpectedly into her mind earlier.

"I named it MAP. That stands for Metaphysical Acceleration Processor. The name just popped into my head. Why do you ask?"

"I was simply curious. Do you regularly have accelerated

metaphysical experiences in there?"

"I really never took the time to think about that but now that you mention it, I would have to say yes. Not only metaphysical but also in some cases paranormal as well. I remember vaguely getting upset at my clock for taking a vision of my former wife away from me. I was so mad at it, I mentally ripped it from the wall. It broke in pieces but the funny thing about it is, I never got it repaired. When I saw it the next day, it was back on the wall."

"What powers the device and what does the processor part of the name mean?" She was asking questions out of the blue now. The hundred or so she had written down while housecleaning were not being addressed.

"You are good, Gem. First, I believe the power source comes from the magnetic fields that are in the earth. It somehow taps into them. The other option is it could be powered by the 'black sun.' This is that dark black hole at the center of our galaxy that causes it to rotate. I think some of Tesla's devices were powered by that as well as some of the UFO craft designed by the German's near the close of the war. I placed rechargeable batteries in this portable unit, but I do not need to recharge them. They continue to operate at peak performance, perhaps being recharged by the forces within the liquid universe. This was a possible new function of this unit that I thought on for a bit. This unit produces more energy than it consumes. It has an element that operates outside of the realm of physics as we know it. It is at least 200%, perhaps even more efficient than any machine in the known physical realm. If the unit stays in there for a short time it is always ready to capture a gray, what should I call it, a gray gate or entry point. So far as the processor part goes, it is in effect its own power source. Thanks for the question. I never pondered on it that much before. Paranormally speaking perhaps this thing helps a person accelerate the metaphysical part of life and even process those things, bring them from the realm of thought into the physical." Art paused a moment then picked his arms up and threw them down a couple of times as if disgusted with himself.

"Now I know why. I know how. Why didn't it register before? It makes sense. But no, that cannot be. No way. It is impossible!" He smacked himself on the head a couple of times. Gem ran over and grabbed his arm to restrain it. She looked scared.

"What? Tell me. You got some insight here. Let us hear it. Don't leave me in the dark now."

"No, I can't. I cannot even go there. It is too deep."

"Art!" She raised her voice in a scolding manner. "We have to be honest with each other. It is the only way this is going to work. If you cannot tell me these things, then we might as well quit before we start. You yourself said you needed to come right out in the open with things. So, let me know what you said can't be."

"Could we set down then, Gem? I do not even know if I can take what I am about to say standing up. If I cannot, then you probably cannot either. I will tell you my story and then get back to your concerns. On second thought, why do not we go in there and look around first. It will help you understand my story better." They entered.

Gem was not as used to the liquid environment within like Art. She felt a great deal of pressure in her lungs. She did not like the feel of it on her clothes. They seemed to cling to her skin like a shirt just out of the dryer. It took her a while to get used to the delayed reaction within also and to the muffled sounds and the darker lighting. Art pointed out the various colors around the living things. He took her to the kitchen and showed her the sink. It had little splotches of color all over it.

"Do you have any Lysol?" he asked while looking around as if he expected to see a can on the counter or something. She pulled some out from a cabinet and he sprayed the sink. He showed Gem how the colors went out when the microorganisms died. He opened her dishwasher. She had clean dishes in it. There were no glowing colors on any of them. Everything was sterol. The dishes from their recent meal, however had colors all over them.

"When I first noticed this, I created an invention. It is a type of scope that enables people to see the colors around germs and bacteria. They can tell when a place is sterilized. A manufacturer is producing it right now. I just got an order from Spiffy Clean for 1,700 units. The income from that one order will be substantial."

"I want to test what I thought about out there before I tell you. If the test proves good than I will know the other could be remotely possible." He went over to the couch and sat down. Gem watched as he did a few breathing exercises, then spaced out. After a while he spoke in a slow relaxed tone.

"I am going to try and move the phone book on that stand over there, do an act of telekinesis for you." Art focused on the book. It wavered then moved. It lifted off the table and he willed it to him. He reached out and took it in his hand. Gem was amazed.

"Some people can move things with their mind out there. Can you?"

"Not out there," he answered. "I will try something else I have never done before so it might not work."

"Tell me so I can know what to expect," Gem pleaded. The purple intensity of the rings around her eyes brightened as she spoke. Perhaps it was a surge of adrenalin or extra energy that came from her excited state.

"I am going to make something with my thoughts.

As Gem looked at Art, she noticed the color of the aura around him change. It brightened and turned almost to a sparkling blue. It was wonderful to see these vivid colors.

I am going to make a white ball." He took a couple of more deep breathes then proceeded. He was at the river now, that limitless supply that fills ones needs and sometimes one's desires. He drew some white plastic from a vein and brought it out. He formed it in his hand and shaped it perfectly, then opened his eyes. He held his hand out to Gem. She saw a plastic ball about 2" in diameter.

"How did you do that?" Gem gasped. Her breath

vibrated, she was facing Art. When the current hit his chest, she noticed it go in and out a little.

"I simply willed it out of the river. Have you ever delved into metaphysical things like meditating, image streaming, lucid dreaming and stuff like that?"

"No, I can't say that I have. My mind is logical. I suppose the closest I have come to what you are talking about is when I see in my mind a picture of what modifications I want to do to some equipment. After I visualize it, I go and do it."

"That is a good start. That is the foundation. From there, Gem, the limits to what you can do are only stifled by your belief. Let us go back out now. I am ready to tell you my story." They left the MAP and settled themselves comfortably on the couch. He started with the story of the murder of his wife and son and how he knew deep inside that the neighbor had done it. He came to his wife's dying request and struggled for a while with it. He tried to remember. Somewhere off in the distance he heard her say. "My only regret is that I could not give you the daughter you wanted." He turned to Gem and with a pleading look in his eyes for her to believe and proceeded with his theory.

"My wife had only one regret she voiced before dying. When I tell you what it is, you probably will not believe it. But please you must. I am not making this up. I now believe MAP has more ability than I had ever imagined. My wife's regret was that she knew she would die before she could give me a daughter." Now it was Gem's turn to respond.

"No way, Art! There is no way in the world you are saying that Kanna is..." just like that white ball, something fabricated from your mind, she thought but dare not mention. "It's just is not possible."

"But it was, Gem and is. One day I was inside looking at an album of family photos and I saw my wife and son. I missed them so much I went back in my mind to a time when Sonny was younger. I remember how the eyes of he and his mother were so real looking. I let my thoughts bring her back. I remember we got passionate and she put the boy down and we made love. The stupid antique clock pulled me back to reality. That is when I got mad at it and with my mind wrenched it from the wall. When I went back downstairs and out of the dimension, Kanna was laying on the couch in the next room. I wondered who she was at first then I knew all about her. I had a thousand memories of her. I remember her birth and her first, second and third birthdays. I remember her playing with Sonny. I remembered when Sandra took pictures of them. One minute she was not and then she was there and now is. It happened because when I was in there with Sandra, she was conceived from that experience. The clock brought me back to my time some six years later. But part of my life had changed. We had created a baby. Since it happened, she had to exist. She can read my mind and I can read hers. I cannot keep anything from her. I really don't know how to raise her."

Gem shook her head. Kanna was real, as real as any little girl. She had held her in her arms just yesterday and cried. They could go to the telephone now and call her and she would answer. The rest of the story was just too weird to swallow. But Art had proved it. He had created a plastic ball from the substance of his thoughts or the river he claimed was there to draw from.

"You say she can read your mind? How do you know that?"

"I just recognized it yesterday on the way home from the daycare. I would think of something and she would talk about it. For instance, I remembered fleetingly just for a second that Sandra had not physically given me a daughter and Kanna asked me what it was like not to be. I thought how she needed a Mom to care for her and she asked if she would ever have a Mommy again. I asked her what she wanted her Mommy to look like and she described you, like you are in there. Let us go back in. I want you to look in the mirror."

They went back into map and entered the bathroom. He pointed out the green spot on her chin. He also showed her the lavender rim around her eyes. Then they exited again.

"After describing you verbally, she pulled out a picture she had painted of her new Mommy. It was a picture like a five-year-old would paint of a person, but the painting had a little green spot on the chin and there was violate around the eyes. I was so rattled by it I missed my turn. Then I tried to see if I could read her thoughts. I could see a picture of my mother and she started talking about Grandma. She told grandma that she needed to stay there for a couple of weeks so, quote 'Daddy and the scientist could work on some secret important things.' I was thinking about that at the precise moment. She also told grandma that the scientist was going to be her new mommy, but she did not know it yet. Mom got on the phone to me and asked if I was engaged to you."

Gem was shaking her head for real now.

"I am a scientist and I have never believed in stuff like this. If your story is true, then when is the wedding going to be?" She asked it quickly and with a little laugh. Art was hurt a bit. He was not expecting that one. Had she become a believer so quickly or was she joking with him?

"You must have had some reason behind that question. Tell me what is between the lines." Now it was time for Gem's story.

"Do you remember when Kanna asked me for a hug yesterday?"

"How can I forget?"

"When I was holding her, some deep emotions that had been locked up way down in a forgotten corner of my being were released. I had the distinct impression that to be her mother was my destiny. When I found out that I could not have children, it nearly killed me. I think that is what really came between Robert and myself. I had so much guilt that I could not give him children. I blamed myself and I must say, took it out on him. After we divorced, I buried all hope of ever having another relationship. But when I saw that little girl and felt her soul cry, the Mommy came back to life in me, and I knew that was my destiny. I knew I would marry you and become a mother to your daughter. I knew it would happen because I wanted it to. I have never wanted anything as much as I want this, Art. And I am so happy that it is happening."

Art reached out and took Gem in his arms. He held her close while struggling to control his emotions. Then it came. All the bitterness, all the pain, all the loss burst from his anguished soul and he started shaking, then sobbing like a baby. Gem was crying too. It felt so good. They cried for several minutes, each letting go of the hurt and letting the healing tears wash them clean. They lay there a long time, finally falling into a restful sleep. Complete, fulfilling sleep that was long overdue for both. There was something about being together that made it so. They slept for hours. Somewhere in the distance a clock chimed. 1, 2, 3, 4, 5, 6, 7, 8, 9.

Chapter 6

It was after 9:00 in the evening when they awoke. Both were surprised at how long they had slept. They kissed for a few minutes then Gem started the conversation.

"We still haven't figured much out have we?"

"Not really. There is a powerful lot of potential setting over there and it is like the thing does not want us to find out any more than is necessary. Do you think this technology came from some advanced form of civilization, Gem?"

"If you mean, do I think it was planted here for some purpose, which some higher form of intelligence is controlling, I will have to say yes and no. No, in that I do not think it is an alien implant. Yes. In that there is a higher form of intelligence here at work, but it is not out of reach for the normal individual."

"So, you don't think that someday we may wake up and find this thing gone?" Art looked at Gem with one of those sober expressions that men get when they are serious about the question they are asking.

"You know more about this than I do, Art. But let us assume that it is here for only a short time. Why would it be here, or why would this higher entity enable you to give birth to, how should we say this? Give birth to a daughter of your thoughts? What would the higher intelligence gain from studying your unique situation?" Gem pulled away from her new friend as if viewing him for the first time from a distance. She noticed one lock of hair at the back of his head that stood up like a duck tail. This brought a slight smile to her face.

"I wish I could think of something, but my mind is drawing a blank." Art really did try to investigate his mind for an answer but there was nothing there at this precise moment. Then he continued speaking. "I love Kanna very much. Sometimes I feel she has only been in my life a few months than at other times I know she has been there for her full five years. Maybe both views are correct."

"What do you mean, Art?" It was Gem's turn to draw a blank as if this strange new machine was begging to be left alone with its own secrets. "How could both views be correct? Did your wife ever have an abortion or miscarriage? If so, this child could really have been conceived while you were physically rather than only mentally with her inside that thing." Art took some time to ponder the question and think back over his life. Nothing unusual or out of the ordinary in her behavior came up so far as he could remember.

"Not that I am aware of, but she was quite modest that way. She could have kept a secret from me but somehow, I do not think Kanna is the essence of an aborted or miscarried child. I believe she is the direct result of that time we spent on the couch. She has been in existence for five years, but the time is split. Most of her life was lived in the subconscious realm. When the timing was right, when I needed her to help me cope with my losses, she came. I think she came to bring justice and perhaps stop more innocent people from being destroyed. On the other hand, I have heard there are an infinite number of parallel universes. In another, parallel universe she could have been created under normal circumstances and somehow I jumped from my current universe into another with her in it."

"As for the other question, I do not think there is a time limit on this discovery either. I have assembled the processor in several different locations, and it has never failed to capture a doorway. That part of this is purely physical. I also have another unit, a stationary one. I have had them both open at once." Gem really looked excited now. The thought of more than one of these gateways existing at the same time brought a flood of new possibilities to the forefront of her scientific thought processes. She always was fascinated by new discoveries in science. This was her element, and this was her soulmate. He was here right in front of her.

"So, there is more than one door?" she questioned as she tried in her mind to envision the stationary unit thought he had not described it.

"Precisely but they lead to the same place. In there." Art motioned to the portable unit as he responded.

"Are you sure?" She was really letting her mind go wild now. "If you went in one and I went in another, could we meet inside at some point?" Art tried to picture this event happening in his mind. He could see the unit's side by side and both disappearing through the doorway only to meet inside and embrace. He really did want another kiss from this beautiful, intriguing woman.

"I think so, but I never tried that because aside from Kanna, you are the only person I have shared this with and, well I haven't had many discussions with her about physics. She is." "Five." Gem cut him off. "I know. What did you expect my research with the particle beam camera to do for you? Help you find your soulmate?" The question came out unexpectedly. She had not been planning to say that at all. What had gotten into her suddenly? Art caught on but went on as if she had not made the blunder.

"I had taken pictures a little ahead and a little behind time with a normal video camera and a digital one. I wanted to see what a different form of image recording might reveal about MAP. I did not realize that your camera was so large and stationary. After seeing it, I do not know how I would set it up to expose anything inside the new dimension. It looks to me like it photographs on an atomic level. I was looking for something that would record a wider spectrum and be much more compact, perhaps even portable."

"It can record on a wider spectrum, Art. It can take x-ray exposers in layers. When you were here, I had the beam focused down to its smallest size. I was also shooting particles at each other with speeds faster than light speed, I think, in hopes of recording explosions on a quantum level. That is something the other cameras are not designed to do. It is very versatile though. It has other features that allow it to do recordings on the level that you are talking about. I would probably be safe in saying that the modifications

I have made have enabled this to do things that no other piece of equipment is capable of, yet. I can pick up a book for instance and take pictures of different pages at different depths with it. In its medical application it was designed to take pictures of different organs within the body. You are right about one thing though; it is not very portable. It also emits radiation. That is why I need to suit up while using it. They do have portable models out now that can be operated without radiation suits. This unit's technology was outdated long ago, that was before I installed some upgrades of my own design. There is something I would like to try. I would like to go through MAP and see how the machine operates in the liquid dimension." It was Art's turn to get interested now. A whole barrage of new ideas where swimming around in his brain since meeting this remarkable woman with her intuitive mind. Sandra was amazing but she had never interacted with him at this level of scientific discovery.

"Are you telling me there are portable cameras like yours available today?"

"Yes. There are three over at the medical building where I purchased this one. One of the units was for sale at the same time this one was, but I did not have the money to purchase it. You must realize the more portable unites do not have the ability to do what this modified unit does. No one that I know of yet has this precise technology in any other unit."

"Did they ever sell the unit you said was for sale?" Art tried to visualize the smaller unit in his mind but could not take this monster unit and get any sort of a vision of what a compact one might look like.

"Not that I am aware of. It is locked in a storage closet." Gem could clearly see it sitting on a shelf collecting dust even as she spoke.

"Let's go and get it, Gem."

"You mean steal it from the hospital, Art?"

"Not steal it, borrow it. We could take it out of the container and they probably would not know it was missing. We could use it for a while and return it with no one knowing any different. If it were used within MAP, it would never be moved in the physical world. It would still be there. If my theory is correct, in this liquid environment we are in a parallel universe something like I mentioned with my former life with Sandra but not exactly. In my own testing I could move things around from inside and they would not be moved outside. The only way I could make the move permanent was to zap the items I moved inside with a few hundred thousand volts to reset them in the same location in the physical universe. I checked it out with cameras. It would be so much better to have a real, live partner to observe in real life." Art's excitement was extinguished shortly though by her response.

"Are you sure about this parallel universe thing? If you are not 100% certain I would not want to try it. It does not fit with the man I think you are. Besides what could a portable unit do that mine can't?" she asked rather defensively as a matter of fact.

"OK, you got me. I will tell you what I need it for. It is a selfish reason, but I think with it I could prove that the man who killed my wife and son was my neighbor. How much are they asking for the other unit?"

"You don't want to know, Art. It's a bunch." Gem thought of her dwindling bank account and how she needed to get her revised unit to the point of producing some serious cash or she would need to go back to work full time, something she did not relish one bit.

"I only need the camera for one day. If I cannot figure anything out in that length of time, then I will let it go. I have, kind of, already but if he preyed on my wife and son, the next neighbor he moves in by could be a victim and the next and the next. I really believe he is a serial killer. If I could link him to the murder of my wife and son, I am sure there are probably others. He could be stopped."

"So, you want to play detective now?" It was a snub remark and she regretted saying it once it left her mouth, but it had happened.

"Yes, I do. There was an unexplained murder in the

city he moved from. Same kind of thing. It was brought up in some of the trial documents, but he had a good lawyer who directed the attention away from those papers about as skillfully as I have seen it done." Art really had studied into this man's background and not all the pieces fit together like they were supposed to.

"How do you propose to 'borrow' the camera from the hospital?" Gem asked, thinking she had him.

"I would need your help, Gem. Getting it out is the easy part. We will just walk in and take it. No one will know we are even there. All we need to do is enter the hospital through MAP. Remember a person within is not seen. They can walk among others unnoticed. In MAP dimension, all movement is absorbed. We will go in, take it. I guarantee it will appear to be there in real time, in fact it will be there in real time. They could even use it at the same time we are using it and it would function in both dimensions at the same time. I do not know that much about it since this is still a bit new to me, but I do know it would be as if it never happened. Do you know how to operate the portable unit, Gem?"

"It is a piece of cake, like taking a walk in the park. There is nothing to it," she responded, remembering back to the time she had looked it over before placing her money on the large broken unit. "If you really believe this guy is a serial killer and we can prevent him from hurting others, I might go along with you, but I don't like your way of going about it. There are too many unknowns, especially with this new technology. I would rather keep things upstanding and legal. Since my recognition in the science article, I am somewhat of a celebrity. I am sure if I were to ask the administrator, he would let me use it, especially if I told him that his medical facility would be mentioned if another breakthrough came up."

"You are right, Gem. What was I thinking? I keep forgetting this great discovery has even greater responsibilities that go with it. Do you think it is too late to ask him now? Could you get on the phone and ask him right away?"

"Why so quick? Can't this wait until tomorrow?"

"It could, but I have just slept for eight wonderful hours with the woman of my dreams and I feel like an adventure. It is good for the soul you know." The old Art was creeping back out of the shell all this technical talk had placed around them. He grinned and winked at her. She caught it and while returning the act proceeded to speak.

"What kind of an adventure are you referring to?"

"If we got permission to use it, we would not have to tell him how we plan to pick it up would we?"

"No, she answered." Now this was a mystery, and she was up to a good one about now.

"We could still use the MAP dimension and when or if they noticed that it was gone, then the administrator could tell them he gave you permission to use it. That would be the end of the questioning. If no one ask, then no one would know the difference anyway. Besides, I plan to use it within the MAP universe. It would only disappear out of its place at the hospital if it were taken into the physical universe through the gray doorway."

"OK, Art, you convinced me. I will call him. This sounds like the perfect thing to do this evening. I can hardly wait to see how you plan to carry it out." She picked up the phone and after a ten-minute conversation procured permission to use the camera. The administrator had only one condition. He wanted a written letter of request from her so he could put it on file in case there was any damage done to the unit. He also told her she could use it if she wanted but if damaged, she would be responsible for the repairs.

Art and Gem got into the van and headed for the hospital. Gem knew where the keys were kept. They were in a room that would not be in use at this time of evening. There would be someone at the information desk and the building had a night watchman but that should not be a problem. She had her own pass so they could get in. They would walk in together, go to the office where the keys were, set up MAP, enter and then proceed to the storage closet. Gem and Art would open the door and remove the camera then walk out in the new dimension with the merchandise. Once outside they could find some secure place to assemble MAP again and reemerge into the physical realm. It would be a good way to test a few theories, just in case an emergency came up some time in the future. One never knew what might happen when dealing with the metaphysical. The lady at the information desk greeted Gem as she entered.

"Hi, Gem. We have heard about all the attention you have been getting lately. Good going."

"It has been interesting, Connie," she replied.

"What concepts are you working with now in your research?" She asked the question but was not committed to receiving an answer. Her focus was on the smart phone in front of her. The scientist felt it was more to make conversation than out of genuine interest.

"I am working on some metaphysical applications with Professor, Arthur Goldstein here. You may have heard of him. He worked in the physics department over at the University."

"Dr. Goldstein? Yes, I remember hearing about him. Let me see what was it that happened a couple of years ago? Oh, Now I remember, yes, um Goldstein, but never mind that now. How do you do Dr.? Connie started to come to life, too much life. She took one look at Art and went through an amazing personality transformation.

"I can't complain at this time. Thank you for asking, Connie is it?"

"That's me, in the flesh." She responded as she shook her chest a bit revealing some not so well concealed curves.

"Nice looking man, Gem! Connie was chewing on a wad of gum and wavered the man, a little on Gem's name. Gem continued, trying to hide her discomfort at the comment."

"We are here to pick up some equipment the administrator is kind enough to allow us to use. I have a letter he requested. Could you put it in his mailbox for me?" Gem handed the letter to the receptionist as she spoke. Connie took it and crumpled one of the edges a bit then proceeded to smooth it out on desk.

"Sure," she replied. She stuffed the paper in an overstuffed box behind her and went back to work. Gem and Art headed for the office where the keys were kept.

"Sorry about Connie, Art. I did not know that this was her night at the desk. She does things her own way." Gem pointed a thumb over her shoulder back toward the office door they had just exited.

"I have no doubt that she does." Art spoke with a bit of humor in his voice and perhaps a tad bit too much enthusiasm.

"What is that supposed to mean? Remember I found you first," the lady queried as she looked at the corner of the hallway up ahead. She opened the door to a small room.

"Nothing much," Art finally responded. "Just a comment. And as for you finding me, I would not have it any other way. Like I said to her, I don't have any complaints."

They set up MAP and both entered. Art followed the lady a step and a half behind. The halls glowed with pink and purple colors. The handles on the doors were badly colored. It was kind of creepy thinking of all the bad bugs that might be lurking around especially in a hospital that was supposed to be sanitized. The worst thing about the doors were, they had to be opened. A door opening of its own accord might be hard to understand outside of the realm of metaphysics but then it wouldn't be seen or would it? Gem still was not completely convinced. This could be complicated trying to figure out with MAP sucking up movement and all. They had success. They entered the storage closet, Gem showed Art the case with the unit and they took it back to the little room. From there they collapsed MAP and proceeded out of the building right past Connie. She never looked up. They were passing through the last door when the night watchman came around the corner. It was one of those delayed ones that met the safety code for handicap people. Apparently, the night watchman never noticed it open and close. Gem sighed with relief then spoke.

"Where do you propose to get back to the real world?"

"It is late, and the traffic is not that bad. We can do it at your house.

"You don't plan to drive in, here do you?" Gem made a complete circle with her hands spread.

"Why not? I have done it before. It makes for a real fun road trip. I have driven into the backs of other cars and they never noticed a thing."

"You have got to be putting me on, young man." Gem was getting more and more skeptical as the evening progressed but was her skepticism based on the facts she was witnessing? So far everything had worked out just as Art stated it would. It appeared they could walk in the same room as people, walk past them, even talk to them or bump into them and raise no response. This was the creepy part of the whole scenario. Just to ease her mind she voiced her concern.

"Be careful!" Art came to close to an iron pole marking the entrance of the parking lot. The van ran into a portion of it. There was a slight delay, and the muffled sound came filtering through the mist.

"I don't think we can be hit?"

Gem was getting used to the liquid state. Her steps were sure now and balance was no problem. They had passed through town and were stopped at the last intersection when a car turned the corner right into them. There was a delayed crash, and the cars head lights were knocked out.

"That is impossible!" Art exclaimed. "How did that happen?" He knew about the taser. Could the car have given off an unusually high electronic pulse that made the vehicle switch universes? He had to act fast. He pulled out the taser and zapped the door handle a couple of times with the unit powered up to a million volts. Then he quickly backed up and bypassed the car he hit making a sharp turn at the corner. There was no other way for Art to communicate with an officer or the unfortunate driver of the other vehicle.

"Are you ok, Gem?" he asked as he turned and saw her slumped back in her seat. She did not answer. The impact had caused her head to smash into the side of the window.

She was unconscious and bleeding. A streak of blood was pouring down from a gash on her face. It trickled down the window and found a small flaw in the rubber then continued down into the center of the door. Art hurried to her house. He took her keys and opened the door. He carried her inside and lay her down on the kitchen table. There was a dish towel, so he dampened it and washed the blood away. The cut was not deep, but she might have a scar. It would probably be best to take her to the clinic, especially with a head wound. He went to the car and got out the case. Soon MAP was assembled, and he returned to the kitchen. Gem was still out. Since he zapped the van into the real world, he needed to get her back inside, and quick. He managed to place her in a recliner. In a few minutes she came to and started talking.

"What happened?" Art did not respond right away but flashed a quick question back at her.

"Are you OK?"

"Aside from a slight headache, I feel great! Is there anything I should know?"

"You got a cut on your face. I was planning to take you to the clinic and get it treated but I would have to do it from out there, so I brought you in here."

"Could you bring me a mirror? You will find one in the bathroom." Art went there and found a blue one hanging on the wall. He brought it out and handed it to her then went around and looked. The cut had stopped bleeding and a scab had formed. Gem looked at it and run her finger over the area.

"I must have been out for a long time. This is scabbed over already. How long was I unconscious?" she pulled her hand back and looked at it. There was a small smear of blood just slightly coloring her finger. That was all.

"About 20 minutes is all."

"Come on Art. It had to be longer than that. No cut scabs over in 20 minutes. Look? It is already starting to heal." She put the mirror down and resumed talking as she ran her fingers over the wound.

"I don't think we need to go to the clinic. When I had

the skin graph on my chin, my scars healed up quite nicely. I will get out the vitamin E oil again and it will be good as new in a week or two. What does the van look like?" She attempted to look out the window as she spoke, but Art was blocking her view.

"I haven't had time to check. You were still bleeding when I brought you in. I washed the blood away and sat up MAP."

"What happened to the other car?" Gem was starting to worry again as she thought of the complications associated with this midnight adventure.

"I don't know. I saw that the head lights were knocked out at least the one on the left. I did not stick around long enough to see. I could not. If an officer came along, all he would see was a car with no one in it or some other strange thing. I would not be able to communicate with him because that is not possible from in here. So, I zapped the van into the real world and took off. If anyone saw anything at least it would be a whole vehicle and not a partial one. There is only one thing that could have happened, something must have shorted out the vehicle but not completely. Part of the van was in the physical world and part of it was in the MAP dimension."

Gem picked up the mirror again and touched her face. The scab flaked off and fell on the table. There was a slight scar where the gash had been, but it was not bad at all. She and Art just stood there in wonder.

"I never would have believed it. This has never happened before. I never was sick, so I never had a chance to see what the differences were in here from a medical standpoint. Do you understand what this means, Gem? A person could make millions, even billions bringing sick people into this dimension and charging outlandish prices. Healing times must be accelerated by at least a hundred times in here." Gem stood up and went over to Art. He opened the unit, and they were soon in the physical world again. Just then there was a loud knock at the door. Gem went and opened it and an incredibly angry man started yelling at her.

"What kind of contraption hit me? All I saw was a frame of a car. Where did you park it? How did you drive it? It did not even have tires. You also killed my buddy. He was thrown from the car. I watched him die right in front of me. I called the police, and they will be here in a minute. You had better have some answers." Art ran the assessment through his mind. What must have happened? Something shorted out in the ground wire that was attached to the frame. The electrical pulse had not been strong enough to completely set the van from the MAP universe to the physical universe. Only part of the rig materialized. He briefly thought of the post he had scraped on his way out of the hospital parking lot. Perhaps? His quick thinking with the taser had finished the switch. Gem had been knocked out. She had not seen a thing. What would he tell the police? Fortunately, the mad man was half drunk. That would help.

"What did you see? Tell me again." Art questioned.

"I tell you it was a floating frame, it hit me and busted out my light. I followed it here." The man's eyes were wide with fear. He was clearly traumatized. The alcohol clearly had taken control of his motor skills. Along with bloodshot eyes he fit the picture of a drunken driver to the tee.

"Was the thing you saw a frame or a van?"

"It was a frame then it turned the corner and all I saw was this van. It suddenly popped out of nowhere. You better have some answers."

Just then the flashing red and blue lights turned into the driveway. Two policemen got out and came up to the house where Art, a confused Gem and the man was arguing on the porch. He was shaking like he had seen a ghost.

"What happened here?" asked one of the officers while brandishing his weapon.

"This man was riding on a frame of a car and hit me in front as I turned the corner. He knocked out one of my headlights. But he has hidden the frame."

"Is that story true?" the officer asked Art. He looked a

bit amused as if he were having a hard time swallowing the tale. "Were you driving down the road on a vehicle frame?"

"No, sir. I can assure you I was not. There is no frame of a car anywhere around here. You are free to look."

"He must be hiding it in that garage, officer. I swear I saw it. Just look at my light. That will prove it is so. Ask him to open up the garage." the man was frantic now, he looked like he was about to go crazy. One never knew with a person who could not be reasoned with.

Art did not hesitate. He nodded to Gem and she went inside and hit the button. There was only her red sedan inside, no frame. The officer took out a breath analyzer and tested the man then drew a line and had him walk it. He did not perform positively to say the least.

"I am sorry this happened to you." The officer shook his head as he spoke. "This one has had too much to drink. We will take him down to the station and let him dry out for the night. A tow truck will be by in 20 minutes to remove the vehicle. Once again, sorry for the inconvenience."

They handcuffed the man and put him in the back seat of the patrol car. They could hear him complaining from inside.

"You folks had better watch out. Once I get out, I will get to the bottom of this. Just you wait and see. I have connections." The car pulled out of the drive and was soon gone. Shortly after a tow truck came and removed the vehicle.

"What was that all about?" Gem asked after all was quiet again.

"One of my theories about MAP just got confirmed again, let us set it up and go inside. I want to show you something unless you think you have had enough excitement for the evening."

"I have got a better idea. You can tell me and/or show me about it later but right now... What are physical relationships like inside of there? If healing rates are a hundred times better, is sex a hundred times better also?" She stood smiling up at him with a mischievous grin. Art looked at her hesitating a little before he spoke.

"Do you feel up to finding out?"

"We might as well, kiddy-O. It would make an interesting climax to a very strange day. We ate, experimented with MAP, cried, slept, burglarized a medical institution, got in a car wreck, I got knocked out, you escaped being ticketed by the police, I got all healed so why not?" She started taking off her top, but Art stopped her.

"Let me do that, but don't you want to do it in there?" They entered the gateway together. Inside he took his time. Part way into it his thoughts were interrupted by the memory of his time with Sandra.

"What happened, Art? You went away suddenly."

"I was thinking about kids. Last time I did something like this I came out and found a four and a half to five-year-old girl in my house. What will happen if we do something in here?"

"Nothing, Art. It is impossible for me to have children. It's ok." Once again, the violet color around her eyes intensified as she spoke.

"Out there maybe, but in here?" he questioned. "If a cut can heal in half an hour, you might be able to bear children after spending some time in here."

"I never thought of that. You might be right. We could use protection."

"It's your call, Gem." She left his arms. He watched her walk away. When she returned, they continued. When it was all over, Art had to admit. Love with her, within was one "Gem" of an experience, at least ten times better than anything he had experienced out there. What made it so was love. In here the physical senses were heightened only a little more than outside but the emotional senses were like being on a run-away train. He recovered a lot faster. They did it again within only minutes. Then they slept for a while, entwined together in a loving embrace that satisfied the need of their lonely hearts.

They awoke late in the morning and made love again

before getting up. Art did not want to get up and neither did Gem but now that their longing had been filled, at least for the time being, there were things to do and places to go. Art wanted to take the portable unit over to his house and get to work. The urgency for him to do this though had somewhat lessened. He no longer had feelings of hatred and bitterness. Now it was a sense of duty. He had experienced life so precious. He had come close to losing this beautiful angel that was fast becoming an extension of his soul. As he thought of someone else, perhaps another pretty woman somewhere being subjected to the inhumane treatment that he felt his x-neighbor was capable of inflicting, he had to prove it and after that, stop it. Yet he did not know what he would do if he found the evidence he knew was there. Would he go through the long legal processes again or find a simpler means to bring justice? With MAP he had the power to do terrible things beyond imagination. He did not want to go there though. Somehow, he wanted to keep this world in the elevated state that had been his experience with it so far. If the good was this good, how bad was the evil? He pushed the thoughts out of his mind and kissed Gem again. He was almost tempted to linger one more time, but duty was calling. They left the opening with its liquid comfort and emotional warmth to return to the real world. They ate a breakfast of cold cereal, milk and fruit then unpacked the equipment from the medical establishment. Gem showed him how it worked. It seemed easy enough to operate.

"How do you plan to use this, Art?" She questioned as she fooled with some of the controls on the gadget. There was a very bright orange one that did not seem to have any purpose so far as she could see.

"When I took pictures from inside the MAP dimension, the cameras I used could not record the auras around the living matter I saw. My eyes could see them but not the camera. I believe that each living species has its own color. If this camera will record the different colors, I want to take it over to the neighbor's house and try to find some living species that will probably be plentiful over there. Those same colors might be rather scarce at my house. The guy claimed he never saw Sonny. He was killed in a room upstairs on the other side of the house. If I can find something in his house, then find a match in Sonny's room, I will prove that he was there. Once I know that, I will know that I must track him down. Then I will probably have to observe him for a while and see if anything suspicious is going on. Once in his house, I can look for things that might give me an indication as to what types of literature he feeds on. If I find even one scrap of child pornography, I do not know what I will do? I might just castrate him then and there and be done with it. I will probably collect more evidence though and turn him over to the authorities."

Gem looked sad.

"What is it dear?" he asked cradling her chin in his hands. He noticed no scar where the cut had been.

"So far my experience with MAP has been blissful. I never knew that such a utopia could exist this side of heaven. I know there is a lot of evil in the metaphysical dominion. I shudder to think of what will happen if you awaken the darker side."

"I was thinking the same thing just a few moments ago, Sweetheart. I know how I must approach it now. I must not go at this through the channels of bitterness, hatred, and revenge. If I meditate and approach this through the shield of justice, I think I will be safe. I will not allow the dark to control me. I will try to keep as far away from it as possible. That is why I need you. Your love, our love, Kanna's love will be my protection. I sense that she has something to do with this, like I mentioned earlier. I need her innocence when approaching this greatest of evils. It is the only way now I can see to keep me from doing something that would change me forever, possibly destroy me. Her childlike trust in me and our love will keep me on the right path. If I had tried this any time before today, I would not have been able to keep the evil from taking control of me."

Gem held him close and lingered.

"I know you are right, Art. I know it just as surely as I knew my destiny when I held your daughter in my arms. It is going to be OK now. I'll try not to worry about it, and I do love you."

"I love you too. I hope I never grow tired of telling you that." Gem tidied up some things around her home. She went into the lab where the camera was and put a cover over it. She had installed sliding, electronically controlled doors to conceal the unit from a casual observer when not in use. A person could go into the room and never see it once the doors were closed. It had its own secret room. After doing that she went to the cupboard and gathered a few cooking supplies and spices. Since it had been a few years since Art had a woman around the house there was no telling if he had the right spices and cooking supplies to put together a decent meal. Plus, she really liked using her own stuff. She had kinda moved more into organic foods after hearing about GMO's and other stuff giant corporations were doing to food these days. A person could not be too careful. She appeared with the sacks and handed them to Art.

"What are these?" he questioned. "I have food aplenty at my house. You must realize I have been Mister Mom for quite a while, plus we have a store only a couple of blocks away.

"No hard feelings, I hope, Art. A woman likes to use her own things especially if she is going to be expected to cook."

"I am a good cook, Gem. I will prove it at our next evening meal."

"I do not doubt that. But how long will we be there? A change in diet might not be bad occasionally."

"You are probably right, Gem. The couple of meals I have had here have been very tasty. Have it your way." He took a couple of sacks from her and headed out the door. She grabbed another.

Chapter 7

It was about 11:00 when they arrived at Art's house. The van had a large dent in the back, right hand side. Art decided that before getting to the detective work, he would spend a little time with it from within MAP and see if he could remove a few wrinkles. He had created a plastic ball there so perhaps a little body work was possible also. There was no hurry on the heading over to the other place. No one had lived in the neighbor's house since he moved away. He took Gem inside and showed her around. Before long she made herself right at home. She told him she would scrounge up some lunch while he worked on the van. It was quicker to activate the stationary MAP unit, so Art opened the panel and punched in the security code and the conductors sprang into action. He entered and left the house by way of the garage door. At the van he closed his eyes and tried to locate the sources he would need to pull the wrinkles out.

Gem finished lunch and went out to check on his progress. She could not see him at work. Art saw her watching and stopped for a couple of minutes. He went over to her and took the liberty to embrace her. She did not have a clue. He could feel her there in the shadows of the future.

Gem left and came out a few minutes later from within. The van was finished so he took her in his arms and laid her down on the lawn. The ground felt cool to woman's back not unlike the warmer body that covered her own. They played for about 20 minutes before going in for lunch. Food tasted better in the physical world so they exited MAP and ate. After lunch, Art and Gem would start to work. First however, he would put the taser up to a million volts. He had modified another one. This one he would give to Gem. She would taser the front of the van and he would taser the back. It might take a few delayed seconds for the charges to meet but once they did, the newly un-dented van would be set in its permanent, revised shape in the physical world.

"How are you going to approach this detective project, Art?" Gem asked as he brought in the equipment. She was still new to all of this and endless questions popped into her mind and out just as quickly.

"I really do not know yet, Sweet. I must find out what this thing can do in there. Perhaps it is a dry run, but I do not think it will be. Like I mentioned earlier, I am in rather good tune with my intuition. I think the time I have spent in there has heightened or accelerated my metaphysical aptitude. I want you to get acquainted with ways to do things with your mind in there also. There might come a time when you will need to know these methods. Perhaps it may even save your life or the lives of someone else. Your strengths will probably lay in a different area than mine, but you need to at least become familiar with the basics. From there you can branch out on your own."

"I would like to try, Art. We can start some basic exercises right after we check things out, hopefully before you launch off on some mind trip that will lead you to the truth."

"Hopefully". He mumbled something but was already seeing the path he would chart in his quest for the killer. They entered the stationary window again and headed over to the neighbors. The door was locked.

"How am I to get in here, Gem?" he asked while trying to figure it all out with his mind. "I am not that great at picking locks."

"Let's try the camera." She took the unit and turned it on. There was a little screen that lit up as the unit hummed to life. On the side there was a lever that moved forward and backward. Gem focused it on the handle of the door. As she moved the lever, the internal workings of the lock appeared one layer at a time. She noticed something strange and pointed it out to Art. This lever started focusing on the front of the lock.

"Do you see how it shows you the different levels of the mechanical workings inside?"

Yes, he replied," while focusing his eyes on the little camera window. He followed the progress of the lens on the door. It passed through the wood and he could see the handle on the inside. He noticed the lock had one of those turn buttons.

"When I move the unit to a point further from the inside handle, what happens?" Art looked. What he saw was very strange. Beyond the turn button there appeared to be a pattern of door handle parts that trailed off into the distance. Gem pushed the lever further, following the trail of parts. They went into the garage and set-in midair for a time, arranged the way one would expect them to be in a package at the store. As she pushed the lever further, the window showed a path leading out of the drive.

"Are you thinking, what I'm thinking Art?"

"Maybe? What are you thinking?"

"Do you think it is possible for this camera to take pictures back in time from within MAP?"

"That is what it looks like to me, Gem. The door handle was purchased from some store and was brought here in a vehicle. It stayed in the garage for a time before it was installed. How long ago do you think that happened?"

They looked at the handle. It was quite new. All the door handles were new. They had just been installed recently. Art looked over to where the "For Sale" sign had been. It was gone!

"It looks like the house has finally sold, Gem. That is good news and bad. Good news in that it will probably give us this guy's new address and bad news in that we do not know how much time we must do what we need to do. We had better get started. Focus the camera back on the door handle. I think I can get us in. Focus on the turn nob inside." She did and he mentally moved it to the left.

"Now focus on the dead bolt." He did the same with that moving it to the right. He turned the handle. The door opened.

"That was easy enough, My Love. You are good." She

mentioned that with a hint of self-satisfaction while intending it to be a complement to the man.

"Thanks for the compliment, My Lady. You're not so bad yourself." Inside they locked the door behind them. There was no power on, so the only light was coming from a window and a flashlight if they needed it. There were several plastic garbage cans strung around the place. Some had old lawnmower and yard equipment parts. This guy had been in the lawn maintenance business. That is how he had come to know the Goldstein's. He had kept up their yard. It was one of several. If he was a serial killer, that was not good. He could come in with his service, do his work and leave without rousing suspicion. The neighbors would not even stop to question a yard man working around a house. Some of his clients even entrusted him with keys. There were other cans that had old pizza cartons and fast-food mocha cups. It was a mess. There were old magazines and trade journals around and Art picked up several, but none were of a questionable nature.

"Focus the camera on some of those garbage cans, Gem. I don't want to paw through all the trash but perhaps there will be something in one of them that can help." She did and some interesting images emerged. Each item of garbage had a trail leading off in one direction or another. As they followed them, all seemed to come to rest about 3 to 4 feet above the garage floor then flow in a straight line and head left or right at the road. After looking through 5 or 6 cans, they decided to go on to other places in the home. There was another, new lock on the door that led into the kitchen. Once the camera revealed the workings of the unit, Art could mentally open it.

"You are going to have to show me how you do that, Art this is amazing!"

"I am sure you can learn, Gem. It takes some people longer than others to get in touch with their inner mind but eventually anyone with a normal brain can do it." They went in the kitchen. It was dirty like the rest of the house. The refrigerator door was open a little and the colors radiating from it proved that the microorganisms within were alive and active. There were some spare dishes in one of the cupboards. They found a couple of abandoned spoons and some empty, cottage cheese cartons. In the living, dining room there was no furniture, but the carpet was half ripped up. Someone had been there recently. There were little piles of it here and there with pieces of padding scattered all over. They pointed the camera at a strip of carpet that was still attached to the floor. The camera had a magnification feature in it. Gem activated it and zoomed in on a 2-inch section. Several hairs grew before Art's eyes.

"That is amazing, Gem! I did not know that it could do that. Wow. I am going to purchase this thing."

"You won't be able to afford it, Art. Remember you are an x-professor." She was quite proud of herself pointing out that he was kind of an average Joe.

"We'll see." Art smiled to himself. He had some inside information on that aspect of his life. "Is there any way to record that image?" Art pointed to the screen. There were about 9 hairs that formed an interesting pattern. At one end of five of the hairs there was a gray, brownish colored, neon glow.

"Either this guy had some hitchhikers in his hair, or some little critters found them here on the floor. Look at that. I have never seen that color before." Gem turned the camera on Art's head.

"My, my. You are hiding some critters of your own. They laughed and the laughter echoed and vibrated throughout the empty house as they moved to the next room. It was a bedroom. The floor contained hundreds of hairs with neon gray, brown highlights. There were several others. They took photos of 3 or 4 different specimen types and moved to the bathroom. It was very colorful.

"This is sickeningly disgusting. This guy was a pig," Gem exclaimed. "Unfortunately, we all are but these bacteria have a job to do and they are doing it. They are breaking this stuff down, eating away the evidence. I want to go down in the basement then we can get out of here. Who knows when the people who are buying the place might come back? Not that they would be able to see us but after that accident, I really do not want to encounter people this close to reality. I found out if I passed through a unit three or four times, I could go ahead or back in time three or four seconds. That gave me more distance from the physical realm. It had its disadvantages though. The closer I am to the physical, the more visible the physical is to me. At five seconds the world out there is not much more than a ghost shadow if ghosts have shadows."

In the basement they saw some more garbage, lots of it. There was trash strewn all over. It was here that Art found his first evidence of pornography. He asked Gem to move the camera around and focus the viewfinder a little deeper than the paneling. The first pass revealed nothing. He had her scan a little higher. They could see the strips of wood where the paneling was mounted. When she did the last, highest pass, they discovered a depression. Art pulled out the flashlight and saw that the paneling was cut. He pried it open and there was a stash of journals. Their content was evident. They were some old detective magazines and other stuff. All the pictures and stories were bad but the "other stuff," was by far the worst. The pictures inside were sickening.

"Someone forgot these." He pulled a pair of gloves out of his pocket and picked a loose grocery sack off the floor. He opened the top and stuck the stuff inside. "If this goes as far as I feel it will now that we have been in his house, I might send these as evidence. A good homicide lawyer can read a lot from the expression of the guy when he sees them." As they were leaving, Gem focused on the rug below where the magazines had been stashed. There were several spots on the carpet. They glowed with active bacteria still at work. It was not too hard to imagine what had caused them.

"For what it's worth, take a recording of that too." Gem pushed the record button and sent the image to the disk.

"Let us have one last look, then we need to get out of here. There is a trash can over in the corner. X-ray it." Gem pointed the camera that direction as she activated the button again. The beam revealed nothing at the first and second passes but the third one showed what looked like a pair of broken glasses. One lens was shattered. The bow on the other side of the shattered lens was missing along with an earpiece. Art reached in and pulled them out. He still had the gloves on. A little off to the side he saw the earpiece and picked it out also. "See if you can see where these come from?" The trail of the glasses led up the stairs.

"What did you expect? Art." Gem had a funny smile on her face that was a tiny bit lopsided causing a dimple to appear suddenly.

"I expected them to go up the stairs." They laughed. Art put the glasses in his pocket, and they left. They locked the kitchen door and looked out of the garage window. A truck was turning into the drive.

"What do we do now, Art?" For the first time the scientist appeared to be fearful. Was she imagining an encounter of some type? Art wondered?

"We have a couple of choices. We can go out that door over there and wait until they are inside before heading to our house or we can stay back out of the way and go out the door they come in before they close it. What do you want to do?"

"I vote that we go out this door." She quickly unlocked it and they exited. There was a row of arborvitae separating this house from the neighbors. They passed between two trees and came to the back fence in Art's yard. He opened the gate using a little latch string that hung down and they disappeared inside. He noticed that Kanna's bicycle was in the yard where she had abandoned it. He picked it up and wheeled it onto the patio under the deck.

Sonny's room had a patio door that opened out onto the deck. It had been a little over two years since they had found his body on the floor by his bed. The detective who was assigned to the case claimed the killer had entered and exited the home by that door. This was the first room the couple went to. It had not changed much. Art had left things pretty much as they had been. Fortunately, new carpet had not been installed. Sonny had been struck with a rod of some type several times. It could have been a pipe or a bat. No weapon was ever found. His blood had landed on a couple of throw rugs. These had been taken to the lab for testing. In the room Gem turned on the camera. She began to check the carpet for some of those hairs that had the neon brown color at one end. No match was found. She turned it on the bedspread but that should not yield anything either because it was a different one than had been on there when the boy had been killed. Art did not know why he did it, but he took the camera from Gem and opened the closet. There was some hair there that had a yellow aura to it. It was fine. Beside the yellow hair there was one with gray, brown. When they compared it to the pictures on the disk, they made a positive match.

The next place was the room Sandra had been found in. One more matching hair was found on the carpet outside the door to that room. The room itself had changed. New carpet had been installed so it would be no good for evidence. They shut down the camera and headed back out of the portal from the standard unit.

"Do you remember that question I asked you, Art?"

"What question? You asked me forty or fifty questions." He smiled as he responded to her query. It was rather ambiguous of her to bring this up, but she certainly had a specific question in mind.

"Can one person enter the portable unit at the same time another person enters the standard one and meet somewhere inside?"

"Let's try." He went out to the van and brought in the aluminum case and in a few minutes had both units operating. They both entered and agreed to meet at the foot of the stairs. When Art got there however, no one was there. Gem found the same thing. She stepped back by the bookcase and looked closely. If Art were there, he was not visible. She was only a few feet from the camera, so she went and turned it on. When she pointed it at the stairs, she could see him on the little screen. He was glowing. She moved the focus lever a little bit and watched as his shirt faded away revealing his well-muscled chest. Putting the camera away she emerged back out of the entrance. He followed not too long after.

"Did you see me in there, Gem?"

"Ya, I saw you alright. You were plain as day." She had a sly smirk on her face as she responded. He looked at her puzzled then continued.

"You are kidding, right?"

"No. I really saw you." She smiled again this time broader than before.

"Perhaps we need to switch entrances then. Why don't you go in the other one this time and I will find out if you can see more from one unit than the other?" Gem laughed. She was pleased that she had pulled one over on him without his knowledge. It was not easy to get the better of him.

"OK, Art, if you insist, but I really did see you."

"I believe you, Gem. I just do not understand why you saw me, but I never saw even the faintest shadow of you."

Inside the portable Art had no better luck. There was no trace of this illusive woman. That set his mind to work. So, each captured doorway led to a slightly different dimension or perhaps a slightly different time. He met Gem out at the front again and asked her if she had seen him this time. She told him she had not. She was smiling but this time she had a very suspicious smile on her pretty face and no matter how hard she tried could not fake the reality of what she had done. Art saw through her. She was not a good liar.

"Did you really see me the first time?" he questioned seriously.

"I saw you alright, in the flesh." She was laughing now but Art did not think it was funny.

"I saw you, Art but I had a little help. I used the camera and well, while I was looking, I took the liberty to move the focus lever. The contents were quite revealing." She was really laughing now and soon Art joined in.

"That is good news, Gem."

"What? The revelation or something else?"

"The fact that the camera can see through the timeline. I do not think we entered at the same milli-second. That would put a layer of time between us even though it would be in the thousands of a second. But it must be more than that. If we enter through the same port, I can go in ahead of you and we will be there together. These dimensions must be layered somehow."

They shut the portable unit down and went up in the kitchen to get something to eat.

"I can move between the layers mentally. I need to teach you some of the basic mental exercises. You know some but since there is a lot of unknown science at work here, we still must be careful. I can move forward and backward in time when I am there. I want to show you how to do at least that much. I will also show you how to select the channels of travel. Once you know that you will be able to move through time also. The main question I have is how easy is it for a person to get trapped, or lost in there? I think there is a possibility of something like that happening and I want us to take measures to prevent it. Those measures need to be worked out beforehand. So, after lunch, we will see what we can come up with." Gem went to the kitchen and whipped up some salad and sandwiches along with some brownies she has somehow managed to make during the short time she was here.

After eating, they chose a comfortable spot in the living room. Art decided to take the portable unit with him. He wondered what would happen if he fired up the portable unit within. Would he be able to even do it and if he managed, what would happen if he stepped out? He decided to try but have Gem keep a hold of his arm. When the process was ready, he exited. He was back in the physical world, in his living room. He checked the clock, and it was the same time inside and out. If there was a difference in time it was minimal. He went back in and shut down the portable unit and placed it in his case. They found a case for the camera also. It was an old army surplus pack that seemed to be made for the unit.

"Gem?" His voice had that gurgling echo sound that was characteristic of the inner world.

"Yes, dear." That was the first time she had called him dear.

"Do you think there is some way to make a smaller camera? Is it possible to take the technology and place it in a unit the size of a small camcorder?"

"It has already been done. In fact, you could probably purchase a unit that size for less than what you could get this one for, but the picture quality might be less." Gem was seeing a selection of similar units in her mind. She had opened a catalog one day and seen them.

"How much are we talking about?"

"You could probably pick one up for under $20,000.00."

"Remind me to go on the Internet and order one this evening."

'And where will you get $20,000.00, Art?" She questioned. For her $20,000.00 was a chunk of change.

"The day I met you I deposited a check in my bank for nearly a million dollars. Spiffy Clean ordered two thousand of my sanitation units."

"Oh," she responded. So besides being good looking this dude was loaded as well. Not a bad thing to find out. "No problem then. You could probably purchase an intermediate unit for around $50,000.00 that would make this unit look like an old Kodak box camera. Techtronic Corporation has four or five models available. I forgot you made that sanitation invention. Once this quest you think you must do is finished, do you think we can go shopping? I can think of a hundred ways to spend $20,000- $30,000.00." Visions of a grand shopping spree briefly streamed through her mind. She just loved to shop. Problem was she never had much to spend shopping so was always looking for deals. What would it be like to just go and purchase whatever you wanted regardless of the cost? Perhaps if she hung around long enough, she would find out.

"Sure, Gem. That sounds ok with me," he answered without so much as batting an eye. "I expect once this unit gets more publicity, thousands of orders will come in. That is just the tip of the iceberg. What we have here presents us with thousands of ways to make money. I really do not think anyone else has discovered this dimension-might I say between dimensions-that enables one to slip anywhere they want to go even going forward or backward in time at will. Let us get to work." They went to an open space and settled in for what could be the start of a long day.

"To start with you need to breathe deeply. Several times. It is harder to do that in this atmosphere. This universe is more compressed. It is more fluid. If our lungs were designed differently, we could breathe under water like fish. Once you have taken a few deep breaths, it might help to fix your eyes on some point and stare at it until you can look right through it. Once you reach that state, you can then close your eyes and think of the back, topside of your head. Once you consciously see that look for pictures that may be flowing through your mind. The pictures should flow by in a stream. This basic process is called image streaming. Concentrate on the images. While you are doing that give yourself some commands to relax. Physically feel all pain, stress, soreness, and weight leaving your body. Come to the point where your thoughts become pure consciousness. So how are you doing so far?"

"I see images flowing by."

"What do you see?" Again, his voice came across the space between them like someone talking and the sound carrying under water.

"Colors, skyscapes, images of things." Gem was watching as all kinds of stuff floated by. The images changed much faster than her conscious mind could recognize them.

"Good, good. Now try to imagine a river." Gem did and in just a little bit one appeared in her mind. It was a vast rive a long way across. Streams of multicolored strands were all woven together. At times she could see objects floating by on top of the river. She felt Art's hand in hers. He was talking to her now but not verbally. They communicated through thoughts, through telepathy. Their minds had merged. He was pointing out some of the objects she was seeing. She communicated back with comments that showed her interest.

"Now we will select one of the streams and follow it. That purple stream looks interesting, follow me." They immersed themselves in it and were soon streaming forward. In time a giant castle appeared in front of them. It looked like it was made from candy. They stopped at it and walked up to the door. It opened automatically. Inside was a fantasy land. There were beautiful gardens of violet flowers that seemed to be made from candy or glass. They passed through and came to an inner garden. There were waterfalls and walkways. They came to an arched bridge that went up over part of the river. It led up to a smaller castle door, a castle within the castle. They tried to open it, but it was locked. Art did not want to take the time to pick this lock, so he went back to the center of the bridge then grabbed Gem's hand and jumped in. She plunged down with him albeit unwillingly. Soon they were back in the river. They swam up to the surface and were back home. Gem was still looking at the river. Art spoke.

"How did you like that first trip?"

"It was awesome. Why did you pull us away from the violet castle? I would like to have stayed there longer and seen more of the sights."

"It was only an exercise in mind travel. We have work to do and that was a way to show you some of the possibilities we can have in here. I want you to go on a trip by yourself now. Take about five minutes. I will call you back after that length of time. Tell me what you find. Before you go though, if there has ever been a place you wanted to visit in this old world you can do it with this. The way to go there is to mentally picture several images of the place in your mind then let go and you will be there. After I call you back, I want us to go back in time and we will then try something I think you will find interesting."

She was off. Gem had always wanted to go to Ireland. She conjured up some images she had seen in books and let herself go. Soon she was there. She had seen green fields and hills but, things were not quite like the photos she had seen. She entered a field. There were some domestic animals grazing there but they could not see her. They had flies buzzing around them and the smell was not pleasant. She headed up to a small farmhouse. The door was open, so she went in. There was food cooking on the stove. This was a much better smell. She could even pick out some of the spices the cook had used in her mixture even though diminished in this realm. By an old sink she saw a crock full of fresh milk. It was probably goat's milk. There was a rather large woman knitting. She was sitting in a comfortable chair humming a tune. In a crib next to her was a baby. Every now and then the woman would rock the crib then resume her knitting. While she was doing this a small lad came running through the door. He had a large frog in his hands. He spoke in a language Gem at first could not understand. She let her mind relax and the interpretation came through.

"Can we have frog legs for supper, Mommy?" Gem could tell the little one was extremely excited about his find. The frog was not though. It squirmed and almost got away. The lad managed to hold unto one leg before getting a better hold on the critter.

"Oh, what a large, beautiful frog. Yes, we can have that with our meal. Put the frog in here." She got up and opened the lid to a large pot. The lad put the frog in, and she returned the lid on the jar but left it open a little.

"Can you catch one more frog? If you can that will be a leg for each of us. Your papa will be home soon, and he will eat two. He will be incredibly pleased with your find."

"OK Momma. I will go catch another one." The lad ran off and the next thing Gem knew she was in the living room looking at Art.

"Where did you go, Gem?"

"To Ireland," she responded. "There was this little farm

cottage at the edge of a field. I went inside and saw a fat lady, her baby and son. He brought her a frog to cook for supper. Then I was back here."

"So, you went to Ireland. Why there?" Art was genuinely interested in what her response would be. He even held his breath in anticipation like she had done a time or two minus the little catch in his voice like hers.

"I always wanted to go there, so I went today."

"Would you go back again if you had the chance?" Art got that question out real fast as he let out the breath he was holding.

"I probably would but not to watch someone boil a frog." Gem wrinkled up her nose as she thought of the unpleasant smell coming from the pasture.

"If you could go back in time where would you choose to go?" Art asked this question very slowly, enunciating each word to the enth degree.

Gem thought about the question for a while then spoke.

"About 18 years ago I left my purse in one of the lady's restrooms at college. I remembered where but a half hour passed before I missed it. When I went back to the stall, it was gone. I would like to go back and get my purse. It had some important things in it that I never can replace. I had some pictures that I was especially fond of. One was a wedding photo of my mother and father. There was also a photo of my little brother who died the year before I went off to college. Plus, there were some research papers and other stuff that is invaluable to me. That is where I would go first."

"Would you like to go back and get your purse now?" Art did not even know if it were possible, but he was sure if he could find a trail back to that bygone era, even to the exact moment, it would be possible to get the purse. It was a leap of faith on his part, but he had every confidence they could and would do it if she wished.

"You mean we can do that?" Gem began thinking of the possibilities as she responded.

"If certain conditions are met. Yes, we can do that." He

had talked himself into it. His faith had become reality in his mind even as making that white plastic ball had become reality.

"What conditions?" The lady was remembering her college days. Would she be able to see herself or be herself, the one who lost the purse?

"You would need something from that time period of your life," he responded. "That class ring for instance that is on your finger. When did you get it?"

"About two years before I lost my purse. Is that too long to work?"

"Not if you were wearing it at the time." Gem thought for a moment then responded.

"I had it on my finger that day. Does that mean we can go back there and recover my stuff?" She was getting excited again. She had again held her breath and that little catch in her voice came back.

"I don't see why not? Are you ready to go?"

"Sure, Art. If I could get that purse back, I would be forever in your debt." Art held Gem's hand and placed his finger on the ring. They were heading back for the great river. Just before they reached it though they struck a wall.

"This is strange, Gem. I did not know there were walls in here. There should not be. Can you see anything stopping us?" Gem looked around and there was nothing in sight. The wall appeared to be made from a glassy substance.

"Do you have the camera, Gem?" he questioned.

"I don't but I think I can reach it. Hold on for a minute." She picked up the camera and turned it on. They pointed it at the wall. Then they saw him. He was off in the distance. It looked like several walls were between them. The man they saw was ancient. He had long white hair and a beard that went nearly to his waist. Though he was old, he appeared to look young at the same time. He was moving his lips and speaking to them, but they could hear nothing. Art tried to read his lips. All he could make out was the word, "come." The man motioned for them to break the glass. The back of the camera had a metal plate, so Art used that to shatter the first wall. The man was talking again. They could almost hear what he was saying. He motioned for them to break the next glass and they did. The first attempt did nothing, neither did the next 10 strikes. They looked at the old man. He held up one finger and mouthed "Once more." Art struck again. A small crack appeared where the back of the camera hit the wall. Then in slow motion the cracks spread in a hundred directions. Little trails went this way and that before retreating on themselves. Suddenly the whole wall burst apart. The glass pieces fell and as they hit the river below, letting off what appeared to be puffs of steam or smoke then were absorbed. They could hear the man now. They moved up to yet another transparent wall.

"Art," the ancient one said. "You need to pass through one more wall then we will be free to talk. Take your camera and focus the beam as wide as you can. Once you have done this move the focus lever all the way back toward you. On your left-hand side, you will find a black square. Push the upper right-hand corner of the square and it will move. Underneath it you will find an orange button. When you push it, a hole will be melted in the wall and you and Gem will be able to pass through. Do that now."

Art followed the instructions he was given. When he pushed the orange button a blue beam came out of the end of the camera. It hit the glass and turned it red. After glowing for about a minute, it vanished in a puff of smoke. There was a perfect circle through the substance in front of them. Art and Gem stepped through it and were in the presence of the old man. Gem looked at his eyes. They were bluer than any she had ever seen. They had a depth to them that seemed to reach into eternity. Then he spoke. His voice was deep and resonated through the atmosphere causing everything to oscillate to the sounds.

"My name is Methuselah. I have come to speak to you about some things. First, Art. I have spoken to you on 3 other occasions. I was sent to communicate with you when you first trapped the door to this reality. I gave you a lot of condensed information. It is still expanding. You know most of the things I shared in that first visit and part of the second and third visit. The fourth time I came, I spoke to Gem. I need to tell you more about this reality and the one you have come from."

"Who are you and why were we stopped from going back in time? Art asked as he searched the ancient one's face for any hint of hostility or danger. There was none.

"I will give you that information in time. What I am asking you to do now is listen. When I am finished, you will have time to ask questions. You have called this place by several names over the last few months. You have called it MAP. You have called it a liquid universe. You have called it a doorway, a gate to the within. You have called it a parallel universe. It is all of these and none. The real name of this place is Eternal Reality. The place you come from is called Earth Reality. At one time everything in existence was Eternal Reality. It was balanced as it is today. Within it everything was in perfect harmony. Then several ages ago an evil asserted itself. It rose to great power in the Eternal Reality. The balance was broken, and the harmony lost. To prevent the contamination of the whole, the evil was banished from the whole. It was placed in several other realities, but the realities had boundaries. The evil could move between the boundaries of the confined realities, but not escape them. These realities had beings who were given the power of choice. When the beings in the Earth Reality chose the evil, it was eventually banished to one reality. That is the place you came from. Down through the ages great men have seen beyond the Earth Reality into the Eternal Reality. Some have even passed between the two as you have." Methuselah paused a moment as he looked off in the distance. Gem noticed that no aura's animated from his form. She looked at Art. The color that had surrounded him was also gone. The old man continued speaking.

"I was once a part of the Earth Reality. I walked your world when it was young. There was a constant struggle there with the present evil. The evil was predatory. After being banished from its glorious state its source of life was cut off. To survive it had to siphon life from living organisms. As it took this life, the living, organic matter it was taken from suffered. Death and decay came where once there was only life. I was given a vision of the eternal and I never felt at home there after that. When my walk was over, I rested for a time then was granted entrance into the Eternal Reality. My son, Enoch preceded me into the Eternal Reality. He never rested but was given entrance directly from earth without seeing death. I have traveled this river for many millennia. I have a home here. It is a beautiful one. Currently, it is beyond your ability to comprehend. You both will be tested. It will be an awfully hard test. Not one in a million who walk the Earth Reality could pass the test. You are being given a time limit with MAP. You could know when that limit will end but, you have not figured it out. In the end you will have passed or failed. If you pass, you will be within the Eternal Reality. If you fail, you will be in the Earth Reality and end up with that which is your portion. I can only speak to you a few times yet. You know how many times, but you are not conscious of it currently. I will give you a few hints now."

"The first time I came to you was shortly after you captured a door. The second time was when you came down and saw your daughter for the first time. You probably remember thinking of how she was not and then you knew that she was and had been. The third time I came to you was when you left Gem's home that first day and discovered upon picking Kanna up that she could respond to your thoughts and you to hers. The time before this visit with you now, I communicated to Gem. I led her to the camera that would allow you to see me and eventually reach me. I will come to you in your journey a few more times. If you need me, call me and I will be by your side to help in any way I can. If you call me though, it will take away from a prescribed visit at a certain, critical point. So, if you do call, make sure I am urgently needed. You have been granted much power.

Your quest for justice is ok. Justice for the wrongs that were committed against your wife and son is a worthy cause, but it has grave dangers. In that quest you will have to view many dark sights. These can draw you down a path where it will be nearly impossible to return from. In all you do from within you need to take extreme precautions. Be careful. Be positive as much and as often as you can. This will aid you in helping to dispense the darkness you will be subjected to.

Be careful when you enter MAP from the other side. There are life forms beyond that reality that would destroy you if they could. They hate humanity and anything that reminds them of that which they once had but lost. Some of these life forms have bodies. The bodies are not the same as living organic bodies. They require sustenance that can only be drawn from living organisms. Others of these you may encounter do not have bodies per say but are composed of consolidated forces of energy. All life forms in these lower realities are predatory. So, tread carefully in those lower realms. If you have any questions, you may ask them now. I may choose not to answer though because it might not be the right time for you to know." Art looked into the eyes of the wise one.

"Tell me a little more about these walls if you can."

"The walls are around both of you while you transverse this other world. They prevent you from contaminating the whole. They also are for your protection. The walls cannot be broken down without your consent. They will allow you to travel to anywhere as an observer and not a participant. If you exit the MAP gate anywhere, you need to realize that what is in that reality will have access to you at that time. That is why you must take precautions when you do this. You and Gem were planning to go back and retrieve her lost purse. A trip like that should not pose much danger if you use the right means to accomplish it. But again, I want to stress that there are other places that could be the means of your destruction if you are not careful. Within MAP, there is only one wall between you and the Earth Reality, not three like you needed to pass to reach me. As you know that first wall can be broken easier than the others. The second is harder and the third nearly impossible. Likewise, in the lower realities, the walls will get harder to penetrate as you go deeper. But I do not recommend that you journey in any reality lower than the first level of the alternate reality. You can travel that reality as an observer. Is there anything else you want to know?" Gem had a question this time.

"Methuselah, you mentioned this camera has some feature that make it possible to see you. When we were using it at the neighbor's house, there were streams leading out of the driveway. Are we to assume those streams or trails lead back in time and if they do, how do we follow them back to various time periods?"

"Art knows the answer to both questions, Gem," Methuselah answered. "The answer to your first question is, yes. The streams lead back in time. In answer to the second question however, there are two ways to follow the streams back. When you accessed the orange button to melt a hole in the last wall between us, you activated the second way to travel back in time. If you focus the beam on the stream of your choice, it will open a tunnel or wormhole you might say to the past. You can physically follow the stream of your choice at lightning speed in that tunnel. You can stop whenever you want and open the gate to that period. The other form of travel is through the mind. You can only travel using this method in the Eternal Reality. Here your thoughts are a substance like everything else. In the Earth Reality, the electrical waves make up the substances in your everyday existence. Some waves make items appear solid, other waves make things appear as a liquid or gas. The camera you have bypasses the waves in the Earth Reality. It also allows you to see the streams. They are invisible to the naked eye and can only be seen through the camera or your mental vision, if you know how to use it."

"In the Eternal Reality the atmospheric makeup is different, so the wave forms are closer together and have electrical charges that make access to places and things much easier. When you travel physically in the Eternal Reality, the shell surrounding you has a negative charge. The camera opens a tunnel that has a positive charge. Since the negative and positive charges oppose each other, friction is nonexistent. This fact enables you to travel at incredible speeds if you want to stay in your physical state. Art was going to take you back in time using the mental state. The mental state is the best form of travel for long distances in time and space because it is in many cases instantaneous. In mental travel your thoughts must become pure consciousness. Everything else even your physical being will disappear until you are at your destination. Both ways have advantages and disadvantages. If you want to retrieve a physical object like your long, lost purse, it is best to use the physical means of travel and go through the electrically charged tunnels. My time is up now. I have to go but I am giving Art another block of knowledge."

Methuselah did something and a small ball of electric light glimmered in his hand. He tossed it in Art's direction. It struck him in the head. There was a moment of brilliant illumination then the walls they had passed snapped back into place. They no longer prevented their travel and became part of the river. They were moving rapidly again, then they stopped. Gem looked around. They were in a dark building. There was a computer screen glowing in the darkness. The two made their way over toward it. They looked at the time in the lower corner. It was 12:45. A calendar on the wall showed the date. Art spoke. His voice coming through the air with that distinct echo sound."

"How close are we to the time you left your wallet in the restroom?" Gem looked at the calendar, again before replying.

"We arrived about a week early, no it is more like 6 days. This is the old science complex building isn't it, Art?"

"I don't know, Gem you tell me. I have never been here before. I was following your lead. You must have been in this room six days before you were in the restroom."

"Art?"

"Yes."

"Do you think we could try the physical means of travel that the old man was explaining to us to move through the next 6 days?" She was mulling over the possibilities in her mind and it told her this would be the best way to accomplish their goal.

"I really do not know anything about that." He searched his mind to try and find even a spark of an answer.

"But he gave you all that knowledge just a couple of minutes ago. I really think that is the way I want to travel in here. This mind stuff is all new to me. When we entered the stream, I lost all sense of being. I did not have hands, or feet, or lips. It is totally weird. At least in the physical I will be whole."

"We can try, Girl. But I am not making any promises." Gem gave the camera to Art. He placed it on his shoulder and looked at the screen. He focused it on Gem's class ring then pushed the orange button. They could see the trail alright. It led out of the door. Over the next few minutes, they were speed walking all over the place. Things were going by so fast it was hard to see what they were. They went into the dorm room and saw where the stream laid down no less than six times then stopped. Those six times were in Gem's room. It was morning. They could see that it was a sunny day at the college. Gem got up and took a shower. Art enjoyed this part. He was seeing a younger Gem. The older Gem took her hands and placed them over his eyes.

"Sorry, Art. I am going out with someone here and I don't think he would like you checking me out like this."

"So, you colored your hair back then. I think I like you better as a blond. You were one foxy chick." Art saw her backside enter the door to the shower. That was one shapely piece of work.

"I went back to my normal color about a month after this, Art. I was walking home from the dorm and nearly got raped by two college guys. They would have succeeded but the campus security came along and saved the evening for me. At that point I changed my appearance. I dyed my hair brown again and purchased some large glasses that made me look old and ugly. I started wearing loose fitting clothes to conceal my figure. After that, my dating opportunities dwindled to near zero. Even the guy I was seeing lost interest in me. This was great! I put myself into my studies and quit socializing with my peers."

"I am sorry to hear you had to go through an experience like that, Gem. While we are-here after retrieving your purse-we could go and work the two guys over if you like. Methuselah stated justice was an acceptable use for MAP."

"Normally I would say no to that, Art, but I think from this new perspective we have of things, it might be a good idea. Two guys matching the description of the ones that came after me did succeed in raping a friend of mine. She left college and never came back. Last I knew she was an alcoholic. Real sad. She had an IQ that was way up in the genius level. If we follow these bustards, we could forget about when they missed me and prevent them from getting to Pam. We would not have to do much. Is there a way to get them in here? If so, we could inject a little something into their groins that would put them on the sick list for a couple of weeks, perhaps months."

"What kind of an injection?" Art asked as his mind tried to picture the color of the solution along with a way of injecting it that gave him the willies.

"There is a chemical we used in biology that acts like a local anesthetic. If I add a little chloroform to it and formaldehyde, it will first numb their privates to the point of making them dead weight, then pickle them. They will not be able to get em up. After the sedation wears off, the next time they have sex, it will feel like they are burning up down there. What would normally be a pleasurable experience will feel like a blistering fire."

"You are wicked, Gem. How do you know about this?"

"I was looking up some stuff on the Internet one day and ran across an article presented by a mad scientist who wanted to get back at a rapist who killed his wife. He entrapped the criminal then tried several things on the guy. He finally let the man go but his appetite for rape was cured. He became a celibate and lived in a log cabin away from everyone for the rest of his life. He supposedly never married. Sex was just too painful. This scientist submitted his findings to the government as possible treatment for sex offenders and criminals. I don't know what they did with the information." The younger Gem was through with her shower. She dressed and exited the room.

After Art and Gem shared several intimate moments, they left the room and followed the younger lady for a couple of hours. Finally, they saw her heading toward the restroom.

"We need to enter into the 'Earth Reality,' as Methuselah called it. Probably the best place is in this storage closet," Art said as he rapped on the door. "We will see for sure that it is not used during the time we need it. The door is locked from the outside, but I think it is the type that you can leave from the inside. You will just have to knock when you have retrieved your purse and I will let you back in."

"Art, are you telling me that I have to go in and get my purse? I thought you would do it."

"It would look pretty strange for me to go into the lady's restroom don't you think? Gem, you are brilliant. We do not even need to go into the storage closet. We do not even need to get out of this realm. All that is necessary is to enter the Eternal Reality, set up the gate right next to your purse and just reach our hand out and take it. Then we can bring it in here and be on our way." The younger Gem entered the restroom. She went into a stall and did her thing then left. Art saw that her purse was left on the back of the toilet. He had the gate set up and motioned for the older Gem to pick up the purse. She put her hand out of the mass and grabbed it. Once inside again they shut the accelerator down.

"That was a good idea you had there, Sweetheart. I think that may have been part of the knowledge about taking precautions Methuselah gave me when interacting with the past."

"You're probably right, Gem responded as she opened her purse and checked its contents. There were some strange items in there. Would the Juicy Fruit Gum still be fresh?

"Thanks. I really appreciate this. I will probably need to go home soon after we get back. There are some things I need to do with this right away now that it is in my possession again."

"May I ask again why this is so important, Gem?" Art was looking at her with a new look. She had not seen this one in their short time together. He acted concerned but was he really? His eyes seemed to say otherwise.

"Yes, you may, Art. One of the things anyway. Inside there is a card with a voice activated code to a Swiss Bank Account my father left me on my 21st birthday. He never told me how much money was in it. I never had the chance to see. If it was substantial as I believe it was, then it is even more so now some 9 years later. Think of the interest that must have accumulated by now?"

"Couldn't you have contacted the bank and told them about the loss of your purse? I am sure they would have issued you a new card."

"Not with this type of account. Some of the big banks back then were experimenting with optic and voice activation, others with fingerprints."

"Well then, if your father opened it for you surely, he could have called them and explained the situation so you could access it," Art injected. He still seemed to think this side trip back to yesterday was a bit frivolous or so it seemed to Gem. Perhaps he had a lot on his mind?"

"Dad was dead." Gem responded as though she had some cold feelings for her dad. Had he hurt her somehow? Art wondered about it.

"I am sorry, Gem. I did not know. Could the person who took your purse have accessed the account and taken the money out?"

"No. This account was one like I mentioned earlier. It

required my father's voice or mine. Besides, since I have the purse, if they did manage to get to the money, it is back in the account now and will stay there until I get it out when I get back to real time." Art suddenly lightened up. She was getting it! Gem was now thinking in ways she had never even imagined before. This adventure was going to be fun! Why not enjoy it? A person needed to just let things go occasionally and enjoy life. They were out of the building and walking on the campus some place near the Art Building. Somewhere in the distance the bells on the old administration building chimed. One, two, three, four, five, six, seven, eight.

Chapter 8

Art and Gem had moved ahead in time to a point about 36 hours before the rape was to happen. They had spent some time locating the two male students. They were roommates. Their room was a mess. It was really sickening to look around in there. Pornographic pictures were pasted all over the walls. Every lewd and disgusting thing imaginable was displayed. They found a list of college girls targeted for rape on the top of one of the desks. The guys had taken a cast and pasted the face of each girl by her name. There were several dates put down. These guys having statlked several of the girls knew when they went out or came in. Pam's name was circled in red and the date and time of the encounter marked. They planned to strike at 1:00 am the next day. She studied late. That is the time they expected her to leave the library.

The two time travelers had discovered a series of tunnels beneath the campus. These tunnels carried the water pipes and electrical apparatus from building to building. The university used steam to heat. At some point all the tunnels led back to the boiler room. There was an access door right next to the Biology lab. Not too far from that tunnel entrance they found a large room. It had the pipes and electrical lines, but it also had some electric panels mounted on one wall. There was a table and a couple of chairs. It was evident that in the earlier years of the university this had been a place for some of the maintenance personal to hang out and put in time. There were some abandoned decks of cards and an old refrigerator in there. In another corner was a trash can half full of empty beer bottles. Art could tell by their shape they were several years old. The two determined this room had for the most part been forgotten. They monitored it for 24 hours before and after the targeted rape date. No activity registered. It was here they set up camp.

Art had an overwhelming feeling that some cosmic clock was ticking down. His time within was limited. The more time he spent in the Earth Reality, the less time was subtracted from his time in the eternal one. If he wanted to, he felt he could hold onto his discovery for a couple of years or more if he only used it when necessary. What he yet failed to understand was what the old man had been trying to reveal without coming right out and saying it. It hung in his mind, heavy like a lead balloon but he did not grasp it. This is what Methuselah could have told him and did had he been able to understand it.

"Art. If you travel through time in the Earth Reality using the camera beam, you will have unlimited access to the abilities you possess while in the Eternal Reality. There will be no time limits. You can go if you like. Just remember though, when you are within, when you enter in to the first level of the Eternal Reality, the clock is ticking. Don't use it any more than you have to." But then Art did not understand that yet although he realized he must limit his time within. In the blast of knowledge he received, Methuselah also showed him how to have unlimited time in the Eternal Reality. He could redeem time. But Art did not choose to focus on this knowledge while in some meditative state. Had he done so a lot of future problems with MAP could have been avoided.

Art and Gem came out the MAP door and were in the physical realm. Davidson recovered several vials of chemicals from the Biology Department and mixed up a potent combination. Now they were planning how best to administer the dosage. They discovered that Jack and Ted had girls over often. Several were repeat visitors. The night before the planned Rape of Pam they had a couple of oldies over. After popping some pills and doing some drugs they were out cold. Art and Gem wanted to get to them before the party. When the time came for the plunge, the boys would be in for the surprise of their lives.

"I am going to take a short trip, Gem. I will be back

before you can count to a hundred."

"Where do you plan to go?"

"I am going into the future to bring back a stun gun. It is a device that throws a beam at people and knocks them out. We can intercept Ted here in the hall when he takes that bathroom break, when he goes to smoke during class, but you know what I mean? I will hit him with the stunt gun and bring him down here. You can do your thing and I will then take him back to the restroom and put him in a stall. When he comes too, he will not know what hit him. He will be numb where it counts but the sensation will not really register until... Once we poke him, we can grab Jack a couple of hours later when he goes back to his room during classes. He takes a nap then and we can just go in and do our thing. When he wakes up, he will be numb also. I'll be back shortly." With that Art turned again toward the unit.

The experienced time traveler entered MAP and in a short time was at a manufacturing plant in Japan. He pulled a unit off the assembly line just before it entered the packaging phase. The grips came down to pick up the unit but when no unit was there, it did not drop the box. Art watched as the next unit came. This time it was boxed. He waited for a dozen units to pass and took another one. The same thing happened. Two of these would be good to have. A person might never know when they would come in handy. He left the manufacturing plant and was soon back in the room with Gem.

"Here they are, Hon." He handed one to Gem. She looked it over in amazement.

"How do they work?" She was running her long slim fingers over the smooth pistol grip. It was fake material but was pearled.

"I don't know. I did not bring the directions. The boxed one might have something inside though. Not that they would have done much good they are probably in Japanese. Here it says stun on this setting and kill on this one. There is a little circular dial that shows a point on one end and a wider area on the other. This is probably a way to set it. I wish there were something to try it on."

"There are some rats in the lab. I could get one for you," Gem suggested.

"Good. Do it." She was about to leave when a rat entered the room from a hole where some pipes were. It was a strange colored creature. Perhaps at some point in the past a few lab rats had escaped or been let loose by a softhearted student. If so, they had mated with wild rats and started their own rat race. Art smiled at him own thought of that pun. Taking aim at the critter, he fired. The rat dropped to the floor like a chunk of lead. They went over to it cautiously. It was still breathing.

"Forget the rat, Gem. This one will do. Find something to put it in. Let us see how long it takes to wake up." Art had the dial set to the smallest charge. It took 20 minutes for the rat to come back to life.

"If a rat wakes up in 20 minutes at the smallest charge how long do you think that would last on a human, Gem?" Art was already calculating sizes and weights in his brilliant mind. He had an answer a couple of seconds after he asked the question. It just came to him.

"It probably wouldn't even register with him. I would play it safe with Ted and Jack. Crank it up to just below max for them. Do not show mercy. Remember these dudes tried to rape me and succeeded in the case of Pam. Who knows how many other girls they have plugged? If it kills them so much the better." A bitterness was oozing out of Gem that Art had not observed before. She could probably be moody at times, he thought to himself.

The time came. Art left the access and stayed in the shadows under the stairs. When Ted passed, he aimed at the back of his head and fired. The guy hit the floor like a rock. Art went and took him under the arms back to the access point and in a few minutes, he was in the room with Gem. She had an angry look on her face that Art would not like to meet had he been Ted. They laid him out on the table. He was breathing but defiantly out cold.

"How do we get to his um... you know, Gem? Thing-a-ma-giggy?"

"You're a man, Art. How do you get to yours?" Her comment was cold, and it hurt. Art did the honors. Ted stirred but did not waken. The ex-professor stood ready with the stun gun just in case he came too. This time he had the dial all the way up.

"Gross," she said to herself as she took up the needle and made the injection. A slight, red, bump appeared where the needle penetrated but nothing more.

"You can dress him now, Art." Her voice was a bit softer this time around. Perhaps she was thinking about the ramifications. Who knows? Can a man ever figure out a woman?

"That went well, I think, didn't it?" Gem was quiet and did not answer. Ted was dressed and in a matter of minutes deposited in a stall in the restroom. They would monitor him when he woke up and see what happened.

It took about 15 minutes before Ted stirred then he woke and rubbed his eyes. He was setting with his pants down on the toilet.

"Weird sensation down there," he muttered as he looked at himself. All appeared normal. He could not go though he felt like he needed to. He stood up and pulled up his pants then looked in the toilet. There was nothing there.

"I must have fallen asleep. What time is it? That late? I had better get to class." He was talking out loud to himself as he left the restroom and headed out of the door to the next building. As Art and Gem watched they did not notice any limp. He walked quite normal. Art addressed Gem.

"Will that stuff affect their going to the restroom?" Art was taking another look at this woman. Now he knew why it would be wise that no other people found out about MAP. It presented a temptation that would have been hard to resist. Suppose a giant corporation-built acres and acres of hardware to spy on everybody like they were spying on Ted now? A person with MAP could plant explosives all over the place and blow it to smithereens. They could assonate anyone, anywhere. Just set up MAP, stick the tip of a pistol out of the mass and pull the trigger. The sound would be absorbed inside, and the bullet would go homing in on its target. No one would know where it came from or find even a trace of the weapon unless people on the outside could see the unit and the door in earth reality. He would have to check out ways to cloak it. He brought his mind back to the question he had asked as Gem started talking.

"I don't think so. The only way it would affect it is if he got an erection before he did his thing. That will not happen for a couple of hours. It will take that long for the numbness to ware off. He will not have any trouble until this evening when the girls come over. Then when they get him hot, he should not feel a thing until he goes. At that time though I really want to be near to see what happens. Poor Ted is going to think he found hades. That dude is going to burn, burn, burn." She ended with that clip to her breath that showed she had been holding it.

"Will I ever dare to go to sleep when you are around me, Gem?"

"If you stay a good boy, Art. That shouldn't be a problem."

"I have a question I have been meaning to discuss with you. Not that we could do much about it now with Ted being done. What will happen to Pam if the rape never takes place? Will she go on and get her degree and with her genus win the Nobel Peace Prize or something like that?" How bad are we changing the timeline here? Will we even know our world when we get back? I have seen movies?"

"Do you think you could find out, Art? If you can travel in time perhaps, we could follow her career for a while. At least 9 years or so to get us back to our timeline. If she does not end up as a drunk, all we will know is this was a good action to take on our part. Perhaps old what's-his-name might even give us a few Browne points." A picture of the ancient one popped into Gem's mind as she responded. Was his beard white or what?

"Good idea. We probably should learn how to do that and monitor the results in the future before we take vengeance into our own hands next time. We could see how this affects Ted and Jack also. It will give us more information on what we are dealing with and how best to use it on future excursions." A couple of hours passed, and they entered Jack's room. He was already asleep on his bed. Art looked at the schedule. Jack had written tomorrow by Pam's name and had drawn an evil smiley face by it.

Art hit him with the stun gun. His head moved sideways and slumped. Both Gem and Art ran to check on him. He was dead.

A sickening feeling crept over Art. He had killed someone. He was a criminal now. He knew what guilt felt like. Life would never be the same again. He looked at the gun. It was still on stun.

"He should still be alive! What do we do now, Gem?" Art was beside himself with remorse. He was wringing his hands in anguish.

"How should I know? Give him CPR, I suppose." Without waiting another minute, she went into action. Two minutes later Jack was breathing normally.

"Good work, Girl. That was close. Should we still do him?"

"What do you think, Art? Will he have the guts to do this on his own if Ted is out of commission?"

"Your guess is as good as mine on that one," he responded then continued speaking while adjusting the stun gun to a lower level. He saw that it was all the way up to the top of the stun level though not in kill mode yet.

"I think Jack is the instigator. If he were not leading, Ted probably would not follow. I think we need to do him. Besides, he is as guilty as the other one. He needs the treatment as well. What is fair for one is fair for the other."

"Why do you think the pulse killed him rather than stun him like on Ted?" Gem asked. She was checking his sleeping form over as she spoke.

"When Ted moved down in that room, I turned the stun dial up to full power. The dial is right next to the trigger. If a person does not fall when the pulse hits them the first time, the gun bearer can dial up without pushing the kill switch. I think maximum stun power is the lowest level of the kill mode."

"This guy must be on pills," Gem stated.

"What do you mean, Pills?"

"They have pills out now that make men larger."

She finished her injection and Art re-dressed him. They re-checked his vitals. He was breathing normally. As they pulled him back up in bed, they noticed a scar on his chest.

"Looks like he had an operation on his heart at one time."

"Could have been that he had a pacemaker installed. The kid must have had heart problems," Gem commented. "That is probably what happened. The stun gun stopped the pacemaker. What would have happened if I could not have brought him back around?"

"Probably he would have been discovered by Ted. And when the autopsy finished, his death would have been attributed to pacemaker failure."

"You're probably right. If your heart stops tonight, Jack, when the fire comes, know this, you had it coming. And by the way, here is that kiss you tried to steal from me or my younger, a couple of weeks ago." She bent and kissed him on his forehead. He moaned but did not waken.

"Why did you do that, Gem?" Art looked perturbed as he asked the question. It was hard to see his woman kissing another man let alone one that was several years her junior.

"Because he's cute. Don't you think he's cute, Art."?

"Not even close," he replied. "Besides, you already did mouth to mouth with him for nearly five minutes. I timed it."

They came back to watch the party. They had seen it once before, but it would be interesting to note the changes this time around. At about 12:00 Jack came in with a brunet.

They kissed a little and had a few beers. Jack was feeling her out when Ted entered with his blond. Jack tossed them both a beer and soon the party got down to the hot stuff. They were playing strip poker. Both girls were nearly naked when Jack decked the pile with the winning card. This is the part Art and Gem had been waiting for. They were within, looking out so could not be noticed. Ted came first and when he climaxed, let out a blood curdling scream. He was rolling on the floor. The action set Jack off and he followed. The girls looked horror stricken. They jumped up and grabbed the first clothes they could reach, half of them were not their own. They literally ran out of the door. Jack and Ted were still rolling around. Both were crying like babies. Jack found a half filled can of beer and poured it on himself to cool his jets, but it only seemed to burn more.

"You sure brewed a hot mixture, Gem! This is one night they will never forget as long as they live and as for your friend, Pam, this little bit of agony they are experiencing now will save a lifetime of agony she would have had to suffer."

"And probably several other unsuspecting girls too," Gem added. "It serves em right."

"What about future encounters with other women, Gem? Will they be able to ever do it again or will this make them into eunuchs?"

"Their sperm producing mechanism is fried, Art. The formaldehyde I believe will sterilize them. But having never done this before perhaps their body will be able to overcome the toxins at some point later. If we use the camera to monitor them a few months into the future, we will know for sure. I personally hope they can never do it again."

"We could do a quick check now, say nine months down the line to see if their attitudes have changed."

"OK. Let us do it." They burned a wormhole into the future and returned to Earth Reality some ten months later. Jack and Ted no longer roomed together. Gem wondered if they were even in college. She took a side trip with Art to the Administration Building and with the use of the camera found the files on both men. Both had dropped out of college several weeks earlier. Apparently without women in the picture-if that were the case-they had lost interest in bettering their education. The couple did not go back to follow up. Whatever happened would have to be.

The team entered the river and were soon back to Art's house.

"Could I talk to you seriously, Art?" Gem asked as she started to chew on a hangnail that was giving her the fits. It was more of a nervous gesture than anything else. It was annoying though.

"Sure! Fire away." You sound troubled.

"I don't know how to put this, but after what we did back there, it would be really easy for you to go back and prevent the death of your wife and son. If you did that, what would happen to us?"

"I have been doing some serious thinking about that same thing, Gem. When the stun gun killed Jack, I was really freaked out. I never had any intentions of using MAP to kill. Somehow, I feel killing gets into God's realm.

If I did manage to stop the rape and murder of my wife, she would not die. Had she not died; I never would have discovered MAP. Once I stopped it, I probably would not exist in here. The lights would just go out and I would still be teaching at the University. I would become me, back then with no knowledge of here and now. I do not think MAP was sent for me to play God. If I even attempted it, I think it would be taken away and mean my destruction. On the other hand, I do not know the real purpose. Meeting Methuselah back there answered at least one question you asked last week. was there a higher power involved in leading me to the discovery of MAP? Now I believe there was. Had I not discovered it quite by accident, a thousand things would change. Add to that if only one in a million can pass whatever test is being given, then what does that entail? Perhaps if I prevented her death, I would pass the test? Perhaps if I did not, I would pass the test? Perhaps the test has nothing to do with her at all? Perhaps after doing all that needs to be done here in this time universe, I will go back. Yet again, perhaps she is just the thing I needed to get to where I am? After considering all these things, I do not plan to stop the death of her and my son. I do not feel comfortable in taking this power and using it for that purpose as good as it may seem. I love you. I have grieved their loss and moved on. Besides, if I held to the past, you would not be in my life and neither would Kanna. I do not think life would be the same again if either one of you were lost to me. I don't know, but I think I might use MAP to, to..." He did not finish but Gem knew what he was trying to say. "Perhaps that is the test?" he questioned softly to himself.

Gem came closer and placed her arms around him. She kissed him on the back of the neck and whispered in his ear.

"Let us go out somewhere and eat a monster meal. I am famished."

"That is a good idea, Sweetheart. After all, if you count all the time that has elapsed, past, present and future, you could probably say without lying that we have been longer without a meal than any others in history. It has been years since we ate, literally. It is just what the Dr. Ordered, Dr. Jackal."

"OK, Mr. Hyde!"

They went to a Chinese place and ordered the sea food special. It was tasty.

"Next time we get hungry, Gem, if we are within why don't we make a meal out of our imagination? It seems like that would be a cook's paradise! We can make it inside and take it out to eat rather than go out to eat."

"Great idea, A.r.t.t.y," she laughed as she strung out the words before asking another question.

"When do you plan to get on the trail of the lawn maintenance guy?" She finally ripped the hangnail completely off her finger. Blood spurted momentarily as she spit it on the ground. She sucked it away and spit one more time.

"Perhaps in a couple of days. I have been in the Eternal Reality so long it feels great to be back on earth. I would like to escort you to your home or wherever you must go to see how rich you have become first if you do not mind. Besides, we have that $30,000.00 shopping spree to go on, remember?" Gem looked sullen.

"Art? Do not take this wrong, but I would rather not have you go home with me tonight. I will come back tomorrow evening after I have done my running around. Then we can plan our spending spree. If you have the time and would not mind? I would like to request that you book us a flight to Canada. They have this gigantic mall up there I have been dying to go to. That is where I want to go shopping." Art looked at her a long time before responding. He was a little surprised and disappointed at the same time.

"We don't need a flight to get there."

"I know, but I want it to be romantic. I have always dreamed of flying off there with my beloved and spending two or three nights in exotic motels. It can be like a honeymoon." A warm, cozy, contented smile crossed her face as she pictured it all in her mind. There would be a fireplace in their special retreat. She would purchase them some big, white fuzzy bathrobes and curl up on a tiger rug in front of the blaze. If it were too warm, they would turn on the air conditioner and light a fire. She knew she wanted the fire.

"OK. That is fine with me. Will you be taking the van, to your house?"

"It's the only vehicle I have. Yours is in the garage, isn't it?"

"No. It is at your house. And yes, it is in the garage, but it is in your garage."

"Oh. I forgot. Then we will go there after the meal. You can pick it up and we will both have transportation."

"OK, Babe. You're the boss." Art tried to sound cheery, but Gem could tell he was disappointed.

"Cheer up, guy. I'll be back before you know it and if that account is even half what I expect it to be, I'll be wanting to spend a lot more than $30,000.00." Her eyes really sparkled as she emphasized the spending part. Art could not help himself. He took her into his arms and gave her a passionate kiss. She seemed to be incredibly pleased, returning the favor with one of her own.

Art was home now and did not know what to do with himself. He missed her. He wondered how he become attached to her so quickly. Did he miss Sandra so much that he settled for the first person who showed an interest in him? No. She was different. But Gem was one in a million. He knew it deep inside like other things he had experienced. He had heard somewhere that each person has 12 soul mates available to them if they could only find them. Most people did not even find one. But there were those rare Romeo and Juliette stories you hear about every so often. Was this one? Hopefully, it would end better. Much better! Then he realized he could choose the ending he wanted in more ways than one. This was the ultimate love story. No, he did not want to lose her and now he need not. He had "Absolute Choice." Neither did he want to go on his quest without her by him but if he hurried, he might get it over within twenty-four hours. Then when she returned, they could plan what to do on their Canadian trip. Canadian trip? That is what he needed to do. He logged onto the Internet and booked a couple of flights. They would be leaving in three days. After the booking, he went down to the stationary unit and fired it up. He picked up a digital camera and Rod's glasses. He also pocketed one of the stun guns. Once inside he put the glasses on. In just a few moments he was traveling through time. He found himself at an optical place. Rod was trying on the glasses. Art concentrated. If he allowed himself to do it, he could see through Rod's eyes. He followed with him for a while then went forward in time. Art did not recognize Rod's house. It was smaller than the one he had lived in next door. As he traveled with him, speeding up and slowing down, he followed him to various houses where he did maintenance. Nothing unusual seemed to happen. He followed the glasses all the way back to the present time and discovered nothing.

He tried again. The glasses went back 10 years. He was

about to give up when he took them off. Once they were off, he realized what had happened. Rod did not need glasses. He had 20/20 vision or better and was using it now. He was peeking through a window. There was about a 12-year-old girl undressing for a shower. Rod watched her for a little bit and took out a book. He wrote something in it. Then he put the glasses back on. Art followed the book back to the point Rod wrote it. He wrote notes about thirteen times. Art marked those times in the timeline. Then he checked out Rod at work. Something had to click soon, or he might as well give up. The day was misty. A light rain was coming down. Rod was cussing under his breath when the mower broke. After a few minutes though, instead of cussing more, a wicked gleam came into his eyes. Art drew off to the side and watched. The mower broke at the 12-year old's home. Rod loaded up the rider and headed out. He went to his shop and removed the blade. It had broken when he struck a rock. The maintenance man took the broken blade to the grinder and reshaped the remaining edge. He ground down the broken edge until it fit in a short pipe.

The little book came out and Art was horror stricken by what he saw. Dancing around the mower man were tiny dark shadows. They would jump in and out of Rod's mind and as they did so, little sparks of fire would flare up. When that happened, Rod got an unholy, wicked grin on his face. Whenever a shadow figure completely disappeared in Rod's head, his eyes would glow momentarily then return to normal. Later that evening he drove back to the house. He let himself in the girl's window and came up to her while she was sleeping. He stuffed a filthy sock in her mouth and taped it shut. Then struck her with the pipe end of the weapon. The black shadows were darting everywhere. Whenever one penetrated Rod's head, he struck. Sometimes with the pipe end and other times with the blade. Art put the glasses back on. He could not stand it. They blocked out the sight. He had been so taken back by the horror of it all, he forgot to use the camera. As much as he hated to do so, he went back to just before the first blow landed and took a picture of the girl's face. After that, this time around, he had the glasses on so he could not see. Only the camera saw. It was enough. Art pulled the stun gun from his pocket. He set the switch to kill mode and pulled the trigger. Rod doubled over and fell face down on the girl. Out of the blast, three fiery shadows entered through the pulse stream and struck Art in the hand. Because he did not have the metaphysical accelerator, the shot from the stun gun did not kill Rod. He recovered quickly, put his glasses on and retreated through the window.

Art knew he had been to slow to save the girl, but he had tried in the only way he knew to help. He followed the truck toward Rod's house when it was all over. Just before the maintenance man turned into his drive, he turned down a dead-end road and walked up a short trail. At its end, he buried the weapon. Art knew he had to get it. It would be proof along with the photos. Somehow, he knew that weapon could not go within. The living particles would be removed. It had to be sealed up in something. If he only had remembered to bring the beam camera, he could have traveled back in the physical realm through time. He decided that is what he would do. He would come back for the weapons later.

The next murder came about three weeks later. Rod's mower broke down at another home and the killer planned another visit. The dark shadows with their fiery points were leaping around him again. That wicked grin was back. This victim was a man. An old man from what Art could see. Rod did terrible things to him. The wheel had broken this time, so the madman made a weapon out of that. During this murder, Art heard voices.

"Art, old buddy. You can stop this guy. You know that. You have the power."

"Ya, man. Do something about this senseless killing."

"You could hack him up like he is hacking this poor old man. He won't even know what hit him."

"Yes, yes, Art," a third voice came into his mind this time. "You could go and get your portable unit. The one you scrapped. You could catch Rod at work tomorrow when he is mowing the neighbor's lawn. You could bring back your ax and let him have it. Could you imagine how funny it would look to see this mower guy riding on his mower and an arm falls off? Swish. It would be so easy."

"That it would, old buddy. You would not need to stop with the arm. Take a leg, take both arms. His head would look groovy. Get it? A few grooves in it from the ax."

"No one would have to know. You could put the pieces under the rider when you were through, and they would think the poor guy had a heart attack and fell off his mower."

"And got run over," another one chided.

"Think of your wife and son, Art. You are a father. You could save their lives. You could end this horror right now."

Art fought off the thoughts and followed the truck as it left the old man's house. Rod again buried the weapon at the end of the trail. The guy was a lunatic. He made little grave markers and placed them over each weapon. Here lies Xpock. May he fertilize the trees. Here lies Xzack. May he live long in our memories causing them to flourish, green. Rod would have a little ceremony for each weapon. After it was finished, he would put the glasses on and become another person. There were seven murders before he got to Sonny. By that time Art was sick. He would not be able to enjoy a vacation with Gem now. The horrors of what he had seen were too terrible. He decided to rest before watching the way his family had been taken. The camera was full of pictures. Art downloaded three or four random ones and looked at them. They were good enough. Rod's face was clearly seen in one of the samples. He took the small memory card out and stored it in a magnetic proof box.

At the car he looked for the camera. He needed to go back for the weapons. There were two graveyards. The camera was not there. Then he remembered he had accidently left it in the van. He would get it when Gem came the next day. He retired and drifted off into a restless sleep. Dark shadows lingered nearby. He tried to face them, but they were sneaky.

They darted at him and retreated as he turned to face them. The game continued for 10 minutes. Art was tiring. Then he was struck. The fire did not burn as he expected but tickled. He wanted to laugh but could not. Then they were gone, and he slept. He was awakened by the antique clock as it struck seven times. He turned over and went back to sleep. This time he dreamed of the purple castle and when he opened the door, Gem was there smiling at him. He took her in his arms and slept some more but she turned into a purple shadow with orange flaming edges. When she struck him, it burned. There were dark violet shadows lurking around him. One took the form of a beautiful angel and began to speak.

"Art? There is something you must know. Do you remember how Methuselah told you about the three layers of reality? He did not give you the entire story. There are six layers you can pass through. The seventh is Eternity itself. You may have heard of the seventh heaven. There is such a place, and it is beautiful beyond description. It is where Methuselah has his beautiful home. No evil thing can exist there. All those bad things you saw will be forever erased from your memory. Come and I will show you." The angel took him to an open field. He saw two gates set up. They were different than his. The units he had constructed were crude compared to these. These entrances were not a dull gray like the ones he was used to but shimmering silver with deep violet hews along the edges. They were beautiful. Sweet music, like the songs of angels came softly to his ears. The scent in the air was that of a garden with a thousand flowers. He was hypnotized by the beauty and serenity of it all.

She led him to the center between the two entrances, then explained to him what he was seeing. She first pointed to the unit on the right.

"If you go through this entrance and the other two within, you will enter the Eternity I was telling you about. On the other hand, if you go through this entrance, you will also get to Eternity. The entrance on the left is easier. You can pass through the levels very quickly. You do not have to pass any test to get there. You can go instantly. Your wife is there and your son. Once inside you will be able to use your great powers to do an unlimited amount of good. In here you will be given even greater power. You will not have to wait for knowledge. I will be near you and you can talk to me whenever you like. Ask me any question and you will get an immediate answer. I am much more powerful than Methuselah. You will be able to think things into existence. Speak and it will be done. You will be a great genie. A powerful magician with eternal realities at your instant command. Come and I will give you a demonstration."

She entered and Art followed. The texture of the place was not as fluid as what he was used to in the realities where he had traveled. It was warmer and cozier. It felt nice to the touch. It seemed to caress his entire body all over, soft, like the kiss of an angel.

"Now, Art. Commmme, commm, mm through this next door, or, or." The echoes were soothing to his ears. "You will like this re-reality even bet-better." The violet angel's wings shimmered with a golden color. Her face radiated as she neared the next inner gate. She had a heavenly, sweet smile on her face. Art had never seen anyone so beautiful. "Commmmmm," she whispered. Art felt himself being drawn toward her, reaching out to embrace her. She looked like his Gem only turned into a goddess of splendor.

"Just a little further, little fur, fur r, ther, r. That is the way. It is so beautiful inside. You will love, ove it." At that moment, Art turned and saw Kanna outside of the gate. A dark shadow with a fiery orange tail had grabbed her and was whisking her away.

"Help me, Daddy! Please," she cried. Art felt himself running toward her, diving through the entrance. He struck the ground and rolled then stood up. Kanna was not there. Then the dream ended, and he slept some more.

Gem did not arrive when she said she would. Art got up and showered. As he looked in the mirror, he saw what looked like blisters all over his face. He got out some cortisone cream and in a few minutes they nearly disappeared. He shaved and showered then gave her a call. She did not answer. She must be on her way, he thought but when an hour passed and she did not appear, he began to worry. He decided to drive over to her house. He would probably meet her coming he thought. But that was not to happen. The van was in the driveway and he breathed a sigh of relief. She was home. He rang the doorbell six times, but no one answered. Then a neighbor came over.

"Have you seen Gem?" Art asked her.

"Yes," the lady replied. "Some policemen came by and took her away in their car. What happened to your face?"

"Police? Are you sure?" Art avoided answering her question about his face. He would have to go inside of MAP for a while and get those pesky things healed as soon as he got back to his stationary unit.

"As sure as I am standing here. She is probably down at their office. If I were you that is where I would go to find her." The woman spoke very matter-of-factly.

"Thanks," Art replied and got in his car. He did not know where the police station was in this town, but after driving around for a while found it. He inquired at the desk if a Gem Davidson was there. The receptionist told him that she was not. They had brought her in on charges of manslaughter and leaving the scene of an accident. A van matching the description of hers had struck a car. A passenger had been killed. Then the van had vanished but not before witnesses had tipped the officers off as to where she lived. When Gem drove up, they apprehended her. She was not there however, because she had mysteriously disappeared from her cell before bail could be posted.

"Officers have seen a lot of strange things, Mr. but Miss Davidson's manner of disappearance beats them all. Once in her cell, she pulled a contraption out of her pants and opened it. It buzzed, she stepped into it and disappeared. Then the contraption disappeared also. I am not supposed to tell anyone about this," she whispered. "But it is just too strange." Art left. Clearly the office was not following protocol. He should have been questioned but they did not even look his direction as he walked out the door. Two of the officers were on the phone. He heard the word FBI. He knew he had to get out of there. Gem was somewhere in trouble and needed him. She had probably tried to call but would not have been able to reach him as he was doing his quest. He went back to her house and looked at the van. There was a dent on the bumper he had somehow missed. It had blue paint on it. So, the car that struck them must have been blue. All they would have to do was check the paint and to see if it matched the wrecked car. He went to his trunk and pulled out some sandpaper. In a couple of minutes, the paint was gone. He finished it off with a rinse of Cocoa Cola. That removed some of the rust from other places on the bumper and made it all blend together. The chances were that they had already matched up the paint. What would this mean? If she came back, they would take her again. This time they would search her and make sure there were no concealed items in her clothing.

Gem watched Art drive away. She was home but locked in the Eternal Reality. They had taken the portable camera from the back of her van. She had taken MAP from Art's case and stuffed it in her pants when he was not looking. She needed to take a trip of her own and go back to where she had last seen her father. He had disappeared over nine years ago. He was never heard from again. Nobody ever turned up. She felt he was alive somewhere and had to get to him if that were true? Therefore, she needed MAP. Therefore, she did not want Art trailing along. Her dad had been with the CIA. Art did not need any CIA involvement with his discovery. They were the last people who should discover what he had. Gem kept the secret of her father's occupation from her mother. When "Daddy," as she called him found out that she knew, he told her about the bank account in Switzerland and gave her the card.

"I could never let your mother know about this, Gem," he said. "It would finish her off. She is not in good health and this would cause her to worry herself to death. You must never tell her. If I go on a case someday and never return, you can access this account. There is enough money there to provide for both you and your mothers needs. It can take care of your college bill as well. But wait at least a year before you access it to make sure I am gone. By then you will be 21 years old. Then it will be safe. If you do not hear from me for over a year, then I will be dead." She could still hear his voice in her head as if he were standing right beside her at that very moment.

The year was nearly up when her purse had been stolen. She had never been able to access the account. She planned to do that the first thing when she got home, but the police had been there waiting. They had posted a steak out. She managed to hide her purse in the van where she was sure they would not find it. When she left the cell through MAP, she headed home and retrieved her purse. She set up the processor, exited MAP and made the call. The account was still active. Money had been added within the last week. If her father was not alive, someone else had access to that account. She had to find out who. After entering MAP again, something had happened. The portable unit had fallen over. A gust of wind coming in from the open window had done it. Some of the conductors broke. It no longer trapped a gray button. She took it within but knew so little about it that she was afraid to work on it for fear of making things worse. She would have to contact Art. He could fix things. They could do something about the accident. Perhaps bring the dead guy back to Earth Reality and plant some alibi in his head. It would work out. It had to work out! She was no criminal. She was to be Art's wife and Kanna's mother. Things like this did not happen to nice people.

When Art did not enter the house, she was at first stunned. After thinking things over she realized perhaps her plight was not so bad after all. There was no way he could even see her with the portable camera down at the police station. She would have to get it. Then she would take a trip to Switzerland and find out what was happening with the account. There was over two million dollars in it. Art would just have to wait.

Art had a lot of decisions to make. He needed the camera. He needed to prevent the accident. That would mean a trip back to warn himself not to drive home in the MAP reality. That would stop the accident but might also cancel a lot of what had taken place since. The trip back to get Gem's purse might not happen. At least not the way it had. In that case, they would not perform the injections on Ted and Jack and Pam would be raped. Art and Gem would most likely not remember the events because they would not happen. Stopping the accident though was a must. It would stop the police investigation and the possible intrusion by the FBI. It would also probably erase the trip back to track the murders Rod had committed. Since he could not go back for the weapons without the portable, particle beam camera, he probably should forget about the whole thing. But the look he saw on the 12-year-old girls face haunted him. This man needed to be brought to justice. He would go back and stop the accident from happening but not yet. He would go ahead in time and see when Rod would strike again. He went downstairs and turned on the stationery unit. Once inside he headed forward in time. Rod had moved back to Columbus. That is where the 12-year-old had lived. As he stalked him from the Eternal Reality, it did not take long to find the next victim. It would happen in 24 hours.

Rod had re-established his business and was caring for the lawns of several of his old clients again. He even was doing the house where the 12-year-old girl had been killed eight years earlier. This was the place where his next strike would be. This time it would be the mother. Art took note of the time and returned to the present. Should he go and record the death of his wife and son? It only took a minute to make up his mind. He would go. He arrived there right on time.

Rod entered Sonny's room through the door to the deck. Art put on the glasses and took the pictures. Right after Rod left Sonny's room, Art passed the closet. As he looked in, he saw Kanna. She was trembling. He bent down and she came close to his ear. She was younger but still had that same look he had fallen in love with. She was crying silently. Giant tears were rolling down her cheeks.

"You have to stop him, Daddy! Hurry and stop him! He is going to kill our Mommy."

"I know, Sweetheart. I know. I am going right away. You stay hidden and daddy will come back for you later."

By the time he got to Sandra's room he knew he was too late. He took the pictures and returned to current time. Over the next several hours he put all the evidence together. The letter read as follows.

To whom it may concern.

I am writing this to you so that you can resolve a string of unsolved murders. What I am about to write is going to be beyond your ability to understand. Do not try to figure it out. The technology in place here is otherworldly. I do not know how to describe what has been done. To simplify it, let us just say I am a psychic who can record the images of my impressions. This I have done with a digital camera. You will find photos of several murders on a memory card enclosed in the envelope. I only looked at 3 or 4 of the photos and they were good. You can clearly identify the suspect in them. You will see the various weapons he used to kill and mane his victims. I will give you the address later as to where they are buried. Once again, do not try to figure out how all this was accomplished. It is beyond human comprehension currently. Only apprehend the killer. He will strike again at the home of one of his first victims this evening at precisely midnight. This is the address. It is 127 Colombo Dr. Columbus, Ohio. The name of the murderer is Rod Johnson. He is in the lawn maintenance business. He made a specialized weapon for each murder. You will find the addresses of each victim at the front of the digital images. All you need to do is compare them with your records and you will find this is all true. The pictures of the victims will match those in your records. There will even be photos like the ones you took when you arrived on the scene of the crime. So please. Go to Columbus Dr. Get their early. Though the law will not allow you to use these photos in a trial, if you follow these instructions exactly, you will catch him in the act of murder. That way you will have the proof you need to put him away for good. This guy should receive the death penalty ten times over.

If you need more proof, there is a path that leads off from Shafer St. Shafer St. is located on the East side of Columbus. It is a dead-end road. A subdivision was started there but never finished. The path goes up to the left. In a small clearing, you will find what looks like a pet, graveyard with little markers. Under the markers, you will find the weapons that were used in two thirds of the murders. The rest of them you will find at an address on the second memory card with the photos of yet another three victims.

This matter is urgent. It demands your immediate action.

Art traveled to the Columbus Police Department in the MAP Reality. When an officer at one of the desks turned around to get a cup of coffee, he put his hand through the gate and dropped the letter down with the envelope on the desk. He had taken precautions to leave no fingerprints or any clues as to where it came from. He decided to stay on and watch to see what would be done. When officer, Handel turned around and read the letter, he called his supervisor over.

"Hey, Charlie. Where did this come from? Did you put it on my desk?"

"Put what on your desk?"

"This letter about a string of unsolved murders and that the killer plans to strike again this evening around midnight."

"What are you talking about? There have been no letters like that in this department."

"Well, there is one now. Look at this. It even gives the guy's name." Charlie read the letter and asked.

"Where did this come from, John?"

"I don't know. I got up to get a cup of coffee and when I came back, the letter was here. The person who wrote it claimed to be a psychic or something. He said he used otherworldly means to gather the information so maybe he made it appear by the same means."

"What do you think we should do about it?" The officer was baffled by the entire thing. He was also skeptical. There had been more than one time his partner had played a trick on him. Perhaps this was one of his April Fool's Day Jokes.

"Check it out, of course but keep this under your hat. Both of us will go. We can see if this is for real if we find the supposed graveyard for the weapons. Look! Here is the envelope with the memory cards. Do we have something we can use to look them over before we take off on some wild goose chase?" Handel asked as he held the card up to the light to get a better look at it.

"There is a digital camera in the lab that takes that same card. Let us check it out." They went to the lab and loaded the second card. In a couple of minutes, the pictures appeared in the little screen at the back. It was the picture of Sonny and Sandra. As the gruesome pictures appeared on the screen both officers colored. Charlie nearly threw up. He had seen a lot of stuff, but this was horrible. They removed the card and inserted the second one. The first picture they saw was of the face of a horrified, 12-year-old girl then there was one of the pipes breaking her arm. Charlie turned white.

"I remember that case, Handel. She was my niece. This photographer is sick. Perhaps this so-called psychic is the one who killed her. How else could pictures like these be taken?"

"Why would he send us the photos then and tell us when he is planning to strike again?" Handel asked as he thought the situation through a bit more. A lot of criminals were stupid but not that stupid. First, they had to see if it checked out.

"Could be guilt. Look at this! Here is a picture of the killer with the weapon right in his hand. He could not take a picture of himself doing this stuff unless he sat up a camera and controlled the shutter via remote. This is uncanny. We have enough information. Let us check out the graveyard. If we find those weapons, we will know this is not some hoax."

The two officers signed out and headed for their cars.

"Let us each take a car. There could be trouble. It could all be a trap. If you see anything suspicious, radio for help Handel, and I will do the same."

Art followed them. It took about 20 minutes for them to get to Shafer St. They had their guns out and ready as they walked up the trail. Just as the letter described, they found the graveyard with its markings of strange names.

"Cover me, Handel. I am going to dig into one of these."

"Be careful, Charlie. They may be mined." Charlie removed one of the markers carefully and begin to scoop away the earth. After about 3 minutes of digging, he unearthed a weapon. It was a lawnmower wheel with a rod and blades inserted into the tread of the tires.

"This thing is for real, Handel. This was the weapon used on the old man if the photos are correct."

Art left them there. He had done what he could. Now it was time to move on. When he re-entered Earth Reality, back at his home, the dark shadows pounced on him the second he came out. This time it was no dream. This time they did not tickle. There were dozens of them hitting him like hornets. They burned and stung. Blisters and welts rose on his skin.

"You didn't kill your wife's, murderer," they screamed. "It is time that you go and join her." A great pressure was pulling at him. He dived back through the opening. They did not follow. Off in the distance he heard the clock strike 6.

Chapter 9

Gem moved into the meditation mode. She followed the trail of the particle beam camera. It was locked in a box labeled, Davidson. There were photos of her van in there too. She could see that a photo had been taken of a dent in her bumper. It had blue paint on it. There were also several photos of a badly smashed Ford Mustang. She saw some guy laying under a tree. He looked Hispanic to her or Asian. So, someone really had died. She shuddered. She manipulated the lock in her mind and opened it. She had to admit that she was getting good at this. She took the camera and made sure to close and lock the lid again. It was then she noticed a pink slip-on top labeled. FBI. Evidence of crime #vb2885403771mt. She did not understand it, but they would really be surprised and mystified when they did not find the camera inside. That would really freak them out. It serves them right, she thought to herself.

Back home she noticed a couple of police cars in her drive. The officers were searching her home. They went into her lab and uncovered her stationary, particle beam camera. They took pictures of it. They went through her drawers and planted some bugging devices at various locations throughout her home. She followed right behind them removing each one and coating the area with some chlorophyll from the crushed leaves she removed from her Aloe Vera plant. This would prevent the items from showing up somewhere in Earth Reality, at least until the living cells died. That would take about half an hour.

A technician came running into the house. He was in full panic mode.

"All of the bugging devices show they are clumped together and following you around the house. As soon as you place one, it is taken down and added to the others. I can track them with the monitor!"

The officers went back to where they had placed the bugs and were surprised to find the guy was correct. They had all been removed. Everyone. Gem decided to have some fun. She went to her closet and pulled out some red watercolor paints. She made a sign in big, red, bloody letters. It read.

"Leave this house at once or I will be forced to take HORRIBLE action!" She put the sign on the floor in the kitchen and zapped it into earth reality then stood back to watch. The tech found it.

"Hey, Guys! Get a load of this. This place is haunted! I'm outa here."

They came in and saw the sign he had dropped, floating to the floor. The technician ran to the van and spun out in his haste to leave. The police followed.

"Let us leave this one for the FBI, Carver. They are supposed to arrive tomorrow morning."

"Good idea. This place is spooky." With that the two exited through the garage.

Gem laughed as they followed the van. Then she grew serious. This was no laughing matter. This was really happening. It had to stop, or better yet, end where it had begun. But that might take it all away? All the stuff she knew might be erased. Her purse would be back where it had been. She had better take the trip and find out about the money first but what good would that do? It could be erased too. She went to where she had hidden her purse. The contents were all there. She found the photos of her parents wedding and her little brother. She found the access card to the bank account and the ruby. It was the largest one she had ever seen. This was what she had wanted to hide from Art. It too had been given to her by her father. He had taken it from an enemy some ten years ago. It was ground to the shape of a lens. A lens that fit in a machine that was hidden somewhere in the archives of some Washington DC storehouse. It was where they stored all those illusive inventions that could change things just a little too much too quickly. She held the gem close in her hand and felt its smooth surface. She had the means now to recover the machine. This ruby had once been inside of it. She could trace the ruby back to the machine, then trace the machine to its current storage place. That, however, would take longer than the time she had to give it now. She would first go to the bank and see what was happening with her father's account, or was it hers now?

Gem flushed the bugging devices down the toilet and tried to take some nourishment. She did not like eating in this reality. The food had little or no taste at all and when some of it got to her tongue, the flavor came too slowly to be enjoyed. Eat she must, however. While she was eating, she heard a clock off somewhere. It chimed 6 times.

Art pondered what to do next. He could not go out because of the shadow stingers. The longer he stayed in the Eternal Reality though, the shorter the time he had left. He needed the camera but then it need not be that camera. He could go and pick one up. He remembered the manufacturer. He went to his safe and stuffed several stacks of 100-dollar bills in it. If he found one that he like he should probably pay for it. After a few mental exercises he was at the showroom adjacent to the plant. There were several models to choose from. He decided a smaller unit would be much handier. He checked them all out. They needed that power surge button or switch if he were to travel in the Earth Reality through time. To do that, he needed only to activate the unit while in MAP. He decided on a small, stainless steel model. It would be nearly indestructible. The display cabinet showed a price tag of $29,999.00. He really was an honest guy. He withdrew 300 Franklins, opened the door into earth reality, removed the camera and placed the bills where it had been. Then he brought his hand back into MAP. It was done. With this unit, he would not be on the time clock and could do nearly everything in Earth Reality. It would just take more time. At home again he remembered a portable prototype MAP processor he had constructed before designing the current model. It worked ok. It just took longer to open than he liked. He could modify it and have another portable unit. Once he had that, he could probably find some place where the fire shadows could not trace him. He went to the scrap pile and found the unit. After working on it for the rest of the afternoon, it was finished. It was about 10.30 in the evening when he fired it up. When he exited however, the fire shadows again pounced all over him.

Art knew he would reverse the auto accident event. The last thing he needed was a bunch of FBI crawling all over the place, getting in the way. Before that happened though, he wanted to see what they would do about Rod. About an hour before the scheduled murder attempt, Art decided to go back and see what progress had been made. He went to the graveyard first and found that all the weapons had been removed. Whoever had done it, tried to put the markers back the way they were just in case the criminal stopped by before he was apprehended. A couple of the markers were out of order. Art spent a few minutes fixing the error. Then he went to the house. He noticed 3 police cars parked in a place Rod would never see them. They had men staked out on three sides of the home. The only part of the home not covered was the front. At 11:55 Rod parked his truck about a block away. He was going to enter through the same window as last time. Soon he was there. He had taken time that day to unlock it. He had asked the lady if he could use the restroom and she consented without question. When he talked to her, he was wearing a new pair of glasses and appeared to be the old friendly gardener personality. He did small talk with her about using a high acid fertilizer on the roses and evergreens to help green them up. He had also collected his monthly check. After tonight he would not get paid. Now he approached the window and removed the screen. He was halfway through it when an officer spoke to him.

"You are under arrest, Rod, for breaking and entering and suspicion of murder. Drop your weapon, now."

Rod slowly retreated from the window and started walking toward the officer.

"Stop, where you are. Rod kept coming. Art saw an arm tense at his side. He had broken a rake at this place so that is what he fashioned the weapon from. Suddenly the rake, dagger was flying toward the officer. Rod was running. Two shots rang out from different directions. The man crumpled and fell to the ground. When the officers reached him, he was dead.

"This is one serial killer who will never kill again," Handel mentioned. "So how are you, Charlie? I see you managed to dodge that rake thing. It is really nasty looking.'

"Ya, that was close. I did not expect it. I guess my reflexes took over when that thing came flying at me. I don't remember making any decisions at all." They called the ambulance and Art made his exit. He went back in time before the accident he was about to erase and mailed another copy of the letter just in case erasing the wreck, erased Rod's death. That way they would get the letter, and this would really happen. He could forget it now and move on with his life. Justice had come full circle. He wondered if the fire shadows were still at his house. He would reverse the accident first and if his calculations were correct, Gem would be back with him that very hour.

Art was back at the medical building with Gem. He tuned in and watched the two of them as they exited the door with the camera.

They got in the van and left.

"It is late, and the traffic is not that bad. We can do it at your house.

"You don't plan to drive in, here do you?" Gem was talking and what she was saying was familiar to him. He could say it in unison with her if he wished.

"Why not? I have done it before. It is a real trip."

"I bet it is. Be careful!" Art watched the expression of the lady's face. She was really questioning this whole thing. He could tell. After this though she would or should have more faith. He crossed his fingers.

"I don't think we can be hit. Remember, we are in a kind of parallel universe."

Art heard a voice in his head. About the time he was ready to stop for a red light.

"You don't need to stop for red lights, Art, remember?"

"That was stupid of me, Gem. I was about to stop for that red light."

"How could that be stupid? You are supposed to stop for red lights." The conversation was familiar this time around.

"Not in here. We could have been hit."

He drove through it and things had changed. Art exited through the MAP unit back at his house. There were no fiery shadows darting at him this time. Gem was sleeping on the couch. She was so beautiful. Tomorrow they would head for Canada, but they still had tonight. He gently lifted her head and set down. He rested back against the couch. Her long hair hung down toward the floor. He began to stroke her gently, petting her head like he would a kitten. She murmured something and continued sleeping. He was exhausted too. He had not slept well the last couple of evenings. He dozed off wondering what changes his actions had reversed. He awoke sometime later and decided to catch the news before going to bed. He reached for the remote. Some lady was talking.

"A man was shot early this morning while trying to escape police. Our sources tell us he was connected to a string of nearly a dozen murders. When interviewed, officers refused to comment on how they happened to be on location at the exact time he attempted another break in and possible murder. Off in the distance the antique clock chimed out the hours. 1, 2, 3, 4, 5, 6, 7, 8. Art slipped into a dreamless sleep with Gem held securely in his arms.

Gem awoke and reached up to caress Art's face with her hands. He awoke and she began talking.

"I had the strangest dream," she commented. "I dreamed that we were driving in the MAP dimension and were struck by a blue Ford Mustang. Some police came out to my house later and put me in a cell. I was taken in on charges of manslaughter. I guess some guy even died in the crash. It was all so real."

"It's good that it was only a dream, dear." Art was fully awake now. He searched his mind and remembered everything. The entire nightmare she had seen was all there. He looked down at her and wondered if they had managed to get her purse.

'Did you find everything in your purse that you expected?" he asked as he stroked her long hair with his left hand.

"Yes, I did," she replied. "I checked on the account and there is over two million in it."

"Wow, Lady. You are rich!"

"I don't know if I am, Art. The account showed activity as recently as last week. Someone is still adding money to it."

"You can be glad they are adding and not subtracting. Any idea who it might be?" Art always had liked a good mystery. This one was turning into a good one.

"Actually, I don't have a clue unless it is my late father. He may still be alive after all these years. I would like to check it out. Did you get the airline tickets all set up for Canada?" she added as an afterthought.

"Sure did. We fly out at 3 this afternoon. That gives us a little time before we must leave. Do you want to go check on that bank account?"

"I haven't decided yet, Art. If my father is still alive, I would like to know before I meet him. I would like to find out exactly what has transpired in the last few years."

"You have all the tools you need to do that, Gem. Feel free to use them if they will help."

"No, I don't have all the tools I need," she responded as she shook her head and looked down at the carpet. "I have some bad news. I broke your portable MAP unit."

"I know you did. Gem." Art spoke with a comforting voice.

"How do you know that? You could not have known. I was home alone when it happened. A gust of wind came in through an open window and knocked it over. Some of the conductors are broken. I think you can fix it."

"The reason I know is that I went and checked up on you, when you didn't get here yesterday as planned."

"Oh, that. There were several complications. I really cannot remember what they were, but things got crazy after MAP broke. I know that much."

"I have another portable MAP unit. I salvaged an old prototype from the scrap heap. I made some modifications. Check this out." Art went and got the unit. He had created a small trigger on it and added a handle. He pushed the trigger and the unit expanded out and ignited instantly. In the matter of seconds, it had trapped another-world button. This unit even dialed down the power immediately after capturing one of those gray cylinders.

"That is really neat," she said as she patted him on the rear.

"Did anyone ever tell you your butt is cute?"

"Can't say as they have. Mine isn't nearly as cute as yours though." Gem looked at him seriously now with her emerald eyes shining like two priceless jewels, then asked.

"How did your detective work go?"

"Good, actually," he replied as he looked off across the room and out the window. The new neighbors had come with a large Ryder truck and were starting to move their things into the house.

"Rod did some awful things. He is dead now. He was shot by Police early this morning at the scene of another crime. They got him before he got the lady."

"That is good, no?"

"Yes, he had it coming. The world will be a little safer place to live now."

"Gem?" Art started spacing out again. His mind seemed to leave his body.

" What is it, Honey?"

"I need to move away from this place. I would like us to go house hunting. We do not need to live here in this area even. In fact, I would like to be several States from here if possible. I never want to come to this city again. We can live anywhere we like. There is just too much, you know, too many memories connected to this place. I would like us to take some time and look around after you see what happened to your father and all. Can you understand?"

"Definitely, Art. That is a great idea. When is the return flight scheduled from Canada?"

"I left that open. We can stay a day, a week, or a month. It is up to you."

"Let us come back in three days and pick up Kanna. Then we will go house hunting, all three of us. We can take a month and travel all over the states, checking out different locations. I do not need to know what is happening with that account right now. It has waited this long. A few more weeks will not matter much. I have felt uneasy about staying around here too. I need to search out some things. I feel like part of me is missing. I know she is out there somewhere waiting. If I can find that part of me, maybe I will understand more about all of this." She moved her arms around in a big circle. "It's going to be fun." She wrapped her arms around Art, and they embraced quietly as he took in the scent of her hair. He loved her. He loved everything about her. This relationship was taking on the characteristics of a match made in heaven, or MAP to be more precise. A strange thought crossed his mind. He spoke it without thinking about the consequences.

"I think my new neighbors would like to buy this house."

"What are you talking about, Art? How do you know?"

"The thought just came forcibly into my mind. They want to be close to their son and daughter-in-law, and there are 3 grandchildren."

"How? I do not understand you sometimes, Art. You have this mind that goes way deep, way deep. It is so deep I can't touch it." She released her hold and walked over to the window shaking a little as she paused in front of it. A car drove up and a younger man and woman got out. They were followed by three children.

"Way too deep, man. Look! There they are. The son, daughter-in-law and their three kids. Art? Your mind just blows me away. Behold, the new owners of your home. She pointed at the kids as they ran around to the back of the house. A golden retriever followed closely at their heals, jumping up occasionally while looking for a ball the boy was sure to throw.

"You sounded sarcastic, when you said that dear."

"You knew this, before didn't you? You met them sometime in the last couple of days and they expressed an interest, right?"

"Nope. I have never seen them before, but I know they will purchase this house. There are some things I just know will happen and this is one of them that is unless we get stuck in some far-off parallel universe or another dimension in time."

"Perhaps old Methuselah paid you another visit and interjected some of these things in that big head or yours again." Gem was thinking back to the meeting with the ancient one as she commented.

"Perhaps?" is all Art questioned about it before walking away from the window.

Methuselah pondered the situation for a few minutes. Since being assigned to these two, he had done quite a lot of work behind the scenes to bring all the events into focus that led up to this point. Most of the problems the couple had made for themselves were resolved but not all. There were now two Gem's in existence. One on her own time zone within, tracking down the mysteries connected with the large bank account, her missing father, and the ruby lens. The other Gem was interacting with Art in Earth Reality. There were also two clocks ticking away the time. Art had recovered a couple of time segments by reversing some of the mistakes he had made. The Gem within, however was a different matter. She had not been given the insight that would enable her to reverse time segments. Art had eight segments left in his Reality. The Gem of both realities only had six. The six within were fast counting down. That is the way it had to be if she remained in the first level of the Eternal Reality. He could give her no further instruction. He only wished for Art's sake that things would change. The ancient one knew what the outcome would be. It was all part of the plan. He just hated to see what these kids would have to go through before getting to the place they were going to end up. Other than that, these two earthly clients were passing the test. Both were intelligent in their own way. By today's standard they would be genius level mentally.

Art had met the darkness and with a little help, had escaped its destructing grasp. The bright shimmering angel had nearly seduced him. Only a moment longer and he would have fallen beyond recovery. He was wiser now and would be less likely to fail in the future. He had even paid for the camera he had purchased from the future. That had given him another time notch. If he would only go back to the manufacturer of the stun guns and pay for them, he could regain more segments. That, however, would speed up his separation from his new love as they would be three-time segments apart.

"Perhaps I can work something out in Canada, or before if I am lucky," Methuselah thought, "to get them back on a closer, time track. He knew before he tried that it would not happen, unless. The ancient one pondered again and ran a hand through his beard as his thoughts streamed by. He was not supposed to alter the plan, but perhaps there was a way to prolong the relationship developing so nicely below him. He would need to advance the Gem within to the second level of the Eternal Reality. This would give her a lot more time to do what she thought she had to do. Time in that level operated at a much faster speed. The only drawback to her being less clarity in viewing those things within the Earth Reality. It would eventually affect Art also but not right away. To launch Gem into the next level, he would have to get the MAP unit she had operational again. If she entered from the opposite side while thinking to exit, she would move to the second level. If he shorted out the circuits again at that time, she would be trapped. This would not be a problem to her physically. In the second level of the Eternal Reality the elements of human existence more closely matched the Earth Reality conditions. Food tasted better. Things were less liquid and more solid. In this level the traveler was nearly immortal. They would age some, but it would take a long time. Already from being in the first level so long, her reproductive organs had regenerated. This level would also keep her further from the darkness. She was not as strong as Art. The added protection could not hurt. He must through any means possible prevent her from getting back to Earth Reality and entering through the wrong side. If this happened, Gem would be in the dimension of the greys and reptilian humanoids. Their advanced technology and way of life would completely mess her up. This was a test Art would have to endure first. It was almost time for that test to start. If certain events could be altered enough, this would help greatly. Methuselah manipulated the conductors on the device just enough to allow them to pass a charge. He also turned the unit over. If she took time to notice, she would realize it but if there were some diversion created, she probably would run headlong into the wrong side, propelling her into level two. In a moment it was done. All he had to do was wait until the next crisis came in her dimension that would cause her to reach for the unit and dive through it. The dye was cast. The ancient one leaned in and waited expectantly.

Gem held the card in her hand. There was a photo of the bank on it. She focused on the photo and did some of the breathing exercises Art had shown her. Then she was traveling. At the entrance of the bank, she paused a moment to be sure it was the right place. The bank's furnishings were very plush. They were all antique. There were indoor gardens with benches and a restaurant where one could get food. Off to the left was a large counter. To the right there were automated machines where people could go to check on their account. She went up to one, but it would not recognize her card. For what it was worth, she had brought the MAP accelerator. She had manipulated the settings. She had gotten a little hum out of it. She would wait for the bank to close and put her hand through and check her balance. She did not need to do that. Just yesterday there was over two million in the account. She did not need to find out what the balance was she only needed to find out who was accessing the account. She located the terminal wires and zeroed in on them with her mind. In time she isolated a call that went to her account. She followed it back to its source. A man had wired the money. She focused on him more closely. In this reality remote viewing was a whole new experience. It had substance. The man did not look like her father although he was about the same size. This man had white hair and a beard. Her father never wore a beard. It was too scratchy he told her. She followed the line back and was standing in a small room. There was a computer and a desk in it. To her left was a door that led into a laboratory of some sort. After looking closely at the man, she could see that it probably was her father. She found some mail but none of it had the right name on it. He was probably living under an alias.

George Davidson was not confined in any way. He lived on what appeared to be a small island in the South Pacific. Tall palm trees swayed gently from side to side while a perfect beach of white sand stretched along an emerald sea. It was beautiful here, almost paradise like. She would try to communicate with him. She fired up the computer and began to write a letter.

"Dear Mr. Davidson," she wrote. That should get his attention.

"This is a note from your daughter, Gem. You will probably be freaked out when you hear from me after all these years. I did not have the means to contact you before. I have met a wonderful man and am planning on getting married soon. He has a beautiful daughter named Kanna. I wanted to let you know this because you will be a Grandpa, finally. You would absolutely love her. I could not access the account you told me about on

my 21st birthday because a couple of days prior to that, my purse was taken. I lost the card and the ruby, but I have both back now. It is a long story how I acquired them. I will not go into detail about that yet. I do not need the money currently. I have done well for myself. You probably know that Mother died about 5 years ago. She was ready. She still felt you were alive somewhere but could not contact us. I love you. I can come and see you personally if you like. I know what the ruby is for. I also know where the machine is that it goes in. If you want me to contact you personally, just type YES on this screen and I will know. The message will stay on the screen until I see that you have read it. At that time, it will disappear. When it is gone, you can write yes or no.

Your daughter,
Gem

George did not see the note for a long time. He was looking out of the window toward the sea. He looked lonely and tired to her. She went up and kissed him gently on the cheek. He felt nothing. Then he turned and saw the computer screen glaring with diminished letters. George walked over to it and peered at the message. He was a brilliant man with a photographic memory. He could have taken it in immediately, but he pondered, taking time to read each word. After checking it out, he looked at the back of the monitor to see where the source of the writing had come from. It did not look normal to him. The letters seemed to float in the air half an inch out from the screen. He sat down and placed his head in his hands. After a couple of minutes, he pulled out a white handkerchief and wiped his brow then placed his fingers on the keys. The message vanished before his eyes and he shook as he wrote.

"I don't know what technology you are using to do this, Gem, but you must not contact me under any circumstances. It is too dangerous. Are you sure no one can intercept this message?" Gem was at the keys. As quickly as he finished, "YES," appeared on the screen.

"No one can read this from any place other than the screen. If there is a surveillance camera focused on the monitor or some inner com system, they could probably pick it out, but that is the only way. Thanks for the word of caution. I will continue in stealth mode. Only you will be able to read my messages in that mode. They could possibly read yours, though? Is there surveillance equipment in your room there?" George wrote back.

"I don't think so, but one never knows."

"I can check for you, Daddy. Just a minute while I do a scan. Oops, bad news. There is equipment in the room. I isolated three sources. Do you want me to disable them? They are not monitoring the screen now. Two are of a revolving type, black and white design. One is at the left of the room the other on the right. The third is in color and has much better optics. It is hidden in the smoke alarm. Right now, it is not watching you but is focused on someone coming up the path." The words faded away as George stood to his feet.

"When can you talk again, Gem?" he typed.

"Whenever you want. You name the time."

"Come back on at 2.00, this time zone. If you can disable the surveillance without them knowing it, do so. I do not want them getting suspicious. Good to hear from you. I miss you and love you. Really wish I could see you again. It seems like a lifetime ago. But it is impossible for you to come. Really, dangerous. Give yourself a big hug for me, sweetheart. Talk to you later. I have a lot of questions. I want you to tell me all about my granddaughter and my future son-in-law."

"You'll like them both. Bye, Daddy. See you at 2:00." Gem walked over to see who was coming to the door. It was a tall, elegant lady. She entered and Gem got a good look at her. She looked for all the world like Pam, but a quite different Pam then the one Gem had known. The lady went into the lab and put on a white coat. There was a high-tech device in some stage of final development. The bottom was saucer shaped. Pam, if that is who she was, soldered a few electrical components together.

"John, Dear," she called. "I think the scale model is ready to test. Do you have a few minutes?"

"I always have time for you, Pam. He went up and placed his arms around her from the back. She stood up and bent to kiss him on the forehead."

"I know you always have time for that, but we have work to do now. We can play later." She seemed to tower over him. So, it was Pam.

"And to think I saved her from Jack and Ted so she could do this, seduce my father?" Gem was furious. She grabbed the MAP unit and opened it quickly. The blue and orange sparks flew into action then cooled. The gray mass was there. Gem thrust herself through it. And headed toward Pam. She must have succeeded in coming back into reality. The ground was hard beneath her feet. Much harder. She ran to the tall woman.

"Just what do you think you are doing here with my father, Pam?" There was no answer. She ran to her father and tried to pull him loose from his grasp, but he never budged.

"Let us find the cover for this unit and get the remote fired up. Did you download those files yesterday on the computer chip, Pam?" George was talking as he brought the cover over to the unit.

"Yes, everything is programed," Pam replied as she packed the extra-long wires into a cover of some sort and screwed it onto the unit.

Gem looked around. There must be something wrong with her eyes. She seemed to be looking at the world through clear plastic lenses. It was not as liquid as within MAP. Things were quite normal. The air was fresher. She must have gone through the wrong direction. She was further in. If old Methuselah was right, she must have advanced to the second level of the Eternal Reality. She walked slowly back to the processor to check. The gray mass was gone. She closed the unit and opened it up again, but it did not even spark. She was trapped, even deeper than before. This was not good. "Art, where are you when I need you?"

Back in the room the contraption was all assembled. Pam was at another computer. There was some sort of map on the screen. She recognized the island of Guam. A light was flashing at one point. Under the light was the word, "destination." Pam punched in some codes and picked up a remote-control unit. She hit the enter button and the computer monitor blanked out. The words "Transmission Successful," appeared on the screen. Another button was pushed, and the small unit hummed and rose about 4 feet above the ground. It hoovered for a moment then vanished in a flash of blue light.

Pam ran over to George and put her arms around him.

"I think we did it, sweetheart!" She went back to the computer screen. The words "Destination Attained," appeared under the blinking light. Where before the blinking light in Guam was in red, now it was green. A box appeared on the screen. "Part #13x being processed. Process completed. Loading part. Transmitting."

A moment later there was another flash of blue and the apparatus was hoovering in the exact location it had disappeared from. It floated down to the floor and a blue light started blinking. There was the sound of humming and a small door opened. Inside was a black component. It had six brass prongs attached to it. Gem's dad took it out and looked it over. He went over to an electrical tester of some sort and hooked up a small, red clamp that was connected to what looked like a glorified ohm meter. He touched another area of the chip with a probe. The needle moved to the far right. He tried each brass prong, and the needle did the same for each.

"Everything appears to be in working order. Let us give the machine a real test now, Pam. Let us see if it can produce some Coco Cola for us."

Pam went to a small cooler and pulled out a bottle. She twisted off the cap and with an eye dropper, placed some of the solution on a pad connected to another monitor.

"Analyzing. Formula charted. Downloading. Ready." The words appeared on the screen almost instantly. Pam took a small chip out of another electrical unit and plugged it into the back of the device. She went to the computer and issued a command. She dumped the Coke into a large glass and placed the empty bottle on the pad. A scanner appeared and passed over the top of the bottle before returning.

"Analyzing. Formula charted. Downloading. Ready." Pam went and pulled another chip from a processor and plugged it into the portable unit resting on the floor. Then she went to the computer and punched in some codes. The unit nearly doubled in size. Gem drew close to see what happened. The top of the unit rose above the base but was connected by what looked like some energy force field. Pam punched in some more commands at the keyboard, picked up the remote again and hit the send button. The unit hummed into action. It went through the same routine as before, vanishing in a flash of brilliant light. It returned about five minutes later with a bottle of Coke, identical to the one on the counter. Gem was amazed!

George was dancing around the room. Pam joined him. They locked arms and twirled.

"Pam and Daddy. I never would have believed it. He is old enough to be her father," she mumbled to herself.

"Of course, he is, Gem. She is your age, and he is your father." Gem paused to listen again. This voice. Where did it come from? She had never heard it audibly before.

"Who are you?" She asked.

"I am your inner voice. At times people call me your conscience. I will be talking to you a lot more now that you are here. I have access to unlimited resources. Ask me a question now and I will show you."

Gem thought for a moment then spoke.

"Pam and Dad just... what shall I say? Faxed a three-dimensional bottle of coke from Guam. Not really faxed it, transported it in that device. What is this unit they have contrived?"

"Good question, Gem. There is a large machine on the Island of Guam in a U.S. Research lab. This machine is a molecular processor. It will analyze any substance and produce it strictly from molecules. The machine your Dad has been working on is a transporting device. This prototype will be in production soon. Navy ships, airplanes, different government offices will have one or several of these units. They will be able to send information as well as solid objects anywhere in the world. The unit your Dad has is small. There will be some that will be much larger. It has taken a long time for them to get here but the project is completed now. It is kind of like a 3D printer on steroids."

"Wow! Technology is that advanced. It is amazing! What shall I call you? What name would you like me to address you by?"

"You can call me, Con."

"OK, Con. Dad did a neat thing. He faxed or transported a bottle of Coke from an island miles away. Can you give me a bottle of coke? I am thirsty."

"Sure," Con responded. "Coming right up. Reach out your hand." Gem did and a bottle of Coke was in it. She opened the cap and drank several swallows. It tasted just like Coco Cola. She could taste things again. That was good!

"Can I get anything I want whenever I want from you?" she asked as she begin to imagine the possibilities.

"Pretty much, as long as you are in this level of reality."

"What happened to me? Why couldn't I materialize in the Earth Reality when I passed through MAP?"

"Because you went through the wrong side."

"Can you fix the machine so I can get back to earth?"

"I can."

"Good. Then will you do it now?" There was nothing more she wanted now but to be back with Art in the earth reality. What would she give for that now? She could not imagine it even. It seemed like a million miles away and it might as well have been.

"I can't."

"Why can't you?"

"I am not allowed to."

"Why aren't you allowed to?" The communication between them was short and to the point.

"Because there are powers higher than me that have placed you where you are for certain reasons that I am not allowed to tell you about. If you only knew how fortunate you are, you would gladly consent to your present condition. It will not last forever. You can do a lot of things from in here. Enjoy this reality while you are given the chance."

"If you say so, Con." Gem went back into the lab. Her dad and Pam were not dancing around anymore. Pam was composing a letter to their headquarters.

"Unit   #PQ3-EER-2957492-M.   Completed and successfully launched." She transmitted the message. In a few minutes, a string of encrypted messages came back. Pam must have known the code by heart. She read through it quickly then turned toward George, or John as she called him.

"The chopper will be here to pick us up at 2:00 this afternoon. We will be taken to Guam. We are to bring the unit with us," Pam told him. Gem looked at her father. He looked sad. He went to the window and looked out across the ocean then turned to the lady.

"Do you think you could get them to postpone that flight for at least half an hour? I have a few things to do here before we leave."

"I can check, John." Pam punched in another message and waited. Soon another encrypted message came back. She looked at it. It was shorter than the last one.

"No can do, John.   Chopper has already been dispatched." George looked downcast. Gem felt sad for him. If only she could get a message to him that would not be seen by Pam, but how?

"Con?"

"Yes, Gem."

"How can I get a message to my father without Pam seeing it?" She kinda liked this short discourse between them, or whoever it was.

"Easy. I will send her to pack. When she leaves, you can put it on the monitor again."

"Can the surveillance cameras pick it up?"

"They could but I can make it, so they won't"

"Do that and then send that woman away. Is she and my father involved?"

"Very much, I am afraid, Gem."

Pam spoke to John now.

"I am going to pack a few things to take with us. We will probably be gone for several days. Henry, and the natives will be caring for the place while we are away. You should probably gather up a few things yourself." She walked out of the lab into the room with the computer monitor then out the door and headed down the walk. George followed her out of the lab. He paused at the monitor and sat down, typing even as he did.

"Gem? If you are watching, you probably know I must go. I will so miss talking with you. I wish I were in a better position to do some of the things I want, but to the world, I am dead. I have a pleasant life. Pam is a comfort to me, and she is brilliant. She is a link to you and that is a help. When she is around, I don't miss you and mother so much." He paused. Gem made his message disappear, then wrote.

"When I first saw you with Pam, I was furious, but I understand, Daddy. Now that I have the means of contacting you, I will do so quite often. The means I am using to communicate with you is way above technology. It is in the realm of the metaphysical. I can communicate with you in numerous ways, totally undetected by even the most advanced technical surveillance systems. That is all I will tell you. Be in touch. Look for me. Your daughter who loves you very much, Gem." The words faded from the monitor.

"I always knew you were brilliant, Gem." The reply came back. "The government is doing a lot of research in metaphysics. I have been a student of that science myself. It has given me access to the latest developments in that area, but I can assure you that they are nowhere nearly as deep into this as you have apparently gone. If they have, they are tight lipped about it. Congratulations, Honey. I will be looking forward to hearing from you. If I need to, how can I contact you?"

"Just a minute, Dad. I will let you know." Gem spoke to Con.

"Just how can he contact me?" she asked. She felt a little stupid talking to this thing. It did not even have a body, only a voice.

"In a lot of ways. I will give you a quick one. Have him write your name on a slip of paper and burn it. I will notify you and you can zero in on him, use what resources he has around him." Gem tapped out a message on the keyboard again.

"Just write the word 'NOW,' on a slip of paper and burn it or wad it up. The message will get to me and I will look you up. I could even be there in an instant if conditions on this side are right. In fact, Dad, I am in this room with you now, right behind you, using the very same keypad you are, but you cannot see me. I saw everything you did with the device you are working on." George turned white and jumped up from his chair. He looked all around the room. He ran into the lab but saw nothing. Then he went back to the keypad and typed quickly, with trembling hands.

"Gem, you are really scaring me now. Are you dead? Are you contacting me from heaven? How deep into this are you?"

"Way deep, Dad. Privileged beyond imagination to be in this position. And no, I am not dead. I am very much alive. Do you have a couple of minutes yet?"

"I think so. I'm just about to have everything packed. Did some already last night. I'm expected to leave today. What do you want to tell me?"

"Your machine transported a bottle of Coke from a molecular processor on the Island of Guam. You are going there in a chopper. The chopper is due to arrive in thirteen minutes. With your transporting device, the government will be able to fax, if you will, three dimensional items of any type to anywhere in the world. Your good but I just asked for a bottle of Coke and one popped into my hand. You will find the half-drunk bottle on the stand by the large recliner." Gem quickly zapped it into Earth reality. It took two hits with the taser to set it though. "I know how Jesus multiplied the loaves and fishes." George was trembling even more now. He looked over at the stand and saw the bottle then turned around to the keys again, looking at a message Gem had written there.

"You don't have to write, Dad. You can just talk to me. I can hear everything. I just cannot talk back to you. Sounds are absorbed."

"I really have to go Gem," he spoke out loud. "Tell me one thing. No tell me two. First how did you know all that information about our work? It is top, top, top secret. If the government knew you knew, they would kill you on sight. But do not answer that question now. Perhaps later when we have more time. Now for the second and most important question. Can you get me out of here, get me to where you are? I am tired of being a political prisoner. I want to come home! I would like nothing better than to spend the rest of my life living like a normal person, with friends and loved ones and grandchildren around. I am so homesick." He looked very tired and incredibly old. As he turned completely around in the room, Gem could see the pleading look in his eyes. She turned and asked Con. The answer came back, and she wrote.

"I can't do it the way you asked, Dad, but I can do something. Go to your appointment. When you get a few free minutes, talk to me. It might take a while, but I will find some way to communicate back. I love you."

"I love you too, Sweetheart. Sorry I never told you that before. I wish I could go back in time. I would do things differently if I only had another chance. Bye Gem."

"Before I say Goodbye, I would like to add one thing. From where I am time travel is possible. After losing my purse with the card to the bank and the other things, I went back in time 10 years to the moment I lost my stuff and got it. Then I brought it back to our time. This is a marvelous opportunity for me. But no one will ever be able to do this except..." Gem stopped typing and the message faded away. George was overwhelmed. He went over and picked up the bottle of coke, took one more look around the room, shook his head back and forth. "I do not understand any of this, someday you will have to tell me all about it." He waved his hand and headed for the door. Just before passing through it he raised the bottle up like a toast then to his lips and finished drinking it.

"This is the best Coco Cola I have ever tasted, daughter. Thanks."

"You're welcome, Dad," she whispered back, but she knew he could not hear her. Suddenly the realm of the supernatural did not seem so supernatural now. What she had just experienced could answer a million questions primitive man had been asking for millennia. What happened when a person died? Could dead people communicate with the living? Could they see what their loved ones were doing any time they wanted? What were ghosts? How could things appear to move without any apparent help from anything? Were miracles really miracles or multidimensional experiences passed back and forth between alternate dimensions or parallel universes? She could list a hundred, no, a thousand that could all be explained now with this new knowledge and universe she dwelt in.

Gem spoke to Con.

"I am homesick too. Can you get me to Art?"

"In part only, but it should be real enough to feel real. Consider it done, Gem."

Chapter 10

Art had a little time before Gem got back from picking up a few things for the trip. There was a concept he wished to verify. Some physicists claimed there were thousands of parallel universes all operating at the same time. Some had even claimed to jump from one to the other. In some parallel existence, a spouse for instance might have died but still was alive and well in another. Some girlfriends a guy had dated in one universe might have turned out to be his wife in another. Why not do a little exploring? Art entered through the standard unit in his basement. He wondered if Methuselah could guide him a little. But how would he call out to the ancient one? He decided to try it on his own first. He went over to the couch and lay down. Before long, his mind was lost in the great divide. He imagined parallel universes. As he let his definition of a parallel universe permeate his thoughts, he found himself in a long tunnel. There were windows on both sides of it. He could travel very rapidly through this tunnel or take it slow and easy. He decided to take it slow. After passing a couple of dozen windows or doors, he entered one to his right.

Art reemerged into that reality. He was still inside MAP. He could travel all over the place in this universe as he did in his own, present to it while not being in it. He had left a marker at the door to his real, reality so he would not lose it. He could go back there and would, once his little expedition be over. In this parallel universe there was still a MAP entrance. He would not exit here, just observe. He saw himself working out in the yard. Everything was pretty much the same. The house had some furniture that was different. There was a lawn mower he had almost purchased resting just outside the carport. So, in this reality he had bought it. He went upstairs. Gem was there. So, in this universe he had hooked up with her. His daughter was also in this reality. She was not at home though so was perhaps at his parent's place or the daycare. Art came in from outside and met Gem in the parlor. The double listened in on their conversation. They were talking about the upcoming trip to Canada. So, in this reality things did not appear to be all that different than his current one. He went back to the couch and was soon back to his entrance. He checked around the home. Gem was still not back so he decided to move ahead in the tunnel by a few hundred windows. Before heading out though he placed a command in his mind to return to the current reality whenever he wanted.

A couple of thousand or so doors to other parallel universes passed before Art slowed down and chose one this time to the left. In this parallel universe there was no MAP entrance. The house was more noticeably different in this place. Art could again walk freely around in the liquid universe and observe everything that was going on. If he wished to come back and enter this reality, he could always bring a portable unit and create a door and enter. This time he went up to Sonny's room. A tall lad was there working on a model airplane. Art moved around so he could see the young man's features. This was his son. He could see him. He was more mature. He even had a few whiskers growing on his chin. Art watched for a long time in awe over what he saw. So, there were defiantly parallel universes and multiple Art's and Sonny's doing their thing in their own little worlds unaware of any other alternatives. After admiring and enjoying his son for about twenty minutes, Art went down to the kitchen. There making his absolute, most favorite dish was his long, lost wife, Sandra. She looked wild and lovely. A thousand memories flooded into his mind. Here in this parallel universe, she was alive and well. The murder had never happened. Were they still married? Art did not have long to wait.

The traveler saw himself enter the home and go up to his lovely wife and give her a quick kiss. He made a few comments before passing into the living room. Art followed Art and yelled at him from inside of MAP.

"You idiot. Don't you see what you have? Don't just give that beautiful woman a little peck on the cheek, take her in your arms and hold her close forever." The Art in the living room paused for a moment and looked all around as if someone had spoken to him from out of the mist. He must not have seen anything or anybody unusual though. After making sure, he returned to the kitchen and took his lovely wife securely in his arms and gave her an extremely passionate kiss then fondled her a bit before letting her get back to her cooking.

"You always were quite the romantic, Arty. What do you want now? Whenever you give that to me you want something in return. What is it this time?" "

" Nothing, nothing at all, Sweetheart. I just wanted you to know how much I love you and that I am the luckiest man on earth to have such a beautiful wife and a fantastic cook also if I say so myself."

Art could not take it anymore. He had to leave. It was too much to take in seeing his first love so vibrant, alive, and well. His emotions were overpowering. He knew he could come and make an entrance to this universe and arrange for an accident to happen to that Art. He could be with her again. He had the ability to make an "Absolute Choice," here if he wished. He could go backward and forward in time, observing all the little details even down to the same clothes. He knew he could do it. But would it be murder? Before reentering the hall of doors, he passed by Kanna's room. There was no little girl in this parallel universe. No sweet little mind reader. In this place she had never been. He decided to teleport over to Gem's home and see if perchance she was in the same house. It took a little doing but soon he found himself at her front door. There was a light on inside, so he tried to enter. The door was locked in the liquid universe but with a little mind manipulation, it opened, and he entered. There was a Gem in this world. She was seated on a couch reading. There was some commotion going on in the next room, so Art entered and saw a very nice-looking guy working out on some portable exercise unit. He was about six-foot-tall and had blue eyes. His hair was blond. He also had bulging muscles. Gem had done well for herself, but had she continued her experimentation in the realm of advanced physics in this world? Before going to the room where the apparatus would be housed, Art paused in front of Gem. She had looked up and was peering out the window. He stole a quick kiss from her unsuspecting lips and exited. She did not even flinch. There was no device. So married life or life with Mr. Muscles had kept her from furthering her studies in this universe.

Art returned to the hallway and gave himself the command to return to his own world. Soon he was there. The door was clearly marked. He entered and found himself back on the couch. Before reentering through the gray door, he paused to think over what he had witnessed. Was there a way to place sensors in those various parallel universes to monitor events that were taking place? The Art of his last adventure had clearly heard the command he shouted. Perhaps there was a universe out there where Sonny would meet with death. If so, Art could perhaps intervene and pull him out of that universe, save his life and have a son again. Possibility after possibility passed through his mind as he lay on the couch. He had a clear view of the door and soon he saw his Gem coming in with the things she had picked up from the store. Thinking possibilities through he realized that he was not ready to trade his parallel universe for another just yet. There was too much potential, right in front of him. First off there was this beautiful lady heading toward him and soon to be his for as long as they wished. No, he would not trade yet but the possibilities? Yes, there were the possibilities, millions of them. He could chart his own course across the universe and make it into whatever he wanted. He truly did have a gate to "absolute choice."

Another thought entered a corner of his mind. He paused and mulled it over. The possibilities for law enforcement were endless with MAP. Injustice could be met, and the terrible atrocities of psychopaths could be countered.

Wicked men could be place behind bars or wiped out of existence. Perhaps there was a place of torment he could find, a place so horrendous it would be like hell on earth? One could capture these tyrants and place them in that reality. A million wrongs could be righted. The terrible events that had devastated this world down through the ages could be altered. Sonny had shown an interest in spying before being eliminated from this world. By now a Sonny like the one Art had seen would be old enough to do that kind of work for real. Surely, there was a parallel universe somewhere that could do without their own Sonny. But then-with the right timing-Art knew he could go back and rescue the Sonny from this universe. He would be here now, alive, and well. Art could bring him into the picture and show him the possibilities. He could save him. But how would that effect Gem and their future together? This might be a good discussion to have. But would it be fair to save Sonny and not Sandra? Would it be murder on his part if he knew he could have prevented her death but chose not to? Art's heart yearned after his son. He saw him there in his mind again in his room finishing up the airplane.

Finishing up the airplane? Yes! He could see, superimposed over his own thoughts the Sonny of so far away. He could trace his steps as he headed down to the kitchen. This could drive a man crazy if he had to ponder it. He could also see what Gem was doing in her home. She had put down her book and was in the room with the muscle man. Art willed it out of his mind and rose off the couch. He needed to get back into his own reality and quickly. He exited MAP and hurried to help Gem bring in the rest of the groceries. In the real world his experience from within seemed like a million miles away and perhaps fifty if not a hundred years ago. It was a relief, really. For now, he would let bygones be bygones. Somewhere the chimes on a clock struck seven times.

Gem and Art were on the airplane heading for Canada. Art had given her the window seat. She was looking down on the tiny city that was passing by beneath them. Suddenly she felt something thrust inside her. She looked at her hands. They felt different. She peered down at the city again. With her mind she magnified it. It grew larger. Below her a small boy was walking his dog on a sidewalk. A Ford Broncho passed by splashing him with water from a puddle. What happened? A conversation started going through her mind.

"There you are Gem. Are you happy now?"

"Very much. Thanks Con. I won't have to miss Canada after all and thanks for helping me find Daddy."

"You're welcome, Gem. Don't forget me now, ok?"

"OK, I won't." The words echoed away in her mind and she was back in the airplane with Art. She did not say anything about it to him but wondered what had happened? The waiter came by and ask what they would like to drink. She ordered a coke and Art got some cranberry juice.

In Canada they checked into a beautiful hotel next to a small chapel. The chapel had a wedding going on.

"Gem?" When Art used that tone of voice with her, she knew he was thinking of something serious.

"What?" It was not quite the romantic answer Art was expecting.

"I have almost lost you three times. I do not want it to happen again. Let us change and go to that chapel over there and get married."

"Don't you need to be in Canada more than 30 minutes to qualify?" she asked.

"I don't know, and I don't care. We do not have to be married by a state or a country, if the preacher is willing, God's binding of two souls in the holy state of matrimony is good enough for me. If he needs paperwork to do it, we will just manufacture it, pull it out of the either."

"I don't have anything to wear. I wasn't planning on this."

"If you are not ready, its ok but I really love you and want to do this right." Gem let her thoughts mull over the proposal.

"I can get you a dress, Gem." The voices were back

again talking in her head.

"Do it, Con. This is a good thing, don't you think?"

"It is an incredibly good thing. I will put your dress in the closet and if you need legal papers, I can plan for that as well. I will get the information to Art. You mustn't bruise his ego." Gem shook her head. What were these conversations she was having with herself? Something was not quite right. She turned and spoke to Art.

"We'll do it. I am sure I can find something to wear. You probably need to talk to the preacher before he leaves." Art headed for the elevator. It was not much of a proposal but then he had never been good at romantic stuff. He was one happy guy. He would not have to go through those long, lonely hours anymore being tormented by memories from the past. Gem would be by his side and he had Kanna. Beautiful, Kanna. He above all men was most fortunate.

Gem spread a couple of changes of clothes out on the bed. Nothing looked good enough to her for a wedding dress. She had her old one at home. She could go through MAP and get it. Art had brought the aluminum case with the revised, portable unit. It was over by the door. That is what she would do. It would only take a minute. She opened the closet and hung up her clothes. She was shutting the door when a dark garment bag hanging from the corner, caught her attention. She was curious. It was heavy. Probably the last people here had forgot to take it with them. They would probably be back for it. She was about to close when a thought struck her. If there was a dress her size in there, perhaps she could borrow it for half an hour. It could be returned, and no one would know the difference. She took the bag off the bar and lay it out on the bed. Inside the first item she saw was a white tuxedo. It looked as if it would fit Art perfectly. Underneath that was a beautiful, ivory colored dress. She looked at it breathlessly. Would it fit? She stripped off her jeans and top and looked in the mirror. She had on a black bra and panties. She could probably get by with the panties, but the bra had to go. She removed it and placed it on the bed. Carefully she picked up the dress. Unlike a lot of wedding dresses, it was made of an unbelievably soft fabric. She slipped it over her head and zipped up the back. She spent the next five minutes putting her hair up and adding a little touch of makeup to her face.

When Art entered the room, he thought he saw an angel again. This one was not dressed in violate though but ivory white.

"Do you approve, husband to be?" she asked while swinging her body around in a complete circle. The bottom of the wedding dress swelled out with her movements.

"Do I ever!" He headed over to take her in his arms, but she waved him away.

"You're not even supposed to see me in my dress before the wedding, let alone touch me."

"I thought you said you didn't have anything to wear. If that was the case, where did you get that beautiful dress?"

"It was in the closet waiting for me. It is a perfect fit too. Your tux is in on the bed. Can the preacher marry us?"

"He needs us there in twenty minutes. I had to bribe him to do it. He put his secretary on the paperwork. We will be married through both man and God. It will be as legal as any wedding and with these clothes, we will make quite a handsome pair."

"Beautiful," she corrected. "Beautiful pair."

Art changed into his tux. It fit perfectly. They took the elevator and were at the chapel right on time. There were even a few people left from the last wedding who stayed on for a few minutes to see the couple happily united. In fifteen minutes, it was all over. Art even had a ring for her. It was a large diamond with seven perfectly matched jewels around it. As they were leaving the church, a boy about 13 years old handed them an exposed roll of film.

"I took this while you were being married. I hope you don't mind." He held it out to the groom. Art found his wallet and drew out a bill and pressed it in the kid's hand. The new husband did not complain that it was not digital.

"Thanks. I am glad you had some film left over from

the last wedding. Here is something for your trouble. It is not Canadian currency, but a bank will change it for you. The kid took the Franklin in his hands. His eyes grew big.

"Thanks, Mr. I didn't expect this much." He rushed down the aisle and out the door. They signed the papers and headed back to the hotel. The garments were soon back in the bag and returned it to the closet where they had been found.

"Whoever you were who forgot those clothes, thanks. Hope you do not mind that we used them. You made two people really happy," Gem said out loud as she patted the garment bag.

"Glad to be of service to you, Gem," a voice said in her mind.

"You are the most beautiful woman I have ever known, Mrs. Goldstein. I love you; I love you; I love you!"

"I love you too. Dr. She came to him and he took her in his arms.

"I wish there were a fireplace here somewhere." Gem commented even as she remembered her imagined fantasy. And could there be that soft blanket to put down before it?

"Sorry, my love," the man replied while trying to get a tighter hold on his bride. "I do not think this room came with that and besides, it is 76 degrees out there."

"We could turn on the air conditioner." She responded as she slipped out of his grasp. A large curtain she had not noticed before caught her attention. She went over and opened it. There behind it was a fireplace. It was not a real one but electrical. It would do in a pinch. On the mantle above it rested two, large, fluffy white blankets. Also, hanging side by side were the softest, fuzziest robes she had ever laid eyes on. They were not linen but what the hay? "Beggars can't be choosers." The old cliché popped into her mind. She punched a couple of buttons to activate the flame and took down the blankets. She spread them out in front of the warm glow. It was perfect.

They were undressed so followed the next, natural step and spent the rest of the evening enjoying the closeness of each other's bodies. Before they were through, Art had memorized every little curve and knew how to touch her to bring deep sensations reeling to the surface of her being. They used no contraceptive devices, and it was wonderful, completely natural to be so uninhibited with each other. The little chapel bells chimed out to awaken them the next morning. One, two, three, four, five, six.

Chapter 11

The morning was sunny and warm. Out of their hotel window, birds were busily pecking tiny rocks off the roof. They could see the mall off in the distance. It was not really the time to shop. They were soon to purchase a new house. Then shopping would be necessary to furnish it. But today they could take their time and look around. Perhaps get some ideas for the future. The future? Arts mind began to turn. Would this mall be here in the future? What would it look like in ten or twenty years? It might be nice to find out.

"What do you want to do today, Gem? It is your call and my treat."

"I would like to look around in the mall, but for the life of me I can't figure out what I want to look at. I really have everything I need. I have plenty of clothes. I have tools to work with. I have a wonderful husband and a beautiful daughter. Oh, that is what I want to do. How is Kanna set for clothes? Winter is coming and she may need some new things for school."

"To be truthful, Gem. I have no idea. She has been a private child, quite independent and grown up like. Do you want to know something? In all the years she has supposed to have been with me I cannot for the life of me remember shopping for even one item of clothing for her. After I found her, the room she uses was filled with clothes, toys, games, and puzzles. I do not even remember purchasing the bicycle we almost ran over with the van. Oh! Pardon me. I remember. Yes. I remember a lot of shopping trips. What is happening?"

"I think the time warp just caught up with you. It was not until you touched those programed thoughts that they were activated to become conscious to you. I will shop for Kanna then," she replied while reaching for her purse. It was the same one that she had recovered from the bathroom long ago although it was not. It was days at best. Funny how this unnatural world was becoming more and more natural with each passing day.

The mall was just opening. The people were starting to come in, but they found they could get around quite easily. Gem and Art patronized several clothing stores and in no time Gem had quite a few bags. By then it was nearly lunch time.

"Let us go back to the hotel, dump these packages off, and then find something to eat. I am hungry. How about you, Art?" Gem's face was flushed with excitement from her trove of treasures. She had never shopped for a daughter and it had been a wonderful thing to do! If the little one was here with them, she would have her do a dress rehearsal to parade all her new lovelies.

"A man can always find time to eat, Honey. What kind of food do you feel like today?" He started to rub his tummy. It did feel strangely empty.

"Mexican. How about you?"

"Mexican sounds fine. Do they do Mexican in Canada, or are all restaurants French Casein?" He asked trying his hardest to make a joke that might get the new bride off her purchases.

"There were a couple of Mexican places in the mall. We could go back there."

"How about going there about fifteen years in the future to see what changes they will make, Gem?" This was strangely creative for Art since typically it could take as long as twenty minutes to get into the groove of time travel to specific times and places.

"Can we do that?"

"I don't see why not. I have gone that far into the future before. I went and purchased a small camera unit, like the portable one I left in the van. It is totally stainless steel. If I use it in the Earth Reality after we travel there through MAP, we can move around in the future without taking too much time off the clock as Methuselah was so kind to inform us."

"Sounds like an adventure to me." Gem responded

as she looked in her purse to see if she had much Canadian currency left. That caused her to ponder if this same currency were used at that future date or if the world would be under the fabled digital currency? "Can we bring things from the future back to the present, like clothes and stuff?"

"Sure, we can. We probably should be careful in our selections but that will make shopping this afternoon kinda challenging. It will also give us a chance to see if food taste have changed much in the future. I would suggest we propel ourselves into the future from this hotel and walk overusing the camera." He went to his case and pulled out the stainless-steel unit and wrapped the little strap around his wrist.

"How will we know if this room is taken then? Won't we be stepping out of MAP into the future Earth Reality?" she asked. Her mind was adapting but had not arrived there as naturally as Art's.

"While in the Eternal Reality, we can check for vacant rooms and export from there if this one is occupied. I believe there are thousands of parallel universes. We the people are existing in all of them. If we do move into the future and do some shopping, it will be in a different universe. I suppose it is as real as the one we will be in, in 15 years but it could never be the same universe. We are in effect creating our own alternate universe. Different people would not be in the hotel room, it would be us. We would create that universe even as we create our own by the choices we make constantly. I think with MAP I can somehow slip from parallel universe to parallel universe. Who knows? Perhaps in the real world there will be no mall here in our universe in say fifteen years. But there will be one with us creating one now. Perhaps in the universe we go to we are married to someone else? I think if we create it now with MAP, we could very well be assuring our existence in the future together"

Art opened the MAP unit and stepped in. The object was to select some item in the room that would be here in the future and follow the trail it mapped with the camera. Art pointed the camera at several items. The door seemed to stay the most stationery. Other things like beds, furniture and fixtures trailed off out the door at independent times. When they were at the approximate time in the future, Art looked at a clock on the desk. He was rewarded with a winner. They had arrived 14.5 years into the future. They checked the room. Then went down and looked at the schedule just in case Art's theory was not correct. They were surprised to find that it was occupied by an Art and Gem Goldstein. The question was, was it them or an older version. Art slipped to the room monitor and mentally manipulated it. There they were unlocking the door. It was the young newly, married couple he saw not an older wrinkled version. But perhaps age extending techniques were prevalent then. They would just need to keep their eyes open. They proceeded to step out of MAP.

The elevator had changed a lot. It was no longer a large bulky box. It was a lightweight unit that went not only up and down but along a horizontal track. At the ground level they stepped out momentarily but entered again when they noticed three underground levels that had not been in the older unit. At the bottom level, they entered a type of subway propulsion system that went directly to the mall. What a change in the place. Rather than neat little signs above the different stores, there were holographic images of all types hanging in the air. Items that were hot sellers were displayed in quick succession and repeated after the cycle of products ran their course. Kids glided around the mall on hoover boards in designated areas. Some sort of computer device kept them from colliding into each other. The elderly had a transportation area where they could set on a moving bench. It had a keypad with the various store locations. The people only needed to punch in the desired number, and they were whisked to that store. There was of course a place for the masses to walk and this is what Art and Gem decided to do.

Gem went into a few clothing stores, but the styles were so different from what was current that she did not purchase anything for either herself or Kanna. There was a small electrical invention that intrigued Art. It would best be described as a photo cube. Somehow you scanned 3D photos into it, and they would appear randomly or in whatever order you prescribed. You could hook it up to a head unit and enter the images. He purchased a couple of cubes and a camera. As they went from place to place, he took several pictures. There was another unit of similar principle in a different store only this one took 3D video. The society would take either cash or credits from some type of smart card. So, Gem's mental inquiry was legit. Art had a lot of cash. Gem liked the video unit, so he purchased that for her. She recorded the holographic images streaming all around them. They found a Mexican place to eat and the food tasted rather good. There was a pair of boots that Art could not resist. When you first looked at them, they were humongous. Once on the foot they conformed to its shape very quickly. If a person needed extra arch support, you could program the boot to give it. They were so comfortable he purchased a pair for Gem, Kanna and himself. She would be the envy of her class at school if they ever found out but then kids her age seemed to be more accepting of each other these days. One added plus to the purchase was the fact that the boot or shoe would grow with the foot. One pair could last for years unless... There were some innovations in the cooking industry. Like several of the science fiction movies Art had seen, someone had designed a unit that would expand miniature packages of food and produce, even entire meals in seconds. A two-inch square of macaroni and cheese could be transformed into a delicious plate sized meal at the touch of a button. They purchased a couple of those units along with a whole assortment of food types. There were vegetables, fruits, meats, potatoes, desserts, all displayed in lavish detail. They were getting quite an armload of things, so Art rented a hoover cart to carry it all.

They passed a hair place. A slogan on the window stated the following. "If you do not have enough hair, we'll put it on. If you have too much, we will take it off. Choose from twenty different styles." Art looked in a mirror outside by the door. He was not thinning on top yet, but this might be a notable place to come if he ever did start too bald.

"Is there anywhere else you want to go in this world, Gem? Art ask as they were being whisked back to the hotel."

"Yes, I would like to get out of this sub chamber and have a look around in the open air. There was a flyer advertising an art exhibit going on not far from here. I would like to go there next. What about you?"

"I would like to check out the entertainment world here in the future."

After surfacing, the exhibit was only a few blocks away. After leaving the things off in the room, they went down to ground level and walked out the door, taking the cameras with them. There were several types of automobiles traveling around. Some were confined to road travel, but others flew on invisible paths two or three levels up in the air. Art turned the particle camera toward one of the tracks. There were long streaks of some type of light that seemed to guide the vehicles. Somewhere between the then and now, light particles had been trapped. They could be sent down invisible tubes to locations all over. Communication was instantaneous to any part of the world. Terraforming was also being done on a planetary scale. The desert was beginning to blossom as a rose. Large waste areas were being transformed into gardens of Eden. Soon humanity would be heading for the stars, but Art wondered about that. Methuselah had talked about an evil that had been confined to the Earth Reality. What were the limits of that confinement? Plus, the idea of creating their own universe was more real than he understood. Would this reality ever exist in their timeline or had they created a future that might never be? He had to ask himself these questions once again. Perhaps there was a block of knowledge he had not consciously accessed. Absolute Choice? But no! The elderly traveler through time had stated that evil would come to an end. Something would happen, perhaps sooner than 14.5 years into the future? Art was still lost in thought when they arrived at the art exhibit. They entered.

The first sculpture they looked at was amazing. You could touch it and it appeared to be made from solid rock, but it was constantly changing shape. At the base was a control panel with a digital readout. You could speak to it and request some art era and the stone would transform itself into works of art from that period in history. Gem punched in Michelangelo and his sculpture of David appeared life size then changed into several of his other masterpieces like some 3D morph unit. A holographic form of the master himself appeared and explained how the feat was accomplished. Somehow the processor manipulated a combination of sound and light waves to form solid images. Michelangelo then led them to some of the other art wonders. One artist had done something with water. There was a waterfall that had multiple streams falling in different directions. The water appeared to come out of the air with no apparent plumbing. It was awesome! Gem recorded everything on her unit. They entered a virtual museum. It was a copy of the Art Museum of Chicago. The spectator got on a revolving conveyer type apparatus that matched his or her step. You could walk through halls and see paintings from the great masters of all ages. Another artist had created paintings of a 3D nature using transparent colors that changed from every angle. Michelangelo explained that if the entire possible surface area of the painting they were looking at were laid out in the format he had been confined to, it would cover a large wall in a person's home. It was quite grand and amazing to say the least.

The couple was intrigued with the 3D virtual guide. He looked and acted like a real person. You could shake his hand, even give him a hug. What they did not know was that a few thousand miles away this technology had far superior qualities. It came into being shortly after Donald Trump, in this reality had been elected president of the United States. The history was interesting but not published. While campaigning for the 2024 election, Donald had received a call that if he were to show up at a particular rally, he would be killed. There were no if's ands or buts about it. He was advised to not go and drop out of the race completely. Unbeknown to his enemies, some human clones of Donald had been created. At this stage of technology brain programming of the double was somewhat limited. It was good enough though. The clone was Donald in nearly every respect. That night in front of all the world and broadcast by all the news media, Donald collapsed and died. He was pronounced DOA. And his enemies rejoiced. There was dancing in the streets. But when special OPS forces stole the body away, Donald made a miraculous comeback. He appeared in public the very next day and gave the names of those who had masterminded the assassination attempt. The press coverage was phenomenal. He surged in the poles and the ones who had rejoiced at his death ran scared. They could not understand it. Now in places where there had been thousands, millions turned out to see the man who had died but now lived.

After that other attempts were made on his life. But he pulled through in each case. They even impeached him in the House so hated was he by his enemies. This led to having him go to his public appearances first as a projected, 3D image. But here, some 14 years into the future, the technology Gem's father had pioneered had transformed into a much larger project. Molecular constructs of people could be sent out in public. No one could tell the real from the false. If a bullet penetrated a molecular construct of a person for instance, they would never fold no matter where or how hard they were struck. This was the way most of the elite appeared in public now. These molecular constructs could go all over while the real persons spent their days in luxury tucked away in fortified, secret hid-a-ways.

Artificial intelligence in the form of robotics was beginning to make its appearance in this age. Nearly everything that could be automated was. Kids could spend hours running through virtual worlds shooting monsters and traveling back to certain time periods of history. Education was mostly entertainment. You did not need books. You could move things around in these worlds with your hands or mind.

Microchips were implanted in the brains of thousands. They could upload data from thousands of sources. If they were manipulated in areas outside of the realm of imagination, the story would revert to the nearest substitute.

The afternoon slipped away quickly. They left the exhibit and were walking back to the hotel when a small lad with a reality unit on his head stepped in front of a land vehicle. It struck him and he was thrown up in the air. The unit on his head flew off and landed on the sidewalk next to Art. Not knowing what to do, he picked it up. It was broken. A siren sounded and soon a medical vehicle appeared. The lad was placed on a stretcher and whisked away. Gem felt something deep inside her. The voices were talking again.

"Con?"

"Yes, Gem."

"Will that little boy live?"

"Not normally but you could help him. Healing is well within the means of your attainment in this reality."

"Take me to him." Gem felt some sensation in her being and that fullness she had felt the last couple of days left her again.

"Art, I have this feeling that part of me went to where they are taking the boy. I think I need to go there and do something. I do not know what. Will you show me how to get there?"

"That is a strange request for a bride but let us try. He turned the beam camera on the retreating vehicle, placed his arm around his wife, pushed the turbo button and they were propelled inside what appeared to be a worm hole. It seemed to suck them in. The paramedics were working on the lad. They had some probes hooked up to him and a monitor was monitoring his vitals. He had lost a lot of blood. Gem let her inner self take over. She reached out a hand and placed it over the wound where the blood was coming from the fastest. She felt a sensation flowing through her. Her hand was transparent. She could see the gash plainly. Right before her eyes it began to close and heal. The blood stopped bleeding out and in less than a minute, the skin replaced itself. She next placed her hand on his leg. A paramedic was trying to set it. She helped him in her mind. She could see the broken bone and knitted it back together mentally. She did the same with an arm that was broken and three ribs. He had a concussion on his skull. She mentally entered and mended the crack then went deeper and restored the damaged brain tissue. The lad stirred and appeared like he was going to waken. She touched a portion of his head and put him into a deep sleep. They would most likely take him into the lab and do heat-rays and all that stuff.

Art and Gem could not be heard from this dimension, so Gem asked Art to give her the beam camera. It was a wonderful unit. Far superior to hers. She turned it on and passed over the lad's small frame several times going deeper with each trip. He had a crushed spleen. She focused the beam on it and allowed energy to pass through her to it. It was amazing. All she had to do was reach into the exhaustless river of cosmos or the zero field and pull forth whatever was needed to heal. The last injury he had was a broken ankle. The paramedics had not noticed this. She set it and again knit the bones together with healing energy from the beyond. It was done. When he woke up, he could go back to life in this sometimes-cruel world. She wanted to give him one more thing. Some bit of knowledge that would keep something like this from happening again. She formed it out of the river and transported it to his mind, just on the edge of the conscious. The next time he got too involved in some surreal reality, the warnings she had planted in his mind would surface and perhaps save him from another fatal accident.

Art watched her work with great awe and wonder. He had never seen anyone that gifted. He knew he could go to the cosmos anytime and draw from it that which was needed to bring restoration and health, but he had never devised a way to use that to benefit others who were suffering in Earth Reality. If he were to do this, he would need to take them within to draw from the resources. Medical knowledge in this era was far superior to what was available in the Earth Reality they had come from, but it still fell far short of the personal touch that Gem had just demonstrated. They left the emergency vehicle and were back at the hotel entrance when he decided to mention it to her.

"You were pretty amazing back there. Where did you pick up these skills?"

"I really don't know for sure, Art. Just lately I have been hearing these conversations in my mind with myself. I am talking to some entity that is called Con. Con told the Gem inside that she had the means to help the boy, even save his life and then it was me, doing all that stuff. There was also a conversation about wedding attire and Con said he could supply it. The inner Gem told him to go ahead and do it and that is when I discovered the clothes in the closet. I really do not know what it is all about. Perhaps that is something we can talk to Methuselah about on our next encounter with him."

"It sounds like you have figured out how to access some of the inner levels of the subconscious and draw substance from the metaphysical to do your bidding. There are ancient mystics who have done this for centuries, but this is way beyond where most of them have gone. Your inner connection is in some way superior to what I have even experienced. I can do stuff like that when I am within, but you can bring those same skills to the Earth Reality apparently at will. I have to say I am a little bit jealous of your abilities. It makes me wonder if you even need a MAP unit or if you have advanced beyond it? Do you know if and or what kinds of limits are set on your abilities to do these different things?"

"No, Art," she responded as she reached her hand up to press it on her skull just behind her ears. There was some buzzing going on in her head. When she applied pressure in this spot, it stopped.

"It is so new; I have not really had a chance to explore all of the possibilities at my disposal." They entered the room, opened MAP, and transported their treasures back to real time. They made a stop at the hotel of the past and exited. Art went down and checked them out then went back up to the room. He and Gem opened MAP again and transported all their things back to Art's house without using the airplane. It had been an interesting adventure into the future and back. They went to bed early, enjoying the companionship of each other as they lay side by side. While he slept, Art dreamed about Methuselah. The conversation he had with him was quite intelligent unlike other conversations he had with dream characters in the past. He asked Methuselah about the skills he had seen Gem use on the boy.

"How did Gem manage to perform those acts of healing?" he asked as he searched the kind face of the elder. There was a purity about this ancient one that did not exist in any other human so far as Art knew.

"Again, I cannot reveal the full answer to your question because it would influence what you do in the immediate future. That would not be according to the plan, but I will share some of what I can with you. Gem accessed elements from the second level of the Eternal Reality to bring restoration to the boy. Time is passing at a much faster rate in that level of reality. A portion of Gem's consciousness is existing in that reality you know, with another portion of her the physical body of the first level of the Eternal Reality. She has what you would call a split personality at this time. It would have taken the boy weeks even months in Earth Reality to heal, if he healed at all, but in the second level of Eternal Reality, since time is much faster, Gem simply accessed it and the wounds were exchanged you might say causing the healing speeding along in that reality to be applied to Earth Reality. The spiritual essence of the lad from that reality was first made whole there before being transported to Earth Reality. Once his spiritual essence was healed, the physical quickly followed. In other words. If a cut took 4 days to heal in Earth Reality, the same cut could heal in a matter of minutes in the first level of the Eternal Reality. In the second level, it is even quicker. And in the third level of the Eternal Reality, it is instantaneous. You have heard of Jesus have you not, Art? He accessed this level of Eternal Reality to do mighty works of healing on earth, even raising the dead. Gem went through some unique experiences that gave her access. You saw some of the advantages she appeared to have from these experiences. There are also disadvantages which I am not free to explain at this time." Art had another question.

"We are going to pick up Kana tomorrow and travel around the country looking for a new place to settle in. Is it possible to settle in a place at some time in the future? When we met up with the boy, we were approximately fourteen and a half years into the future. Could we go there and settle, or would you advise us to stay in our current earth period? "Methuselah thought for a few moments then answered.

"You could settle into a new home in the future if you wanted to. You have the tools to do that. I would recommend that you do not go too far ahead though. Perhaps a maximum of four- or five-years tops. If you do that however there will be missing periods of your life that you will have knowledge of but will have missed living. It is like Kana. You have only had the physical privilege of associating with her for a few months even though you have the memories of being with her for her entire lifetime. It is a little different than that, though. You would not be any older say five years into the future, but you would have five years of mental living added to your mind. Your mind would be older with more life experiences in it. That could be confusing at times when conflicting thoughts and feelings collided with each other. You would also cut off real time that you could spend with your parents and friends. If you jump five years into the future, they will be five years older because they do not have the means to skip through time as you do. Your I-ness or self-awareness would jump, but there in the past you would have been doing things in a parallel universe, you would be existing, but you would not consciously know about it even though you had memories of it." Art talked with the guardian for a while longer in his dream. He asked a question about the parallel universe subject Methuselah had mentioned.

"Are there thousands of parallel universes going on at the same time and am I am acting out different things in each one?"

"To answer your questions, I would say 'yes and No.' Each person has been granted the power of choice. They make thousands of choices each day. Had they made a different choice; their universe would have been different. There are these universes running parallel to your own. But there is only one moment of reality for you. That living reality is what charts your course through all the parallel universes. You only exist in one universe in the present Earth Reality where the spark of life meets the actions of your choice. This would be called your Present Reality. Your Present Reality is reality for you. Your choices are your reality."

Art was having a hard time figuring that out, besides, he was dreaming, or was he? He asked another question.

"Suppose I had ended up with that red head I dated for a few weeks. Are we a thing in some parallel universe, or are their several paths where we are together doing who knows what somewhere out there?"

"The best way to describe that is to say yes, but in that parallel universe you and Ellen are only shadows of reality. It would take the spark of present reality, your spiritual essence, your soul that makes you, you to jump into that parallel universe to make it present reality for you." That was a little easier for Art to grasp. So somewhere out there he and Ellen, Sandra, Gem, etc. could have been existing and indeed were but with the absence of self-awareness, the I-ness that made that reality the living reality. Of all the possible Art's out there, only one had a present soul with life throbbing through it. It was the self-aware Art of the here and now. The very one talking to the ancient wise man. The others were only shadows of the possible choices he might have made or could make in the future along with the results of those choices.

Art remembered his travels to those two other, parallel universes. Things had seemed so real there. If he had taken the portable unit with him, he was sure he could have entered. But what would have become of the Art in that universe? He would ask.

"Has a person ever jumped wide, multiple streams of parallel universes to enter into an entirely new reality different than their present one with new players in the field?" Methuselah's nodded his head, yes. He did not hang around to explain the answer though but was gone. The conversation had ended.

The dreaming man paused to remember his travel to the world where Sonny was still alive. What would become of that Art? This Art would become that Art or that Art would become him. He would not have to murder him. Where he to jump into that parallel universe, his self-awareness would jump with him. That reality would become the reality with the soul, I-ness that was his current Earth Reality. Those memories would be his memories. That life would be his present life. He would be there in the present, Earth Reality. It might be nice to swap places with one of those other Art's sometime, but would he still retain his current memories, or would they be forgotten? If they were forgotten could he ever come back to his present reality of the here and now? If that other Art were Art, then who would that Art be? It would be risky to say the least or if the ancient one was still here; he could ask him one more question. But what question would he ask? He had at least a hundred of them on the tip of his tongue right now. But Methuselah was nowhere to be found. At least he knew more now than he had before. The question was, would he remember later what he knew now in this land of limbo?

Art eventually slipped into a lighter state of consciousness. He felt Gem stirring next to him. She also moved into a more conscious level of awareness only long enough to hear some chimes ringing out. One, Two, Three, Four, Five.

Chapter 12

Art awoke before Gem. He decided to let her sleep if she liked. He was up for an adventure, however. There was only one time he remembered entering MAP through the backside. What would happen if he tried it now? He retrieved the portable unit and soon had it operational. He decided this would be best because if he did much traveling in this other, parallel universe, he might want to exit quickly. He also took the taser. Perhaps he might need to use it, but what would it do in this other reality? If one stepped through the front of the unit it led to the first phase of the Eternal Reality, would one step in through the other side lead to a Hellish Reality? He decided to find out. He entered and passed through the door into the garage. He went over to the window and looked out. There resting on his front lawn was a triangular shaped aircraft. It was not as large as he would have imagined. It was perhaps large enough to carry four people tops. But even people would have a hard time squeezing into it.

Shortly after spotting the craft Art saw two grey alien creatures pass underneath. A little door opened, and a white light appeared. The creatures under the craft disappeared. They were beamed up into the craft. Shortly afterward the unit sprang to life and started humming. It rose slowly off the lawn and before he could count to three, shot up into the air and went out of visual range. Art looked at the road and saw lots of strange vehicles moving on it. Some of the vehicles had windows. As he watched he saw what looked like humans, greys, reptilian, reticulan humanoids and other creatures with differing physical characteristics. The more human looking creatures could have been real or different phases of genetically modified human and alien constructs. A couple of greys started up the sidewalk to the front door. He hid behind the corner and watched as they entered his house. He went into the kitchen. They seemed right at home in there. He looked around and the furniture was different. There were strange gadgets all over the place. He picked up a black, electronic unit of some type. It was vibrating or buzzing. It was hard to tell in this environment. A little antenna was sticking up. A small red light was on. He had no clue as to what it was. He decided to move MAP to the pantry off the kitchen and watch to see what the greys would do. Would they notice him? If so, he must be ready to dive through the door into Earth Reality and collapse the unit before they followed. After watching for a while, Art ventured out. He would have to be seen if that were possible to answer the question if this reality were like the other one. If so, he should be able to walk among these strange creatures without being noticed.

There was a cooking timer on a counter not more than five steps away. Gem had used it earlier to time the boiling of some eggs. If he could get there and set it, when it rang, he would know if they heard it. Art looked all around. None of the greys were watching so he went over to the timer and set it for 2 minutes. He went back into the pantry where MAP was open and waiting. After the designated time, it went off. No creature came to investigate. He tried a couple of other things and still could not rouse any interest in the inhabitants of the house. It was interesting to note. He could see his own items and move them around like the timer. He could also see the inventions of the aliens and move them around and they seemed not to notice. After a while he found he could walk around unnoticed by them. So, it must be like the physical aspects of the other reality. In the first level of the Eternal Reality, he could move around unnoticed. He could move things around, and they would not be reset in the Earth Reality without applying a charge from the taser. In this reality the items of the Earth Reality existed in a semi-liquid state along with the items of the alien reality. To physically be seen by them he decided he would need to go through The MAP door one more time to get into their physical reality. This was incredibly good news! He ventured out of the door and started walking on the sidewalk next to the road. None of these otherworldly inhabitants noticed him. A small grey about 4'2" passed right by him and never even flinched when brushed up against.

Art followed the sidewalk up town. He went by a fast-food joint. The humans from earth reality entered and so did the aliens from their reality. The alien waiters served a different kind of food than the human waiters. The reptilian humanoids preferred some type of soup to more solid food. Sometimes they would rub the soup on portions of their bodies. Their skin could absorb it Art supposed. This seemed strange to Art since they had carnivore style teeth, teeth that appeared like they could rip flesh to shreds. These reptiles were more sophisticated than the lizards, frogs, and alligators in Earth Reality. They were intelligent beings. They appeared to communicate with each other although in this reality Art could not hear much more than a muffled vibration. It was not audible. There were flying vehicles of all types mixed in with Ford, Chevy, and various other foreign vehicles. Some of the humans drove the vehicles Art recognized and the humanoids operated the others. Art found a bench and sat down to observe. What could he learn from this?

He watched the flying saucers zoom around. At times they would disappear into an invisible gateway like MAP. They would pass through and the portion of the craft that entered the doorway, would disappear. Other vehicles would appear through similar gateways in other locations in the air. The gateways were invisible to Art. There was no structure with conductors around them such as MAP, had. There was one gateway that rested next to an antique shop Art and Gem had visited not less than a week earlier. He decided to go over and have a look around inside. Perhaps that would give him some more information.

Inside he could see the antiques arranged just like they were a week ago. He had at that time been looking for an old pair of glasses that looked like the ones he had found at the maintenance man's home. There had been a pair and he was able to replace the shattered lens. The other antique glasses appeared not to have been moved from where they were earlier. Alongside of, in and around the other antiques were several from the world of the humanoids. These were possibly future human inventions mixed in with useful items for the aliens of yesterday. Art found another black electrical unit that matched the one he had seen back at the house. A grey came and picked it up then took it over to a reptilian that appeared to be at the counter. There were some hand motions and audible sounds passing between the two. With his pointed nails, he or she pushed in on the side where there was a little indentation. The unit sprang to life. A 3D holographic image of one of the national parks appeared to float in the air. There were people walking around in the park. Suddenly they all looked up and a triangular UFO appeared to be hoovering above the gift shop adjacent to the ranger station. Art watched as a flash of light came out of the craft and it was gone. The people went back to what they were doing apparently having forgot what they had just witnessed. The grey took out some black, shiny stones and pinched each one with his fingers. They all lit up. Perhaps these were some type of advanced power source. The reptilian took them from the gray and opened an electronic box that could have been a substitute for a cash register. He put the black stones inside and the grey walked out with the unit.

Art decided to head back for the house and examine the unit he had first seen. Perhaps if he put pressure on the indented area like the humanoid, it would open, and he could examine the holographic image it produced more closely. Would it also be a national park where a UFO was sighted then forgotten, or something else?

On the way back to the house he decided to return on the other side of the street. He was just about home when he saw what appeared to be a large dome covering up a small building. He walked over to it. It was solid. He could not budge it. It did not appear to be glass or even plastic. It was much more transparent. It would have been hardly noticeable under foggy conditions. He walked all around and tried to see if there were some entrance. He found none. He crossed the street and noticed a grey come up to the dome. The creature had what looked like a white remote in his hand. He pressed a button and a red door appeared in the balloon. The little creature passed through and in a few seconds the door closed. Art was intrigued to say the least. It was close to the house and that was a plus. He could watch the activities and see what developed.

Inside the others were seated on some furniture of their own design. They were moving their long fingers over some screen on a unit that could have passed for an iPad of kindle reader. They did not notice him. He went into the room where the black gadget was. The antenna was not up now. There was no red light. Art picked it up, went into the pantry. He placed it down by the MAP door on a counter and made his way to the bedroom where Gem was sleeping. She was resting on her side with her face facing a counter. On the counter Art noticed a small, egg shaped gadget. Little streams of purple were being drawn from Gem's eyes, nose, and mouth even her ears. A small yellow light was blinking like in a camera battery charging unit. Art saw one on his side of the bed also. It was not activated.

Art decided to go get the map unit and reach his hand through it to remove both units. In the earth reality, a couple of levels away from these others, he would have more time to examine them closely to determine their possible purpose. He did it. He managed to move the unit by the bed on Gem's side then reach out and remove the one from his side to hers. Gem stirred. The egg-shaped unit powered down and shut off. Two minutes later Art had it along with the other one in each of his pants pockets. He made his way back to the kitchen and removed the other unit. This one he would not remove in the alien reality but take it back from the lower MAP reality. That way the others would not notice it was missing. Art entered MAP and was soon in Earth Reality. Gem was still sleeping. She had gone back into a deep sleep, so he took the first unit out to the garage. He chose the area where there were no cars. The other units were placed in a drawer.

The professor placed his fingers on the indented areas of the unit. A 3D picture sprang to life. It was the diagram of one of the domes he had seen across the street. He could rotate a little ball that appeared at the top of the unit upon opening and see the dome from all angles. He also could see what was happening underground as well as above. There appeared to be four, metallic, electrical units that were anchored some four feet into the earth. A diagram showed them aligned exactly with the four points of the compass, north, south, east, and west. There was some strange language that he could not read that possibly explained in detail what was happening.

Art was good at guessing. He determined these units somehow tapped into the electromagnetic fields of the earth and when power was supplied, formed a force field. That was the barrier he had run into across the street, the one the grey had breached with his remote. Perhaps these units could download diagrams of all types of things in this other world? Perhaps thousands were stored within? This could be a wealth of knowledge if he could figure out how to make it do all that it could.

Art moved the ball around and saw there was a large round unit in the middle of the four corner elements. It had a series of controls on it. Within this display he could push certain buttons and turn dials and watch the changes that took place in the force field. Sometimes it enlarged, sometimes it contracted. He found he could alter its shape from circular to rectangular or square. He determined to watch the occupants of the dome across the street from inside, perhaps follow them around even. Was there a place where they could purchase these units or trade for them with those little black rocks or whatever they were? If the little rocks were some advanced power source, could he use them to make improvements to MAP? He would find out. He pressed the sides of the unit again and the diagram shrank back inside. Interesting, interesting indeed! Perhaps something like this could be put to good use in Earth Reality or even in the first level of the Eternal Reality?

He was placing the unit down when his little finger accidently activated it again. This time a type of Table of Contents popped up. In place of words though there were thumbnails of various inventions. Art went from top to bottom. One item caught his attention. It was an egg-shaped mechanism like the ones he had removed from the other reality. He moved his finger and a pectoral with all the parts showed up. He widened his fingers and it got larger. The language was not recognizable but by allowing his mind to absorb the images, the meaning came through. These units were placed by the bed of every human. While they slept some of their life forces were siphoned out and stored somehow within these units. There looked to be a small drawer that held the valuable stuff. Art brought one of the units to the counter and by touching it in two places at the same time, a small drawer opened. Stored in the drawer was processed life force. He would call it that for lack of a better name. It was in the form of an ointment. The others who chose to inhabit a body needed to keep those bodies alive. This salve or liniment contained a processed form of the life force it had taken from the humans.

The scientist had to think about this. The ancient one had told him these others were predatory. Those who chose to live in bodies made those bodies do things an energy or spirit version of the others could not do. These bodies were possessed by these otherworldly entities. The bodies were composed of genetically engineered, biological organisms. The organisms did not have a life or soul of their own. They could not sustain life themselves without applying the modified life force of humans and or animals. In fact, all living matter fueled these parasites. It was kinda like the alchemists of old for example. They were given the secret of how to create the philosopher stone. This stone had life giving properties far beyond anything we know of today. Some of those with these stones lived to be hundreds of years old. The elements of the stone prolonged their life. Likewise, this ointment did the same for the greys and their counterparts. Their genetically propagated bodies, having no ability to sustain life in and of themselves had to steal it from others. Humanity was like cattle being bread for the sole purpose of sustaining the lives of these beings.

Even the others who were in a more energy form or spirit form had to continually steal life from living plants and animals. There were billions of them. They would in mass pass through areas of living green and draw life force from the plants, insects, reptiles, and birds. Therefore, they died and were susceptible to death and decay, their life forces were constantly being siphoned away. The bodies these others possessed had some organs like the human body. If a grey for instance started to die, sometimes it was necessary for them to abduct humans and take substances such as organs from their physical bodies to be applied to or in some cases transplanted within their own body. The abductions became more frequent as time passed. The alien bodies were wearing down so needed replenishing more often than in their infancy. Art and Gem did not need to apply the ointment to sustain or prolong their life. They only needed to enter MAP and stay within one of the levels of the Eternal Reality for a while and the life-giving forces in there would rejuvenate them. Humanity was not so fortunate though. Art put the egg-shaped unit away. He now had access to what one might call the fountain of youth. Multiple possibilities and applications for this substance were germinating in his mind. The commercial applications were phenomenal to say the least.

His little adventure thus far had answered a lot of questions. For years, the UFO phenomena had posed the subject of many debates. Were their other beings that existed on this planet that were not in the known realm? Did they come from far, distant galaxies? Did they occupy the same space? How were they able to appear in Earth Reality? Thousands of people had claimed to have been abducted and treated horribly at the hands of alien humanoids. Some said they had traveled to other parts of the universe in flying saucers. They had seen strange things and a lot of what they had seen had been erased from their memory. The technology these others possessed was advanced a great deal from that of humans. Within the large heads of some of the others was an intelligence far in advance of humans. They could process information faster than the most modern computers. Yet they were closer than anyone realized. They walked among us unnoticed in a different dimension, a parallel universe of sorts. Methuselah was right in a way. The realities through MAP on either side of Earth Reality were not true parallel universes, they were a place where the fourth dimension of time and the fifth dimension of matter or the cosmos were combined.

Earth was inhabited by millions and millions of creatures other than humans. It appeared they could enter Earth Reality through invisible gateways or doors. What wonders might Art find if he could explore their space? He determined at first chance to see if upon entrance again to this new domain, he could travel backward and forward in time, go anywhere in their strange new world and capture some of their intriguing technology. If he could, would it be considered stealing? If he had heard anything about greys and reptilians it was that they desired earth all to themselves. They did not like sharing with humanity. They wanted to dominate them, make them subservient or eliminate them completely, but if they did that their primary source of sustaining life would be limited greatly. Their mastery of genetic manipulation was improving greatly though. They were now producing bodies that could sustain more of the life forces. There was still room for improvement though. In time it would happen, then humanity must be stamped out forever. These beings with their creative minds were becoming a threat. The more they learned, the more they dominated. The others must never be dominated by their cattle.

Then there was the matter of-what should they call him-the self-existent one? He had a fondness for these creatures.

He had his forces stationed around them in certain cases, protecting them. Eons ago in an age long gone the others had lived on a large celestial body of vibrant energy. From this planet-if one could call it that-the others had been free to travel to all parts of the vast universe. Billions of galaxies were open to them. On this planetoid, life giving energy pulsated and thrived. It was the hub or center of the whole. From this central point pulsating, cosmic particles flowed out to everything. They sustained everything, kept the forces at work in the universe from failing. In that place of glorious energy, the others drew their life forces from this source of power. It energized them. Their forms radiated with living particles. A rebellion had occurred though leading to a great battle. A portion of the others were driven from their home and confined to a small sector of the universe. The self-existent one had placed a barrier around them they could not pass through. He had further confined them to seven levels of the Alien Reality. There were entities or forces confined in the lower realities that had the potential to destroy the small solar system planet earth was part of. But the self-existent one would never allow these to escape their confines. Separated from the source of their life, they were forced to take it from wherever they could get it. But one day that would all change. Events were about to transpire that would free them from some of the levels of their confinement. Once victorious they would move to the next level, and the next until once again be free to transverse the universe as in the age's past. Expectations were running high. Victory was within their grasp.

Art had a lot to ponder as some of the information that had been given him by Methuselah begin to decode. His mind was exploring areas of thought completely foreign to his understanding. He did not like a lot of it. It was disturbing and unsettling. There were forces at work in the cosmos that humanity had no knowledge of. Some of those forces were so dark if one were to encounter the blackness, there would be no escaping it. It would be a giant black hole that would suck everything in, even the light. The new husband must never venture into that dark territory. He would be destroyed.

Before exiting, Art fiddled with the object a bit longer. There was a lot of new technology held within. Again, he could not understand the language, so he relaxed and let his mental powers merge with the device. Information started to pour into his mind. Some of the other topics explored in this device were: Age regression technology, hyper dimensional beings or entitles, time travel methods and procedures, teleportation techniques, wormhole travel and ports, anti-gravity technology. Art would have to spend some time with that one. It would jump start his own studies in anti-gravity propulsion. The list went on and on. There were topics too advanced for his human understanding. If physicist could get their hands on this information, it would change the nature of the universe and how it operated forever. The student in him wanted to study every topic there. If he ever got the opportunity, he would lock himself away for a few weeks and gain understanding through what was presented. Somehow this device tapped into a vast reservoir of information stored somewhere outside of the unit. He would have to highlight the topic of interest somehow and get the device to download it. Somewhere on this unit was a little antenna that would pop out and cause lights to come on while downloading the information. What fun awaited him!

At home Gem was still sleeping. Art wondered why she was so out of it. This was not like her. Had he really known what was happening to her in her own Eternal Realities, he would have feared for her life. She was even now venturing on dangerous ground, virtually unprotected. But the good doctor could not know. He decided to return to the space between Earth Reality and the alien world. This time he would use his highly developed mental powers in MAP to follow one of those saucer crafts to see where it went.

It did not take him long to get in a position and select a craft not far from his house. The creatures that entered it were different than the Grey's that inhabited his home. They looked a bit more human. Their eyes were only half as large as the Grey's eyes. In Earth Reality they could even have been passed off as pale humans. Perhaps some young people who had been on meth for a long time or were spaced out on marijuana or some other drug. They entered their craft and remained there for about ten minutes before the engines started up and the whirring, humming sound intensified. Soon they were off. Art had brought the glasses with him this time. They had allowed him to trace the movements of his murderous neighbor. As he placed them on his head, he could see trails of where the craft had been. When it rose vertically and shot off into the stratosphere, it left a yellow, green line of matter that was easy to follow. By using his mental powers, he could easily keep up with it. The craft traveled to a distant place on the planet. Just before it entered down through a circular hole in the ground, Art paused and looked around. There was nothing surrounding the entrance. It looked like a vast snowy desert. Was it sand or ice? He could not tell. In this state of the Alien Reality his senses were diminished even as they were in the first, second and third levels of the Eternal Reality.

The opening was exceptionally large, several miles across. He could see what looked like an entire continent below the opening. There were trees, rivers, and lakes. He saw hills and mountains. Here and there were cities with people. He even spotted what looked like a wholly mammoth herd complete with both adult and adolescent members. Did the famed saber-toothed tiger also co-exist with these extinct creatures of folklore? He continued following the trail as it went subterranean. It must have traveled miles underground before coming to rest in some sort of a hanger. The doors opened and the humanoids exited the craft. They were on a high balcony overlooking a vast city. It stretched for miles and miles in all directions. In this city there were thousands of humanoids of all sizes and shapes working on various projects or going about their routine business. It was what he would have imagined an underground ant colony might have looked like if all the chambers were illuminated. There were crafts of all types in this underground wonderland. Art remembered hearing rumors of a hollow earth theory where advanced civilizations existed underground. Could it be true? Was this all a part of his imagination? It could not have been. Never in his wildest dreams had he ever seen anything remotely resembling this!

The traveling observer ventured into the beehive. There were gadgets and gizmos unlike anything he had ever seen or even imagine before. In one room he saw what appeared to be a genetic birthing house. There were glass tubes all over with various types of creatures being propagated or incubated. Some were a mixture of reptile or insect bodies but with intelligent brains placed in their heads. The grey genetic technicians were using some sort of light plasma process to splice the genes of the various species together. In another room some of these amalgamations were confined. There was a battle going on in one place. It appeared that the occupants of the cage were in a battle to the death. On the outside hominid observers were making notes on electronic tablets. When one creature would meet its demise, the carnage would stop, and the tattered remains removed from the scene. Then the battle would commence again. Art shuddered. If any of these abominations were released into the world, they would be nearly unstoppable. Most every one of them had an exoskeleton like an insect or reptile rather than the skin of a warm-blooded mammal.

Some of the humanoids were shooting metallic bullets, even laser like bullets at some of these creatures. Some penetrated, others bounced off as if they were hitting solid steel. It was sickening. Art moved on.

In one area he entered a large dome. It was lit with some form of unnatural light. The light came from the top. It was pink and radiating. There were all sorts of plants growing in the dome. Art remembered a few botany classes he had taken in his undergraduate studies. There were plants here that did not exist above ground. A lecture he heard a long time ago came to mind. Out of curiosity the student had gone to a debate between a creationist and an evolutionist. The creationist believed a flood had covered the entire earth some five thousand years earlier. He gave an account like that in the Bible. He also stated that the world before the flood had a ring of water around it high up in the atmosphere that made the entire planet into a tropical paradise. He told how he believed some large asteroids had broken up that ring of water. The water above the world had come down upon the earth and caused the flood. But this creationist had also stated that 95% of the vegetation of that early earth had been lost. The fossil records showed thousands and thousands of lost species. Here in this large dome some of that must have been recovered. There were plants and fruit unlike anything Art had ever seen. He was surprised to see a very tall, totally human man checking out each of the plant types and placing notes on an electronic pad. The man was not typing though. He would talk and the pad would translate his words into language. Art moved in close. It was in a foreign language he did not understand. Perhaps German.

An exceptionally beautiful, tall slender, totally human woman came up to the man and started to converse with him. If Bo Derrick was a perfect 10, this woman was a perfect 100 if such a creature really existed. Just one look at her and her beauty was intoxicating. She would stop any red-blooded man dead in his tracks just to get a glimpse of her. Her features were chiseled to absolute perfection. She had all the right curves in all the right places and then some, like an ancient goddess. Art was holding his breath as she came toward him. Could she see him? No. Thank goodness! She passed right through him and continued making her way to the door Art had come through. He had been so scared, he realized he had been holding his breath to the point of almost turning blue. He let it out now in a long, lasting whew.

"That was a close one," he uttered out loud. The tall botanist suddenly turned toward his direction as if he had heard something. He walked over and stopped directly in front of Art. He kept his eyes focused on something and made a complete circle around the traveler. Then apparently seeing nothing out of the ordinary, returned to his studies. Art again held his breath as that giant circled him. He must have sensed something. Art would have to be careful from here on while traveling in this window dimension. Apparently, some of the advanced humans in this place had extra sensitive, acute senses beyond anything imaginable to the humans that lived above.

Art wished he could have conversed with that botanist in his own language and found out some of the secrets he held in that large super, intelligent mind of his. Even now he came close to a plant that had large leaves. They were at least six feet long and two feet wide. The man uttered a high-pitched sound, and all the leaves on that plant turned toward him. They begin to sway back in forth in some sort of rhythmic motion. Then they responded with a high-pitched sound of their own that mirrored that of the scientist. It varied in pitch and intensity. The liquid waves in Art's universe lined up with the sound waves. Was it possible that this man could carry on some sort of conversation with that plant? The questions were too many to count. Art would have loved to stay here for hours and take in more and more of these underground wonders, but he feared Gem would awaken and get worried when he was not in bed with her. It must be getting late. He decided to take one item from this underground empire back with him to Earth Reality. He started working his way back toward the hole where he had entered. On a table there was a small device that caught his attention. It was in the shape of a perfect pyramid. There were small, red gems embedded at each corner. It would easily be able to be concealed within his hand. When he went to pick it up though, even in this liquid universe, it was exceptionally heavy, far heavier than a similar sized unit of lead would be. With a little ingenuity, Art was able to slide it off the table. The corners were sharp and cut into his hand. He put it down quickly and saw blood coming from a puncture wound. In this universe though it quickly clotted and within a few seconds the puncture started to heal. He saw a small metallic cylinder on a desk not far away. It was not much larger than the triangular object. At the top of the sphere, there was a triangular hole about the same size as the first object. There was also a box that had a triangular pocket to set the unit in. Within a matter of seconds Art successfully transferred the object to the box and pocketed the sphere. He placed the glasses on and was about to retrace his way back home when his attention was drawn to a craft just landing. He watched as it made its way to an area where there were at least a couple of dozen similar craft.

The physicists had always had a curiosity that never quit. It had gotten him into trouble many times. This might prove to be no exception, but he had to do it. He could not resist the urge. The saucer shaped unit came to rest about seven feet above the floor and just stayed there. There was nothing it appeared to be resting on. It was suspended, floating in midair like a hovercraft only no air or sound was coming from it except a slight whirring that got less and less as the craft powered down. After all, went quiet a small door opened in the base of the craft. Two greys came out first followed by two humans. The grey's appeared to be naked. The humans however had on what looked like space suits of noticeably light construction. Once on the ground they pushed a couple of buttons on the suits and they opened. The humans took them off and placed them on hangers. The headgear was placed on a shelf. There was a man who was shorter and a woman who was taller about the same size as Art. The woman was again incredibly beautiful in terms of females in the Earth Reality. The greys went one direction and the humans another.

The 'Curious George,' or in this case curious Art meandered over to the craft. The door was still open, and a small ladder hung down from the opening, ending about eighteen inches from the floor. It was the moment of decision. Should he? Yes! He might never get an opportunity like this again. He would go in and check it out. Carefully he climbed the ladder. The craft did not even wobble. As his head emerged inside the craft he was struck with amazement. There were six seats. In front of them near a set of controls was the piolet's chair. Art drew closer to it. It was resting on some type of a socket. He tried to spin the seat, but it would not budge. The controls seemed almost primitive. There were two joystick controllers and two peddles. These appeared to be able to rotate. Above them at about head level were a few switches. Art went and carefully sat down in the piolet's seat. No sooner had he done that then the door he had entered begin to close as the ladder retracted. The craft shuddered slightly as an engine of sorts automatically came on. What should he do?

The amazed man jumped up from the seat and the engine started to power down. He never expected to take this for a test ride. But why not check it out further? The door to the ground was opening again and the ladder extending. He went down it and looked around. No one was in sight. The starting up of the craft had caused no suspicion. But that was probably normal. Craft like this probably started up all over the place. Whatever time it was down here must have been after closing hours. Nobody was around. Art walked over to the suit the lady had abandoned. Again, should he? He would. He examined it and in short order stepped inside. He tried a couple of buttons and something like a zipper but different caused the seams to come together so tightly that no air could possibly escape. He was sure of that. Next, he donned the helmet. It was very lightweight. Once in place Art squeezed a small ball that was at the base of his palm. The helmet sealed. Some type of ventilation unit activated, and he was breathing very, very fresh air. It was intoxicating!

With the suit on he took one last look around. Nothing appeared to notice him. Ascending the ladder, he again took his seat in the piolet's chair. Again, the ladder retracted, and the door closed as some type of engine powered up. A small light to a switch came on right above him. Not knowing what else to do he reached up and flipped it on. Some pumps started up. The air inside the unit was changing. Art was used to moving from Earth Reality to the first level of the Eternal Reality or in this case the first level of the Alien Reality. The atmosphere within was under more pressure. It was more liquid. As the air or whatever it was began to circulate, Art could tell it was heavier, more liquid than earth atmosphere, even more so than in those realities. He punched his gloves together and they responded the same as punching his hands together from within. In this environment it was even more apparent. His two hands almost passed through each other but as he closed his fingers around the joystick type controls and placed his feet on the pedals, the objects became solid to his grip and touch. It was uncanny. The suit seemed to anticipate his every move. By this time, the whirring had stopped, probably gone into a frequency above the ability of the human ear to hear. The entire craft vibrated only slightly enabling the new piolet to know it was alive and running.

Art instinctively pressed on the pedal that would have been like what accelerated a car. Some electrical current started to charge the outer hull of the craft. As he continued to accelerate, the inner portion of the craft also began to take on a charge. The inner shell became translucent. It was followed by the outer shell. Art could look out from all sides of the craft now. Ahead of him he saw the other craft. He applied a tiny bit of pressure to the right and the pilot seat spun so he could see the craft that had been to his right side. He did it again and could see the craft and the area that had been behind him. His seat made a complete circle. Again, as he looked out over the hanger area, nobody or nothing was in sight at least in this garage.

He pushed the joystick in his left hand forward ever so slightly and the craft rose a little in the air. He released the lever, and the craft came back down to its resting place. Art was back facing the way he had started again. He accelerated more and the area around him went from translucent to transparent. He no longer saw the seats; he only saw himself sitting about ten feet above the ground in something that was alive and anxious to be on the move. It was now or never, right? Wrong. Art was not going that far, not now, perhaps not ever. He decelerated and the craft became solid again the seats appeared. When the whirring attained a level where his ears could again hear it, he flipped off the switch, rose from the seat and the door opened with the ladder again going down. The new pilot descended. He did not need a flying saucer to move around in the first level of the Alien Reality. All he needed were the glasses to retrace his trail back to more familiar ground. Once down he pushed several buttons until he got the right combination and the suit opened releasing the head gear. He placed them back where they had been. Before exiting this underground city, he noticed another of those small black units resting on a shelf. He would take this back with him along with the sphere and the boxed pyramidal unit for further examination. He donned the glasses and in a few moments was teleporting back to the real world where he hoped to find Gem awake.

Art looked at his watch. Something had happened to the time. It was nearly ten in the evening. His time in the other dimension had either lasted longer than he expected or had changed the clocks. He went to the room. Gem was still in bed sleeping. He undressed and got under the covers. Whatever had happened he would try to figure it out tomorrow. An alarm on his watch rang four times.

Chapter 13

It was good to be home even though Art's uneasiness seemed to be growing. He had a lot of memories tied up in this place. Some he would cherish forever, others he wished he could forget. The first item on his agenda that morning after she awoke was to take Gem over and meet their new neighbors. As usual she got up first. She showered and had breakfast cooking when he came down. She was so exceptionally beautiful this morning. Her hair was still damp and clung to her cheeks as she turned some pancakes over in the skillet. He went up behind her and encircled her with his arms. He kissed her under the ear then whispered something to her.

"You are very pretty this morning, Mrs. Goldstein. And I love you very much." She put the pancake turner down and turned to face him.

"I love you too. Mr. Goldstein. You are very handsome this morning. Where did you get these muscles? They are so uncharacteristic of an ex-college professor." She reached out and took his arm in her hands.

"I work out," he answered. "Haven't you seen my weight room?"

"I don't believe I have." She released herself from his grasp and turned over the last pancake. She put a plate of them on the table and microwaved some hot chocolate.

"This will have to do for breakfast. I was thinking for lunch we could set up one of those processors and try out some gourmet food from the future." Art and Gem sat down at the table and in a few minutes polished off the meal.

"I would like to go over and meet our new neighbors. After my work-out and shower. I plan to bring up the fact that we will be house hunting this week. I am hoping they express an interest in purchasing this place."

"That would be convenient wouldn't it?" she responded as she looked out of the window at the place. Although being owned by a former maintenance man, no one passing by would have guessed it.

"Yes, it would. Do you want to take a personal tour of the weight room, Dear?" Art flexed his muscles as he spoke trying to get her attention again.

"That depends upon how personal." Art laughed and so did Gem. After about five minutes they headed for the room.

"It felt so good to laugh, Sweetheart. I haven't done that for months." In the room Art went through his exercises while Gem left to clean up the breakfast mess. A strange thought occurred to him. If he worked out from within, he could probably generate some decent muscle mass. If he added a little meta-physical weight training only heaven knew how the results would turn out. Wasn't there a Gem existing somewhere in a parallel universe with a blond haired, muscle man as a partner? If she like muscles on her man in that universe she might appreciate them on him in this one. He went over to the standard unit and soon had it powered up.

Art entered and went through his routine a second and third time using the power of his mind to mold his body into a man of steel. He exited, powered down the unit and looked at the results in the mirror. It was amazing. He looked like a Navy Seal solder or someone in the U S Marines. He wondered how long it would take Gem to notice. He would try to conceal it with some well selected clothes. Was there anything that was not possible in this realm of the Eternal Reality? There was a shower in the basement off the rec room. He used that one rather than head up to the master bedroom. After dressing he took half an hour to tidy up the place. He went into where the stationery unit was and put a screen in front of it. If the neighbor were interested in purchasing the place, he probably would want a tour. He must never even get a glimpse of this contraption. For an extra precaution Art placed a tarp over the unit and tied it up. From here on out it would always remain covered unless in use. There was a sloping drive that led down to the lower level of the home. If asked the unit could pass for something else. A vehicle of some type. He placed a spare wheelbarrow wheel in front of the tarp for cosmetic appearances.

Gem found him there in the basement. She made no comment about his physic. That was good news! Perhaps he had concealed it well enough by putting on a long-sleeved shirt. They walked out the double doors up the ramp and knocked on the door of the neighbors. A small, elderly woman answered the ring.

"Good morning, we are your neighbors and decided to come over and introduce ourselves. This is my wife Gem, and my name is Art. The lady looked at them and made some motions with her hands. She formed some words with her mouth. Art thought he could make out what she was saying.

"I no speak. I am deaf. Wait, I go get my husband." Art nodded and in a couple of minutes she was back with an elderly gentleman. Art repeated his statement to the man.

"Good morning, we are your neighbors and decided to come over and introduce ourselves. This is my wife Gem, and my name is Art."

"Good morning. I am Ron and this is my wife Wilma. Pleased to make your acquaintance. Do come in. I suppose you have figured out by now that my wife is deaf and cannot speak. She was born that way." He led them into the living room and pointed out some chairs.

"Would you care for something to drink?"

"No thank you," Gem and Art repeated in unison. "We just had breakfast not too long ago. Thanks for asking. You have fixed this place up real nice. The former owner left quite a mess."

"You don't have to tell me about that," Ron commented. "It took my son and I all weekend to paint the rooms and put the carpet down. The wife and daughter-in-law organized the rest of it. Even the grand kids helped a little. They cleaned up the yard as well as they could." With this comment he looked out the window and made some motion with his hand to let his wife know what they were talking about. She was watching their lips very closely.

"You have done a nice job with everything," Gem commented. The conversation went from general to more specific. The two families seemed to hit it off quite well for a first meeting. During the conversation, Art mentioned that they were planning to move but the elderly gentleman never indicated that they might be interested in his place. Art was feeling that perhaps he had read his intuition wrong as they returned home. Inside, Gem asked.

"When should we go and pick up Kanna?"

"I was going to call right now. Funny that you should mention it. I was just thinking of the same question." He went to the phone and dialed his parent's number. His mother answered.

"Art? Is that you, dear? The two weeks isn't up yet is it?"

"Almost, Mother. It will be two weeks the day after tomorrow."

"How was your trip?"

"Great, Mom! Gem and I went to Canada. We had a nice time there. We even said the magic words. I am a married man again."

"Are you now? I am so happy for you. When shall we expect the pleasure of your company?"

"How about this evening? We will take you out and have a celebration supper at the Country Kitchen. I'll treat."

"Don't you even think of it son. Your father and I are very capable of treating you to a Thanks-giving style, home cooked meal. We would not have it any other way. It is the least we can do to help you celebrate your new life together?"

"How is Kanna doing?"

"You wouldn't believe her, Art. She worked some magic on that pony and has him trotting around, following her commands like he had been doing it for years. Dad has never seen anyone so skilled with animals. Even the ranch collies think she is Cinderella and would pull her around in a carriage if she wanted them to. You will not believe it until you see it! What time shall we expect you?"

"How about 4:00 in the afternoon? That will get us there in time to see a demonstration of Kanna's horsemanship." As he spoke his mind recalled the small pony. He tried to imagine his little sweetheart on it calmly riding around the correl. In time he got it.

"That will be perfect. Looking forward to seeing you and your lovely wife. Goodbye, Son and tell our new daughter hello for us."

"Will do, Mom. Thanks. Bye." Art hung up the phone and took Gem in his arms again. He kissed her on the lips and spoke.

"Kanna seems to have a gift for horses. We might have to find a ranch to purchase. It seems like she has taken a liking to animals."

"That sounds great, Art!" Gem grasped his arms to draw herself closer to him then pulled herself away quickly.

"What have you done to yourself, Man? I never felt that before. The last time I did this a couple of eggs popped up, what did you do, put potatoes in those biceps?" Art played innocent.

"What did you say you felt?"

"Potatoes where before there were eggs."

"Maybe the eggs hatched." Art smiled as he thought of some baby chicks running around in his arms.

"And what you have under your shirt. Something big. Why do you have a long-sleeved shirt on anyway? It must be 75 degrees in here at least? She unbuttoned his shirt. Well defined abs rippled where his beer belly had been.

"OK, Sweetheart. Let me explain. I got this idea that if you could do wonders with the human body from within perhaps I could too. I used myself as a test subject. I have never been in better shape in my life."

"He took his shirt completely off and displayed his new look.

"Wow, Babe. You are sure full of surprises." She ran her

hands over his muscular arms and chest. "You keep working out like that and you will be a rancher." They laughed and embraced again. Art went out and checked on the mail. There were orders for a couple of thousand more cleaning units. He would have to forward them to his sales agency. A couple of the envelopes had checks in them. He paused at the address of one. It was from the manufacturer.

"Dear Dr. Goldstein. The demands for your product have been exceptional. We are about out of the glass filaments. We will need 10,000 by the end of next week. Please ship them as soon as you can." Ten thousand units? Were the orders coming in that quickly? He would have to check it out. He had only received confirmation of 5000 units max. When he entered the house, Gem saw the concerned look on his face.

"What is it, Honey? You look like you received some bad news."

"I don't know what to think, Gem. The manufacturer of my product is requesting 10,000 glass filaments by the end of next week. I have only received confirmation of 5,000 units. It does not add up. I sent them 8,000 units a couple of weeks ago. They should still have a bunch left. My sales agency has not communicated any differently. I am afraid I will have to go and check this out. Perhaps we can do it during our house hunting. I really need to go there and do a quality check on the product anyway. I want to be sure they are not leaving anything out. I did get some good news though. There are a couple of checks for nearly a quarter of a million dollars here. I need to get down to the bank and deposit them. Do you want to come along? We have the time. We don't need to leave for moms for an hour and a half yet?" He was holding the checks in his hand as he spoke. He paused to look at the largest one. It looked mighty fine, mighty fine indeed.

"Sure," she responded. "I need to pick up some fresh vegetables and we are running low on burgers." They got in the vehicle and headed for the bank. After depositing the money, Art mumbled something to himself under his breath.

"Now that these checks are in, I really need to go and

pay for the stun guns."

"What was that you said, Art?"

"Oh, nothing important. I was just talking to myself. I have been alone so long I guess I got in the habit of talking to myself. But now that you are here, I will try and break that habit." They turned into the store and purchased the needed groceries. Art made a call on his cell phone to the manufacturer and decided for them to ship the 10,000 empty filaments to him. He put overnight delivery on them. It would take nearly a full day to fill 10,000 units unless he had some help. Then a thought occurred to him. He could get help. He had Gem and Kanna. If they worked with him, he could fill the order in half the time. Back at the house they packed a few gifts from their Canada trip and headed for his mother's home. It was another beautiful day. Indian summer just kept hanging on. Out of the corner of his eye Art caught sight of the log home again. Why not check it out?

"When I headed to your house that first day, Gem, I noticed that home over there for sale. I do not think we will buy it but perhaps since we are here, we could check it out. Would you like to do that now?" Gem looked at the place and nodded.

"I have always wanted a log home. This one is beautiful!" They turned into the driveway and looked out across the hillside. It was a ranch home with several acres of pasture. There were no animals visible though. The grass did not appear to be eaten but grew thick and tall. The barn was also built with logs. It complemented the rest of the place. There was no one home. The house was in fact vacant. There were no caretakers. It did not even appear to have a security system. Art and Gem got out and looked around. No one had been there in a while.

"I wonder how long this has been empty?" Art asked as he walked up to a window and looked inside. There was a thin layer of dust over the floor. More than a year he thought to himself.

"There is no way of telling, Honey but by the looks of

the dust, it has been a while. Let us have a look around." They walked around the house and really liked what they saw. The former owners had done a wonderful job landscaping the place. Though the grass had not been mowed all year, Art could see no weeds in it. That spoke well of the former owners. The newly weds looked in two large windows. There was a spacious kitchen and dining area. The living room had a lovely, rock fireplace. They went to another window and looked in. The master bedroom was on the main floor. They could see some stairs off a hallway.

"This place looks nice, Art," Gem commented. "It has a barn and plenty of pasture for Kanna's pony. We could all have one."

"I like it, too. But I still want to travel around and check out some other parts of the country."

"That would be a good idea. We can keep this one in the back of our mind though and if we can't find anything, we like better this will be home sweet home." They headed back to the van and were about to drive away when they saw a little red car coming up the road. It turned onto the drive and stopped in front of them. A short bald man got out.

"May I help you?" he asked while pulling out a small comb.

"Yes, as a matter of fact you can," Art responded as he wondered if this man thought he could comb a bald head? "We saw this house for sale and came to check it out. Are you the owner?"

"No, but I have a key. Would you like to look inside?" Art answered no and Gem answered yes at the same time then they looked at each other and laughed.

"So, what will it be? Yes or No," the man replied as he looked first at Art then Gem.

"I suppose we could take the time. We have another engagement, but a quick look around shouldn't take too long." They got out of the vehicle and followed the man to the door.

"My name is Jason, by the way. I am the caretaker of this place. The owners put it up for sale a little over a year ago. They had to move to another location closer to a medical facility. Their youngest child contracted leukemia. They really hated to leave here. They had horses too. Had to sell them all to pay for the medical bills." He opened the door and they entered. The workmanship was excellent. Everything was put together very tastefully. They entered all the rooms they had seen from the windows and went upstairs. Kanna's room would be here and there were a couple more if other children came into being. Gem still did not know if she could get pregnant. She made a note to herself to go in for a checkup soon and see what may have transpired.

"Sorry for the dust. I must come back tomorrow and clean it up."

After the tour Jason gave them his card. The price was too high but then it always is. Money was not a problem for Art and Gem, but they still would like to feel they were not getting exploited.

"We are just looking around for now, Jason," Art mentioned as they headed for the van, "But we do like the place very much. We'll be in touch."

"That will be fine with me. I don't think it's going anywhere and with that price tag, not too many people in this area have that kind of money if you know what I mean?" He handed a second card to Gem. Whenever you want to make an offer or have another look around, just give me a call." He got into his car and they drove out of the driveway behind him.

The trip to Mom and Dad's house was uneventful after that. They arrived shortly after the projected time of 4:00. Mom was just putting a couple of pies in the oven. Kanna came running up and jumped high into the air. Her daddy caught her and boosted her up, so he was looking directly into her eyes. He blanked out all his thoughts but what he was about to say.

"How is my little, Pumpkin doing this glorious, fall afternoon?"

"Just fine, Daddy. Take me to the corral quickly. Hi Gem, I mean Mom. Grandpa told me you married my dad. So, you are my Mommy now. You are a very pretty Mommy. Let me down, Daddy so I can hug Mommy." Art lowered the little girl, and she ran to Gem's side. A flood of emotions came over the woman as she bent down and opened her arms. A tiny girl bounced into them and smothered her face with a dozen or more soft warm kisses.

"There! Now you are my official Mom. I have planted kisses all over you and Adam told me that kisses seal two people together. He wanted to seal with me, but I would not let him. I am too little to be sealed in with a boy's kisses but not you. I wanted to be sealed with you, Mommy. We are going to have the best life together." Kanna planted another kiss on the nose of her new mom then took her hand and started pulling her toward the pony.

The colt came to the edge of the fence and nuzzled the little girl.

Kanna gave him a mental command. With her mind she told him to go to the center of the coral and nod his head 3 times, sort of like you would expect to be greeted if you were in Korea or some eastern country like that. The little pony did and returned to its mistress. She gave it a mental sugar cube and watched as he dissolved it in his mouth. She made an especially sweet one this time, one that would last a long time. Before the show was over, she rode the pony around the corral a couple of times and did some more tricks with him before the group were called in to supper.

Art never was much of a social person. Over the years he usually had so much on his mind that he cut conversations short as well as his visits. This evening though he decided to just enjoy his family. The supper was simply wonderful! Mom made a lot of his favorite food. There was her satisfying meatloaf, her famous mashed potatoes, three of his favorite vegetables, and a couple of delicious salads. Desert was the best! It was Mom's melt-in-your-mouth, apple pie with real whipping cream straight from the cream of Dad's prize jersey cow. Art let out a couple of notches on his belt just so he could have a second piece. Dad noticed the change in his muscles and asked what he had been doing to get those kinds of results. Art told about his special workout place and mentioned he was trying a new scientific approach to body building with good success.

After supper, the men went out and brought in some wood for the fireplace and before long a warm glow filled the room. Grandma, Gem, and Art played Candy Land with Kanna. She won every time or did the adults let her win? Well with Candy Land it is very seldom that one person wins more than two games in a row. But Kanna won five in a row. Art wondered if somehow, she was able to mentally manipulate the dice. If so, what about the cards. That was another matter. Kanna seemed to get all good ones. Grandma got out the camera and had Grandpa take lots of photos. Art and Gem took Kanna up and put her in bed. They read her a bedtime story and had a wonderful half hour with her before she drifted off to sleep. Just before she slipped into dreamland, she suddenly opened her eyes real wide. She looked into the eyes of her new mother then said out of the blue.

"How big is my little brother now, Mom? I know he is in there," she pointed to Gem's tummy, "but I can't see where." Gem flinched a bit as the reality hit her. Could it be true? She pondered being a mom, not only to Kanna but to a child of her own. She sent a question to Con.

"Con, am I pregnant?"

"Yes, Gem," came the reply. "You know you are." Art was looking at both the little girl and his wife. He was going to be a father again? Unbelievable! All in all, it was one of the best days Art had experienced in a long time. It ended well, too. Almost too well.

Art was awakened by the grandfather clock chiming; 1,2,3. After breakfast the three headed back home. They stopped and showed Kanna the log home. She loved it. There was a place for her pony and a place for a dog too, even a cat or two might keep the mouse population down. Art and Gem wondered if they should make an offer but decided to wait until their house sold. It was not on the market yet, but would they need to place it there? Art felt certain the neighbors would buy it, but nothing had happened in that direction so far. The ride home was not like the ride down to the old home place. A cold front was moving in. Dark clouds were brewing on the horizon. The road was covered with lots of leaves from the trees. Winter would be here before long. At the house they unloaded and fixed a light lunch. It was good to be home with Kanna. After lunch she took her favorite dolls and Teddy and played with them in her room. She was telling Teddy a story.

"I love you, Teddy. I can talk to you and tell you stuff that Mommy and Daddy do not need to know. Do you know what, Teddy? Something bad is going to happen soon. You and I are going to be on our own for a while. We need to get ready. Down under Daddy's machine is a big room. It has a couple of beds, a kitchen, a bathroom, and another room that could hold things. We need to start taking food down to that room. As soon as the grownups go out today, we will start." She started humming a little tune Grandma taught her and changed all her doll's clothes. She packed a little suitcase full of spare ones and put in a couple of changes of clothes for Teddy. Then she pulled a suitcase out from under the bed where her brother had slept. It had a few of his clothes inside. She left them there and put several of her own outfits in on top of them. She looked out of the window and saw her dad and new mom working in the yard. Dad was doing some fall pruning and mom was planting bulbs. It was nice to have a Mommy again."

"Mommy will have to go away, Teddy. And Daddy will go looking for her. He will forget about us. You see, he is going where most people cannot go and once, he gets in there, he will be trapped. That is why we need to hurry and get ready." She tugged at the suitcase and it moved a little. Then she saw Sonny's skateboard in the closet. She got it out and put the suitcase on it and pulled. It went much faster that way and she had less work to do. She found the door behind the machine. It was hidden.

"Daddy doesn't even know this place is here, Teddy."

She opened it and there were some stairs leading down into the dark. She hit a light switch and things looked better. She got the suitcase to the stairs but pushed a little too much. The skateboard and suitcase tumbled down landing in a heap at the bottom. She ran down and pulled the suitcase off to the side. Then she went back up and started taking food down. She found a little box just the right size for her to carry and took loads and loads of stuff down. There was a lot of food in the house. Her real mom had believed in keeping the shelves well stocked. Some of it was kinda old though. Kanna made certain to leave the food in front, sort of like it was before removing the food further back. After the twentieth load was in place, the little girl rested. She ate a snack and began to look around. The kitchen had not been used in years. Spiders with their webs were in every corner. The bathroom was also dirty.

Kanna was about to head back upstairs for more things when she saw a button on the wall with a red glow to it. She went over and pushed it. Another door opened and inside she saw long rows of shelves. She turned on the light and walked inside. There was a lot of food there. This food was all packaged up in aluminum foil or special, plastic cases. There were names on all the packages. There were also cans and cans of fruits and vegetables. The food that Kanna had brought down was of the more perishable type. She had chips and cookies some breads and crackers, but this newly discovered food was well packaged. It was dehydrated and had a long shelf life. Perhaps years and years?

"What do you think of this, Teddy? We will have enough food here for at least a year. I sure hope it doesn't take Daddy that long to find our new Mommy after she gets lost in time." The little girl went to the far corner and saw a chest freezer there. She could barely lift the lid, but it too was filled with food, still frozen. There were some good things in there if only she knew how to cook. On the way out she saw a strange machine and wondered what it was. It had buttons and switches on it. She would have to check that out later when she had more time. Somewhere within she vaguely realized that in the future she would have lots and lots of time.

After trimming all the bushes and raking some leave, Art decided to go in and get something to drink. Kanna had just closed the door to the secret shelter when he entered. She looked down at her teddy bear and made a "shisss" sound while placing her finger over her mouth.

"You won't tell Daddy will you, Teddy?"

The order of 10,000 glass filaments had come in. To make his units work all Art needed to do was take them inside the first level of the Eternal Reality, open them up, place the clear plastic rings around the edges and screw them back together. All that was necessary was for them to be filled with the liquid atmosphere of that reality. This was sealed within the filaments when they came back into Earth Reality. That was what made the lenses in the machine capable of seeing the living organisms. The employees of Spiffy Clean could look through the eye pieces of this invention and see how sterile counters, windows, floors, carpets, and anything else was that needed cleaning. All they had to do was bring in their sterilizing cleaner and apply it to the area until all the colors representing living organisms lost their aurora.

Art uncovered the stationery unit and turned it on. He got out the hand truck and transferred the filaments inside. The manufacturer shipped them open. This time he noticed with satisfaction they had even placed the plastic rings on the bottom of the lenses. How long would it take to screw 10,000 units together? He called Gem down and explained the process to her. She grasped the concept quickly. He then asked Kanna if she would like to help. She said she would.

All three of them entered the next reality and sat at the tables Art had set up. Soon they had a system worked out. Gem and Kanna screwed the lenses together and Art tightened them down. He had developed a small torque wrench for this very purpose. In no time the 10,000 units were completed and packed for shipment. Art took them out and placed a call for FedEx to pick them up the next day.

Back in Earth Reality, Gem went up to the bedroom to read more in her book. This gave Art a little time. He went to the room where the stationary unit was and pulled the little box from the drawer, he had placed it in. He opened it and placed the triangle object on a card table. At that moment he heard a commotion on the stairs so turned that direction. Kanna's skateboard had been resting up against the bottom step and slipped to the floor. When Art turned back to the table the pyramid object had dropped to the cement floor. It cut a perfect triangular shaped hole through the card table. The professor examined it. No damage appeared to have been done to the unit but one of the rubies was starting to glow. It was followed by the other corners. A laser beam shot up from the top and started to burn a hole in the ceiling. Three other beams shot out from the bottom. Not knowing what else to do, Art grabbed the little box and placed it open, above the beam shooting up. The material in the box did not melt. In fact, it caused the red beams to shut down again. Art breathed a sigh of relief. He placed the object back in the box and put a board on the card table. He picked it up and placed it on the board. It supported the weight. So, this device was a laser of some sort. He pulled out the metallic sphere with the triangular hole. It was perfectly sealed now. There was no evidence of an opening. What other secrets did it hold? Someone was coming down the stairs, so the physicist put the box along with the sphere back in the bottom drawer where he had gotten it from. He would have to explore its unique features at some future date. Kanna appeared and ran over for a hug and a kiss. Then she and Teddy exited the door.

"I am going out to ride my bike, Daddy. Don't worry about me, I will stay in the driveway and go no further than the sidewalk." She flashed him a huge smile causing her dimples to show.

"What a beautiful girl she was," he thought to himself. "How can a man be so lucky to have the two most beautiful girls in the world living with him together in the same house?" He went back to the drawer and pulled out the projection device. It was a bit smaller than the first one but had the same features.

He pressed in on the sides and a picture sprang to life in the air above the unit. Just as he suspected the picture showing was of a saucer craft. Who knew what other inventions or technological advancements the unit held? The craft had two layers forming the outer shell. There was the outer hull and an inner one. Art expected the air between the two was of similar composition as that of the air within the various levels of the realities. In the center of the craft there was a metallic sphere. Inside of that was a smaller one. The plans for this craft had only four seats and a pilot's chair. The controls appeared to be the same as Art had seen on the other unit underground. Apparently, the power source charged the outer hull with a positive or negative charge and charged the inner one with the opposite charge. Like two magnets that repel each other the inner and outer hull repelled each other. The outer hull once charged ionized the air. While going through the atmosphere here on earth the ionization process created a vacuum around the unit. This reduced friction to near zero, sucking the unit forward at impossible speeds.

The circular sphere within the sphere served as a gyroscope, stabilizing the craft during flight. It could pass-through hurricane-force winds without even being budged from its course. If the unit was like the triangular object he had retrieved from the underground city and the sphere, perhaps the inner shell of the sphere repelled the laser like lights of the pyramid shaped object. This would cause the unit to spin at incredible speeds. This unit did not have a triangle within a sphere however but a sphere within a sphere. Perhaps several triangular objects could be placed together to form a sphere of sorts. Their combined power most likely accounted for the gyroscopic action. It would also enable the craft to have a gravity field inside if the saucers went interstellar.

The suits the humans used were pressure suits. The greys did not need them. Because of their existence in the Alien Reality, the pressure within the craft was like their natural environment. The humans however, using the modified, heavier, liquid atmosphere inside along with the suits enabled passengers within the craft to travel at tremendous speeds without feeling any effects during rapid acceleration or sharp turns. Say for instance the craft was generating 8 Gs. The occupants of the craft would experience nothing. An opposite amount of pressure equal to the acceleration was applied automatically. How fast could the craft go? It depended on the amount of acceleration placed on the petal or handle. The more it was pressed, the greater the charge applied to the hull. More air was ionized creating a greater vacuum around the craft. As the vacuum became greater around the craft it could go faster, perhaps even reaching near light speed. Rather than meeting resistance while passing through the air, the vacuum created around the craft again sucked the unit forward. A sharp turn to the left or right would instantly result in turns impossible for any other type of aircraft. For rapid turns like that the occupants would not feel anything. Amazing! This technology, why wasn't it out there being used for transportation? It would transform life as we knew it on earth. With a craft like this a person could be to the moon in minutes or Mars in a matter of hours. The ionization taking place on the hull of the craft with the gyroscopic, stabilizing unit would enable it to enter the atmospheres of the gas giants in our solar system. A craft like this could even go underwater. This was phenomenal! So, this is how the reports of UFO sightings had the craft doing impossible maneuvers? The technology did exist but who was squelching it? Who was keeping all this secret from the world? It was quite possible that the elite ruling class, perhaps a few people at the top were using this to control the world while taking vacations to Mars, Jupiter, Venus, Saturn, Uranus, even Pluto. The reports of bases on the dark side of the moon as well as on Mars were most likely true.

Interstellar travel was possible with this technology. Man could easily go to the stars. Perhaps he already had that is if the self-existent one would allow it? It sounded like he was confining the dark, parasitic forces to a smaller area than they used to travel in? What would be the effect though in Earth Reality? If these flying craft were as prevalent as they appeared to be in the Alien Reality, the tremendous reactions during their flight, going on at the quantum level most likely leaked through various dimensions. For instance, a saucer craft operating in the Alien Reality could cause effects in the Earth Reality. Suddenly crop circles and other unexplained phenomena did not seem so mysterious. A person in a field directly beneath a landing of some craft in the Alien Reality might feel the effects, even see them in Earth Reality without seeing the craft. Art pressed in on a couple of areas of the unit and the projection closed. He now knew that his goal of developing an anti-gravity craft was within reach, but someone had gotten there first and did not want the technology out there for whatever reason. The only thing he could think of was power. Whoever was holding the technology, keeping it from getting out, wanted to keep it that way where he to develop such a device or perhaps several applications to the principle, some organization would swoop down and confiscate it from him. He would most likely be killed or placed in a chamber somewhere deep underground with four walls, never to see the light of day again. This was discouraging. Suddenly he saw his life goals melt away right in front of him. Somewhere in the distance a horn honked two times.

Chapter 14

Wilma had wondered all her life what it was like to hear. She and her husband had kept up on the latest scientific and medical advances in hearing, but nothing had looked promising. When she woke up on this morning however, she could hear clearly. She lay in bed nearly holding her breath, thinking it was a wonderful dream but when fifteen minutes had passed and the sounds kept coming, she was a believer. At first, she wanted to shout but a warning came from somewhere back in her mind to let no one know right away. Over the next several days she listened and learned. She purchased a talking, English dictionary and used her husband's tape player to listen. When the grandchildren came over, she made a game with them pointing out various objects in the home and having them pronounce each one. As the days passed, she became proficient in pronouncing different words. She practiced into a tape player. One day she would surprise them all. There were hurts associated with hearing, though. Her family often said things they would not have said had they known she could hear. One morning her husband found her crying over some comment that had been made. When he tried to comfort her, she shrugged him off. The gift of hearing far outweighed the pain.

The Gem from within had paid Wilma a visit the night after Kanna had come home. She was confused a lot of the time about what was happening to her. At times it seemed that she was with Art and Kanna then she would be off doing something away from them. Today she would take a trip to the US patent archives and locate the machine that went with the ruby lens. She had laid out a plan. She would follow the ruby back to the time when it was last in the machine, then follow the machine to its current resting place. It seemed easy enough. From within the second level of the Eternal Reality she could move about quite quickly. Had someone been able to trace her movements, it would have seemed like she was speeding circles around everyone. When she finally got to the place that housed the machine, she was somewhere in Russia. It looked cold outside. From where Gem was though it was warm. She decided to continue going back in time until the machine was used. She did not have long to wait. The machine was pointed toward the moon.

As she watched, an old reel tape was loaded with some information. The information was fed into a machine. It transformed it into a series of pulses. The pulses were shot to the surface of the moon. There was a telescope set up not far away. When no one was using it, she went over and looked through it. The red pulses appeared to hit some type of receiver. From there it looked like it was redirected to the left. After several minutes, some blue pulses came back to the reflector on the moon and were bounced to some type of receiver at its base. A group of scientists, at least that is what Gem though they were, collected the information and talked about it. If only she could understand their language. Then she remembered she could. There was a perfect interpreter in the great river. She tapped into it and was soon listening in on the maze of conversations. The words being spoken were those coming from the blue pulse.

"We are watching the sun rise on Mars. It is beautiful. The planet is green this time of year. The lichen grows very rapidly in this higher carbon dioxide atmosphere. It puts off a bit of oxygen. There are some living organisms there besides plant life. These little animals can withstand very cold temperatures. There is a dark ring that looks like snow at one of the polar caps. We have reason to believe there is water on this planet at its warmest season." There was a pause while the machine pulsed another charge of red to the reflector. Five minutes later the blue pulse started up again.

"We will be ready for the relief astronauts the day after tomorrow. All our notes are in order. The plants we brought seem to be doing fine. It has been interesting, but we will be glad to come home." The transmission ended and the scientist closed the station as the sun started to raise. Then something strange happened. A large saucer shaped craft hoovered over the transmission station. Two extremely bright lights came on. A small craft appeared out of a small hole in the side. It came down to the door. Some of the scientist appeared with high powered weapons. They fired at the craft. A blinding light came from it and the scientist were vaporized. The weapon was then aimed at the door where the armed men had come from. It too was vaporized. In less than fifteen minutes the entire place was emptied of all its equipment. The large craft rose vertically into the air for over five thousand yards then sped sideways and disappeared. Gem took the beam camera and pointed it at the point of departure. A violet-colored streak was all that was left to point her the way.

She had gotten good at following lines. This should be as easy as the rest. Soon she was on the trail of the saucer. It ended in a large building somewhere. She would have to look around and see if there was a map. Whatever this was, it was controlled by Germany. Their flag flew proudly in the air of the great dome. She located the machine and watched as the Germans set up the equipment the following evening and beamed some messages to the moon. In time the blue pulse returned asking for code numbers. There was some confusion among the people working with the equipment. They sent a message back and were stalled again. The Russians were still demanding a code. Gem went back in her mind and recorded it at the first transmission she had seen the other evening. With her mind, she fed the information unto the reel and pushed the button. There was a surprised commotion in the room as the machine came on and sent the red pulse. Two men went over and tried to see what had happened. They pushed some more buttons. By the time they realized there was nothing they could do the blue pulse was coming back.

"Code confirmed." The two men and a lady seemed to breathe a sigh of relief. The Russians responded with a series of messages. They told them the transport ship had arrived with replacements. They would leave the dock the next morning. Gem followed the machine ahead in time. Several weeks passed in earth time. Then she recognized her father. He was talking to one of the men who had been in the room when the German's had made the first transmission. Later, that evening, he gained access to the station with a special card, and personally removed the lens from the machine. She could not believe it. Why, if her father were working for Germany, would he steal the lens from them, or was he a double agent? She would ask him next time she saw him. Now she must follow the machine to its current resting place and steal it from there. After that she would assemble it and see if she could still find the point of transmission on the moon.

It did not take long to find the building that housed the laser. It was in a huge underground cave. There were thousands of items in the cave. Gem decided to go back to the current time while still in the cave. In a few minutes she was there. She returned to the stall where the laser was, but it was nowhere to be seen. She was surprised because she kept her eye on it while skipping through the years. She moved back in time again trying to isolate the exact moment it left. In time she was there. She rotated back and forth between the seconds it took to disappear and could not understand what happened to it? It just vanished without a trace. She took out the portable particle beam recorder Art had purchased from the future and took several takes of the disappearing machine. Then she decided to return to her counterpart who was with Art. She would need 100% of herself if she were to solve this mystery. By this time, she realized that though she knew what was going on in both Gem realities, the other Gem did not. The other Gem could only catch a scattering of her activities while in a lucid dream state or in a deeper state of sub consciousness when her brain, wave activity was at or lower than six cycles per second.

Art and Gem decided to do a very strange thing. They wanted to know if the neighbors would buy their home, so they decided to go into the first level of the Eternal Reality and traveled ahead in time somewhere around 36 months. In this future time, the house was still theirs. They decided to exit and have a look around. Not much had changed. There was different furniture placed here and there. Gem had done a little redecorating. The kitchen had been remodeled. It had some nifty things from the future and the lady of the house talked her husband into hanging around for a meal. According to the calendar, the Art and Gem from this time were away on a trip. The visiting couple supposed Kanna was with them. They had a pleasant evening together. Before venturing into the future, Art made a trip to the basement and retrieved the little box with the laser object, the sphere, the egg-shaped units, and the black projection gizmo. He placed them in a fanny pack around his waist. Perhaps he would find some time to examine them more closely during this adventure. After checking things out the couple fell asleep. Somewhere off in the distance a clock struck two.

Gem awoke early in the morning and went to Art's lab. In this future world she ran across a small disk. She did not remember seeing it before and needed to analyze it. She opened the particle beam video camera to compare the disk with the one inside. The one inside was larger. It held five times as many terabytes as the card she had just found. Then she remembered. There was a little box her husband had put some things in and sent home from Canada during their honeymoon. This must have been the chip in the camera they had taken in the Canadian future. The videos of the future world were utterly amazing. The images of different things hung in the air just as if they were back there. There were several shots of Art and several ones he had taken of her. Her favorite was one where Elvis had picked her up and held her while singing "Love Me Tender." Yes, Elvis was still around in the future. She supposed he was one of those timeless legends that would never die.

Suddenly she became very tired. She yawned and was soon in dream land. In her dream she was still looking at the particle beam video chip, but the movie playing was no longer in Canada. There was this large machine that looked like her obsolete particle beam camera. This unit dwarfed hers though and made it look like a toy. As she watched the video, the camera started to shimmer around the edges. It was trimmed in a yellow green light. The light slowly encased the unit than in a mille-second was gone.

From somewhere in infinity, Methuselah looked in on Gem. She was about to enter a journey that would be most difficult. She had not been prepared for this one. It had been a mistake for these two travelers to go ahead in time. Had they remained in the regular zone; they could have been better prepared for this crisis. There would have been several mini tremors before the big one. Most circumstances in the Earth Reality were predictable but a few random happenings seemed to pop up every now and then. This circumstance was not one of those. The higher power had been preparing for this occasion for millennia. The entire world would be rocked beyond anything in history save perhaps the deluge that had ravaged the planet, destroying life on every front. Methuselah had never lived long enough to see it. Noah had preached for 120 years about it. He had even built a great boat to protect hundreds of species of animals. Methuselah had died the same year the flood came at the ripe old age of 969. He had lived in a world that was much different than the one Art and Gem were a part of. In his day, a large canopy of water surrounded the earth high in the heavens. It was nearly a half mile thick. The early earth had a lot more oxygen in the atmosphere. Instead of blue, the clear sky was more of a pink color, like it occasionally is just prior to sundown.

The people were bigger also. Noah was over 12-foot-tall and he was small compared to some of the giants that had been produced through genetic manipulation. Methuselah had seen one that was close to 30 feet tall. There were reports of taller ones but who knows if there really were? The ancient one had never seen any while on earth. That was back then, now the world was about to enter the middle portion of the series of disasters that enveloped it. For this journey Art would need a guidebook. The ancient one brought down a Bible from a shelf in the closet and placed it under the arm of the dreaming lady. It was a literal English translation of the Bible.

Gem used the other camera to record the split second the machine disappeared. After replaying the video 5 times, she finally caught the exact time it went. Focusing on this split second, she mentally went there and hung unto the laser as it was whisked away. There was a loud explosion with a vibrating echo that caused her ears to ring. She sensed an immediate pressure change. Somehow, she knew she had jumped another reality. What direction was it this time? Before she could recover from the shock another one came and still another. She had traveled in the different realities enough to realize how each felt, but the one she was in now was different. A violet angel that looked ever-so-much like Art came to her and put his arms around her. In this reality he, Art or it was totally liquid. It was like a liquid but very dry and very comforting.

"I finally got you back, dear," the voice soothed." This time I have all of you and intend to never let you go it alone again." She was inside of this Art angel. His substance surrounded her. She felt another shock wave, but his essence cushioned her from the impact. She imagined or dreamed that she was floating in a cloud of feathers. They were so soft and wonderful. Her being was as light as the feathers themselves and she floated in limbo enjoying the comfort of it all. She looked around for the laser and saw it a short way off. She thought to go to it and was there. It was not solid like the one in the cave. This laser was like a giant balloon with an exceptionally soft shell. She remembered handling some squishy balls in the mall back in Canada and attributed the substance of the laser with the same feel. Her Art angel was guiding her to a very bright light. She was in him yet out of him riding on the machine. His hand if you could call it that, reached into her purse and pulled out the ruby lens. While they were still moving, he fitted it in place. He simply opened the side of the laser with his hands like one would open a hole in silly putty, inserted the lens and closed the hole back up. He touched the switch, and the machine came to life. A beam of brilliant green burst from the lens and fed into the brilliant, white light. She was inside the Art angel again when the last explosion came. Somehow before her thoughts went out, she realized she had passed into yet another reality. She thought of Art. He was in trouble. She reached for him. Then all was dark.

This hyper-dimensional creature smiled to himself. Finally, it was done! The barriers that had for so long existed between the Alien and Earth Reality were finally opened. Now billions of hyper-dimensional beings could converge upon their common enemy and start the annihilation process of humans. Not even the omnipresent one himself could stop the Archons and other demonic forces from the destruction and bloodshed about to be unleashed. The dimensional prison or abyss-the omnipotent one had entrapped them in for millennia-was finally broken. First however, they would torture and torment these pathetic creatures. They would bring them right up to the point of death then revive them for weeks and weeks, perhaps even months. The Art Angel uncloaked his assumed angelic form and returned to his hideous, natural self. He gnashed his teeth together several times with anticipation.

Art missed Gem. They loved to spoon in bed. Sometimes he would curl around her and other times she around him. Once upon a time he had read that men are slightly positively charged in their biorhythms and women slightly negatively charged. When a man and a woman were close, often the charges attracted one another. In some cases, a lot more than others. Love at first touch was attributed to this concept. It had even been proven until some same sexed people came and were tested. They blew the theory right out of water, you might say. They found ladies with negative charges and others with positive charges. They even found some who could bounce back and forth between negative and positive charges. These were people who could attract lovers-if that is the right name for it-from both sexes. Art had felt the charge of her touch leave. He had reached out to hold her from going but she slipped from his grasp and he dropped off to a restless sleep again. Then he was wide awake.

Art and Gem had been sleeping in earth reality three years into the future. Now earth reality was being tossed around like a cork on a violent ocean. The house was swaying back and forth. Windows were breaking. Sirens were going off outside. Truly this was an earthquake of a magnitude seldom experience. Art got up from the couch. He was calling Gem's name. He somehow made his way down to the lab just as a large beam in the home fell, blocking the stairs behind him. Then he saw her. She was slumped over the video reader he had cobbled together to look over the particle video photos he had taken in Canada and after. He could see the stationery MAP machine behind the wheel he had placed there in front of the tarp. He waddled over to the apparatus and ripped the canvas off. He found the switch and flipped it. Thankfully, he watched as the unit came to life. The power had gone off, but this unit had a backup power source. He remembered seeing-while looking out of the broken windows-electricity arching from the downed wires. Now that the unit was in operation, he knew he had to get Gem through the opening not once but twice. In the back of his mind Art knew that somehow the barrier between Earth Reality and at least one level of the Alien Reality had been broken.

A wall collapsed and the entire front of the house fell outward causing the roof to be ripped from it. Art grabbed Gem and managed to pull her through the opening. He dragged her around again. He had to repeat this two times at the least. Three would be better if he had time. He was just about to reenter the barrier when a hundred fire shadows grabbed Gem and tried to rip her from his arms. They stung, tormented, yelled, and screamed at him. His ear drums popped. The pressure of the blood within his being increased multiple fold. Blood started pouring from his eyes, nose, and mouth. Then it came out of his ears. He kept pulling, struggling against all odds. Slowly he made it to the entrance. With literally the last ounce of his strength, he managed to push her through the opening. Some of the fire shadows had gone for reinforcements. The remaining ones were tugging at him now. One slipper flew off then another. His t-shirt was whisked from his body. Eventually he clung in only his pants with the belt and fanny pack to the rim of the opening. Then a soft, feminine hand locked onto his wrist and with super woman power pulled him in. Inside all was quiet. The house was in shambles as was the rest of the city, perhaps the world for all he knew.

In the final moments before her thoughts blanked, Gem remembered the real Art. She reached out to him. She felt his hand. She latched on to his curled fingers and then found his wrist. The Art angel assumed his beautiful form again and was embracing her, crying in his sweet voice. I love you Sweetheart, do not leave me. You came to me, remember. We promised ourselves we would be together forever. Do not gooooooooeeee.

Art lay panting for a long time. Gem was slumped on the floor beside him. She was unconscious. Somehow when he grabbed her, she had held unto the camera, and a Bible. There was a sharp popping sound and Art watched the door to Earth Reality crumple and fall. Then the unit was gone, smashed by the remainder of the roof. He was trapped in this dimension with no way to exit. While wondering what to do, he thought of Kanna. In his haste to save Gem he had forgotten his own daughter. Then he realized something else. She was not in the reality they were in but in another one back some thirty-six months in the past, abandoned, alone and so noticeably young. It was too much. Art started crying like a baby. It had been a while since he had done that. He went over to his wife and laid his head on her still form. She was breathing but was comatose, somewhere a million miles away in who knew what reality. In her hand she held a book, no it was a Bible. Of all the books in the world, why did she have a Bible?

Art believed in God a little, but all his scientific, educational training promoted the belief of evolution. He had always gone along with the curriculum, teaching whatever they gave him. Now he wondered what the Bible was all about. Was his wife a Christian? He had never asked her about her religious beliefs. He just assumed she held the same views as his own. He was tired. He needed sleep to recover from the battle with the fire shadows. This reality was cooler than Earth Reality. He wished for some covering, perhaps a blanket. He found one but when he placed it over the lady and himself, it was useless. He felt no weight at all; besides, it was translucent. But there was a bit more warmth. While he slept, he dreamed the clock wanted to chime again but it could not. Something had stopped it. Finally, a distant ding came back almost like an echo.

Chapter 15

When Art awoke, he was still in his home some 36 months into the future. During his sleep, his body had healed of all the bleeding he had suffered at the hands of the fire shadows. It took him a while to remember what had happened. He got up and looked around for a shirt. There were none in this reality that would work. He looked at Gem. She had a long sweater on, He could use that for some covering. Without the portable or stationery units used as doors between realities, Art could not enter the real world to get clothes from it. If he placed clothes on from this reality, they would not function as clothes. He decided to take the sweater off from Gem. As he did, he realized that the other Gem, the one traveling in who knew what reality, had one of his portable units. If she were conscious in that reality, she could use it to get to him. How would he communicate with her though to tell her he needed her to come back to him?

The camera Gem had would work in this reality. He picked it up and turned it on. As he looked out at the shambles around him, he could see that world as if he were in that reality. There was still a fire shadow in the house but as he looked through the camera, the fire shadow was no longer a shadow. It was a real, living, walking monster. It was very tall, well over 10 feet in height. It had some interesting characteristics. This creature had long, blond hair. It had some sort of a band around its head to hold the hair in place. The band appeared to be made from gold but was brighter than any gold Art had seen. It was illuminated with a light that dazzled. This creature had red eyes, a bit of a nose and a mouth like a person except for his teeth. They were sharp and pointed, like the teeth of a possum. It also had on a strange looking suit of clothes. There were lights of various colors on the clothes. In its hands it carried some sort of a weapon that was connected to the suit at the back, perhaps even the body.

Art could walk freely around in this reality. He looked at Gem again. He really should place her somewhere where she would be more comfortable. He picked her up and placed her on the couch. It was far more liquid than it should have been. Gem sank halfway into it. It was raining in earth reality but in this reality rain was different. It was slower, gravity was less in here. All the substances were linked closer together. Rock was not as hard as rock. A sponge was not as soft as a sponge. In this reality thoughts could be made into substance.

Art could still travel anywhere in this reality at thought speed but when he tried to go forward or backward in time, it was not possible. Somehow when the earthquake came, when what Art feared as the fracture of some of lower realities happened, earth reality was opened to the fire shadows, or the greys and reptilian humanoid.

He decided to follow the fire shadow around for a while. Before he did though, he went into his meditative state and manufactured some clothes for himself. He wondered why he had not thought of it earlier. He still had his pants and the pack with the triangular sphere plus an assortment of other things. He took the sweater off and put it back on Gem. After a bit of practice, he had a complete outfit with a waterproof jacket. Perhaps he could create a portable MAP unit from his thoughts? He tried for half an hour but the units he conjured up in his mind and crafted with his hands would not power up.

Out in the street looking through the camera, Art saw his neighbor lying down. A fire stinger was torturing him. The weapon he had was placed on the man's hips. From time to time the fire stinger would move the end of the weapon at different places on his body. Ron would scream and writhe with pain. He would try to get up and run but the stinger would touch him again and he would fall to the ground screaming. The fire stinger would give Ron a command and if he did not obey instantly, he would get stung again. Art walked all over the city. There was terrible destruction everywhere. Hardly a house was free from harm. Many people had died. Art calculated at least a fourth of the population of this city had perished in the quake. There were fire stingers or large, sharp teethed angelic beings all over. They were torturing anyone and everyone who would not obey their commands. Art decided to teleport to the log home to see what had happened to it. In a moment he was there.

It was in surprisingly good shape. The logs had survived the quake very nicely. He decided to go outside. He could only go so far. There appeared to be a barrier that prevented him from moving more than a hundred feet out from any side of the home. This was strange or was it? Somewhere in the back of his mind Art remembered purchasing this place as a second home. The sales from his cleaning units had provided more than enough money. He had made some revisions. Then the vision of his adventure into the realm of the greys came back to mind. He remembered the machines that could place force fields around buildings. He must have at some point in the three years between then and now have gone into that reality and removed the grey technology. Yes, he had brought it back to Earth Reality. Then he had gone one level into the Eternal Reality and installed this force field around the log home, their log home. Yes! They had ended up purchasing it. The temperature under the dome was perfect. The wind outside appeared to be traveling at near gale forces but inside all was calm. This would be the perfect hide-a-way until he could figure out what to do.

Art went back to his home. He rigged up a car in this reality. It would not support the weight of Gem no matter how hard he tried to conjure one up from his thoughts. Had she been conscious, she could have traveled with him wherever he went. Finally, he carried her to the log home. It took a couple of hours to get there but at least she would be more protected. Although he did not know of anything here that could harm her. Somehow though seeing her in this home of their dreams was more comforting during this time of trial. If only he had remembered Kanna they could have been together as a family in this new home. Where was she? Where was his little girl? How would she survive in the world all alone? As he thought about her, he wondered if things were still normal, 36 months back in time. They must be. She would at least have a house to live in for a while until someone missed them and came looking. Perhaps she would call Grandma. She was a smart child. Somewhere into the cosmos he placed several thoughts of wellbeing for his beloved child.

After seeing that Gem was comfortable, Art took a trip around the world. Every country he looked in on through the lens of the particle, video camera was in various stages of ruin. Some cities were worse than others. The fire stingers were everywhere torturing the people who were yet alive. Some of the leaders of the nations though, had made a truce or cease fire agreement with the stingers. They were like pawns in the hands of a master chest player. They did everything the fire stingers asked. In exchange these villains did not torment them. These creatures from the underworld had the men and women in their control do terrible and disgusting things. They also commanded them to raise an army. The various nations were organizing men in arms to help control or curb the chaos of people. Those who could, were looting and plundering whatever was left of the world. They would rape women and children and try to kill them or others but whenever any person attempted to kill another, the stingers would nearly fry them senseless with their deadly weapons.

Then Art noticed someone who was different. It was a man, a human person who was walking around untouched by the fire stingers. Many of these aliens or whatever they were, would rush up to him to shoot their hot, burning poison into his body, but they could not touch him. Art drew in closer. The man was talking. He was telling the people that they should return to someone. The name of that someone was foreign to the physicist. It was in an ancient dialect. This man condemned the leaders of the armed forces for forcing the remaining populous to conform to the martial laws that were being drawn up. Every now and then a family or a person would ask the untouchable man what to do. He would tell them, then he would look up and speak some words. At that time, these people would become like him, untouchable by the fire stingers. This made the stingers terribly angry. They would try all kinds of ways to destroy these people but to no avail.

On closer examination, Art could see what appeared to be a shield of light around these untouchable men and woman. It really looked like they personally were in level one of the Eternal Reality but somehow unlike his former experience, in sync with the time and actions of Earth Reality. They might be in a different dimension, but they could experience all of what was left of the world. He saw them in several cities around the globe after knowing what to look for.

In his travels, Art noticed that some cities along the coast had been completely washed from the face of the earth. At some time, either during the earthquake or before, giant waves had come in from the ocean and wiped these cities away. There were portions of the earth that were smoking. Uncontrolled fires had broken out on much of the land. As far as the camera would allow him to see, there was destruction. It made him sick. He decided to return to the log home and Gem. In a moment he was there. He wondered again about Kanna. If she were alive, if she had escaped this devastation, if he could somehow contact her, perhaps she could rummage around the old house and find his portable unit? If she did and turned it on, she could enter and... He took a quick trip over to his parent's place. They were there but to his horror, Kanna was not. He had to find her. But perhaps she had perished in the destruction. It was useless to even hope that little one could survive in a world this crazy for long. He hit himself in the head trying to knock some sense into it. Had he passed into an alternate reality, a horrible parallel universe? Was this all a dream?

Back at the cabin, Art lay down next to Gem and slept. When he awoke the next morning, his waste was soar in one spot where he had laid on the fanny pack. It was like he had slept on a rock or something. He turned to his wife. Gem mumbled something incoherent. Art shook her a little to see if she would waken. She did not. He opened one of her eyes and saw it moving around, following some images in her reality. Where was she? Where was his Sweetheart? There was food in this reality. He could eat it, but it did not fill the stomach. He wondered if he would live long without going back and eating regular food. He had neglected to bring any with him through MAP. He was lucky to be alive. A few more moments in earth reality and he would have been a victim of those fire stingers in person. Not knowing what else to do Art picked up the Bible that had come with Gem through the MAP door.

As he paged through it, his eyes came to rest on a Bible text in Haggai 2:6. For thus said Jehovah of Hosts: Yet once more-it is a little while, and I am shaking the heavens and the earth, and the sea, and the dry land. If there was a Jehovah of Hosts, he really had shaken all those things, violently. Art continued thumbing through the Bible. A long time ago he heard that Revelation, the last book of the Bible talked about terrible things happening on earth. He turned there now and started scanning through all the stuff. There were so many strange, symbolic creatures in this book. None of it made sense to him. How could anyone understand any of it? Perhaps one of the gospels would be easier reading. He turned to Matthew and read the story of Jesus multiplying the bread and fish to feed 5,000 men. Then he realized his problem of food would not be a problem at all. He settled into his meditative state and manufactured a subway sandwich. Within a matter of seconds, it was in his hand. He bit into it and was relieved to find that it had real, nourishing substance, something he could really sink his teeth into. It was delicious. All he had to do in the future was use his memory or imagination and manufacture whatever he wanted to eat.

Looking on from his place in time, Methuselah wished he could come to Art and answer all his questions. It would be so easy, but he had been told what he could and could not do. He could not go and talk to this troubled, lonely man. Perhaps he could help him find some answers though from the book. He watched over Art's shoulder as he thumbed through Revelation. When he got to chapter 9, he highlighted some of the passages. Art was scanning through them quickly when some of the letters and words seemed to rise from the pages of Revelation 9.

> *And the fifth messenger did sound, and I saw a star out of the heaven having fallen to the earth, and there was given to it the key to the pit of the abyss, and he did open the pit of the abyss, and there came up a smoke out of the pit as smoke of a great furnace, and darkened was the sun and the air, from the smoke of the pit. And out of the smoke came forth locusts to the earth, and there was given to them authority, as scorpions of the earth have authority, and it was said to them that they may not injure the grass of the earth, nor any green thing, nor any tree, but the men only who have not the seal of God upon their foreheads, and it was given to them that they may not kill them, but that they may be tormented five months, and their torment as the torment of a scorpion, when it strike a man; and in those days shall men seek the death, and they shall not find it, and they shall desire to die, and the death shall flee from them. And the likeness of the locusts like to horses made ready to battle, and upon their heads as crowns like gold, and their faces as faces of men, and they had hair as hair of a women, and their teeth were as of lions, and they had breastplates as breastplates of iron, and the noise of their wings as the noise of chariots of many horses running to battle: and they have tails like to scorpions, and stings were in their tails; and their authority to injure men five months; and they have over them a king, the messenger of the abyss-a name to him in Hebrew, Abaddon, and in the Greek he hath a name, Apollyon. The first woe did go forth, lo, there come yet two woes after these.*

To Art this passage from Revelation was a breath of fresh air. He could relate to this, symbolic or not. If this chapter gave some answers, there must be others elsewhere in the Bible. He somehow knew deep within that the so-called locust in this Revelation passage were the fire stingers as he had chosen to call them. Before the messenger had been given the key, they had been confined to some of the lower, Alien or Abyss Realities. If there were seven Eternal Realities, it was possible that there were seven Abyss Realities. Art had traveled unhindered in the first level of the Abyss Reality. The greys and reptilian humanoids had dwelt in the second level of the Abyss Reality. Perhaps the fire stingers had been there also or in some of the lower levels. With the camera he could see some of these creatures with long hair like women, teeth like a lion and weapon like tails that stung like scorpions. Most likely somewhere down there these creatures from the abyss had been genetically produced. Somehow in this future world the one with the key had broken through some or all the lower realities. It was possible they had even destroyed the barrier that existed between earth and the first level of the Eternal Reality. That was perhaps why he could not travel back and forth in time. If this Jehovah of Hosts had seen the levels of the Abyss Reality broken open, he quite possibly could have halted time travel in the first, second or more levels of the Eternal Reality to prevent the fire stingers and greys from going into the past and destroying the world before it got a chance to live. Whoever the fire stingers were, they had a leader over them called Abaddon. If he could find Abaddon, or Apollyon as the Greeks called him, he might get some answers to the questions that were screaming at him all through his mind. He ventured out one more time to look for the greys. Were they part of the pack tormenting the remaining humans? Art focused the camera on a stinger that appeared to be seated on a stump outside of the force field. He adjusted the lens. There within he saw a reptilian humanoid or was it a Reticulan? So, they must have come from the same place? Was that second level in the Alien Reality the abyss, John the

Revelator described in the book of Revelation? Where was Methuselah when a guy needed him or some other guide who could chart a path through this maze?

Art got an urge to go to Gem. Something was not right. When he got beside her, she was not breathing. Her body was not stiff, so she had not died. He did the only thing a man could do in this situation; he gave her mouth to mouth. But there was a problem with that. When inside this Eternal Reality, objects touching each other merged. Everything was in a semi-liquid state, so his efforts were of no avail. Finally, not knowing what else to do for this woman who he had come to love more than life itself, cried out "Methuselah! Help! If ever I needed you before, I need you now! Gem is not breathing! Hurry! She is about to die."

Somewhere in the distance a clock tried to strike but could not.

So, what will happen to Art, Kanna and Gem? Will they ever get back together? Will Art be able to break out of the reality he is locked in? Will Gem be able to escape the seduction of the, Art Angel from the abyss? Is she dead? How will a 5- and 1/2-year-old girl survive, alone in a world that will soon be changed forever some thirty-six months into the future? Look for some answers in the next book by Donielle, in this M.A.P. Phenomenon series entitled:

"The M.A.P. phenomenon, Until Infinity."

OK! I will give you a little teaser.

Until Infinity
BOOK TWO

THE INFINITY
TRILOGY
TEASER

Art thought back over the last several weeks as the door into the mother ship closed behind him. It had been quite a journey. Instinctively he reached to his side for the aluminum case but just as quickly remembered it was no longer in his possession. The standard MAP unit had been smashed in the earthquake and Gem had taken the only working portable unit. Gem! Just the thought of her ripped a fist sized hole in his heart. Was she even alive? He had left her un-breathing on the bed sometime in the future in the log home they must have purchased. She had been like that for half an hour before the message came from Methuselah to leave immediately. Funny though, her body had remained warm. He had lifted her closed eyelids and still seen the spark of life there. How could a person not breath and remain alive? But then it was a different world in this eternal reality. The strangest things had happened within its liquid environment. As his scientific mind was dwelling on the hundreds of anti-physic happenstances, the big fellow spoke him out of his daydream.

"Art! You are thinking about her, again aren't you? I assure you when our mission is over here, you will be propelled back to the point in time where you decided to go traipsing off into the future. None of this will have happened yet. You only will retain the memories of this. Gem will not. She will have forgotten all future events. You will hold her in your arms again and probably with more appreciation for her might I add. You will see Kanna again also. So now that we have gotten that straight can we focus on the tasks at hand. Remember the clock is ticking." Art let the words soak in until he finally got it. He paused now to look at the giant. How could a human body be so large? Though ancient, his face had no wrinkles in it. Though white his beard did not look like those on elderly people Art knew. One could say in earth terms this ancient one was an immortal. His skin shown with a luster unlike the millennial's so prevalent where the scientist came from. Little electrical sparks pulsed over his skin. He shown with an unusual light. And when he smiled, time seemed to stand still. What a masterpiece. He thought of Gem again.

"I will see her again!" At the mere thought of it he took gigantic leap. He was a bit too ambitious and his head started quickly closing in on the ceiling of the craft. With another instinctive move he put his hands up to stop his ascent then with a gentler push, propelled himself slower now, down to the floor again. In this monstrosity of a ship there was a slight gravitational field but not anywhere near as strong as he was used to on earth. To move about from one place to the other he sort of hop, skipped, and jumped over to the craft of his giant partner. Fortunately, the air was breathable. The old giant started pulling several boxes out of his craft and stacking them by the ramp. Art pushed a few buttons and his own suit opened allowing him to step out.

"Load these into your craft, Art. There are hundreds of thousands of motherships up here that need to be serviced and we only have a few months to get it done." The elder entered his door again. Already fifteen boxes were stacked ready to go.

"Get what done?" Art opened a box as he questioned the ancient man before him. It contained several hundred black gemstones. They were cut like diamonds each with seven planes. The bottoms were flat. A purple luster went deep into the interior of the gem. They were beautiful!

"Be careful when picking them up, Art. You can get cut really easy." It was too late. Blood was already coming from the long slash on his finger.

"These things bite, man. Why didn't you warn me?"

"I did but you were too eager to see what was in that box. Always the curious one, aren't you? But then I expect that is one of the many qualities about you that had a part in his choosing you." Methuselah bowed his head slightly as he referenced the "him." The scientist closed the box back up and put his finger in his mouth to suck the blood from the wound. Then he spat it out of his mouth. A big red spot formed on the floor but just as quickly turned to a steam like smoke and evaporated. The young man looked at his finger then at the box. There was some type of fabric tape holding the flaps of the bottom together. He ripped off a strip and used it as a bandage around the wound. He drew it tight using his teeth before securing the sticky portion onto the top. It was not a bandage but would work in a pinch. He pulled some gloves from his pocket as he carried a box into the craft. Art stashed the box in a compartment at the back of the craft and returned outside again. He did not use the stairs but jumped. One box was feather light. He could carry six or eight at a time. The ancient one had a stack of ten times that many already unloaded from his craft. Six boxes were as easy to maneuver as one had been and before exceptionally long the pile inside his ship was quite sizeable. What time was it? Art thought to himself? I am getting very hungry.

There were only a few boxes left. What would they eat up here if this task-whatever it was-were to last for months? Art was pondering this when the large door they had entered started to open on its own accord. He looked at the elder. The giant turned quickly at the door of his craft and shouted.

"Get in your ship, quick. They are coming."

"Who is coming," Art replied as he grabbed up the last five boxes and bounded for his door but there was no answer from the sister ship. The door was closed. Art realized he should not have taken the time to grab the last few boxes. Through the doorway came a large starship. The scientist had no other description for it. The craft looked like something right out of a science fiction movie. It was surrounded by five fighter drones. Balls of light came out of one of them just missing him. He did not wait for any others but dived inside throwing the boxes ahead of him. He hit the floor and rolled. The door automatically shut behind him, but it was not enough. Balls of light entered through one side of the ship and passed out the other. One just missed his ear. He hit the floor again trying to avoid any closer calls. His mind was screaming like a thousand crows. ***GET O'UT OF HERE! MOVE FASTER THAN YOU HAVE EVER MOVED BEFORE!*** The ship responded as if it had a mind of its own. It fully powered up and in a matter of seconds, the sides became transparent. The craft of his giant companion was nowhere to be seen. On the floor of the mother ship, he saw his suit crumpled in a pile. In his haste to board, he had grabbed the boxes instead of the outfit. Could he even travel in space without a suit? The five drones surrounded him. Balls of light started flying into the ship from all directions. One passed right through his knee but most of them targeted his heart. The skin above it was burning.